S.K. EHRA

In the Service of Shadows

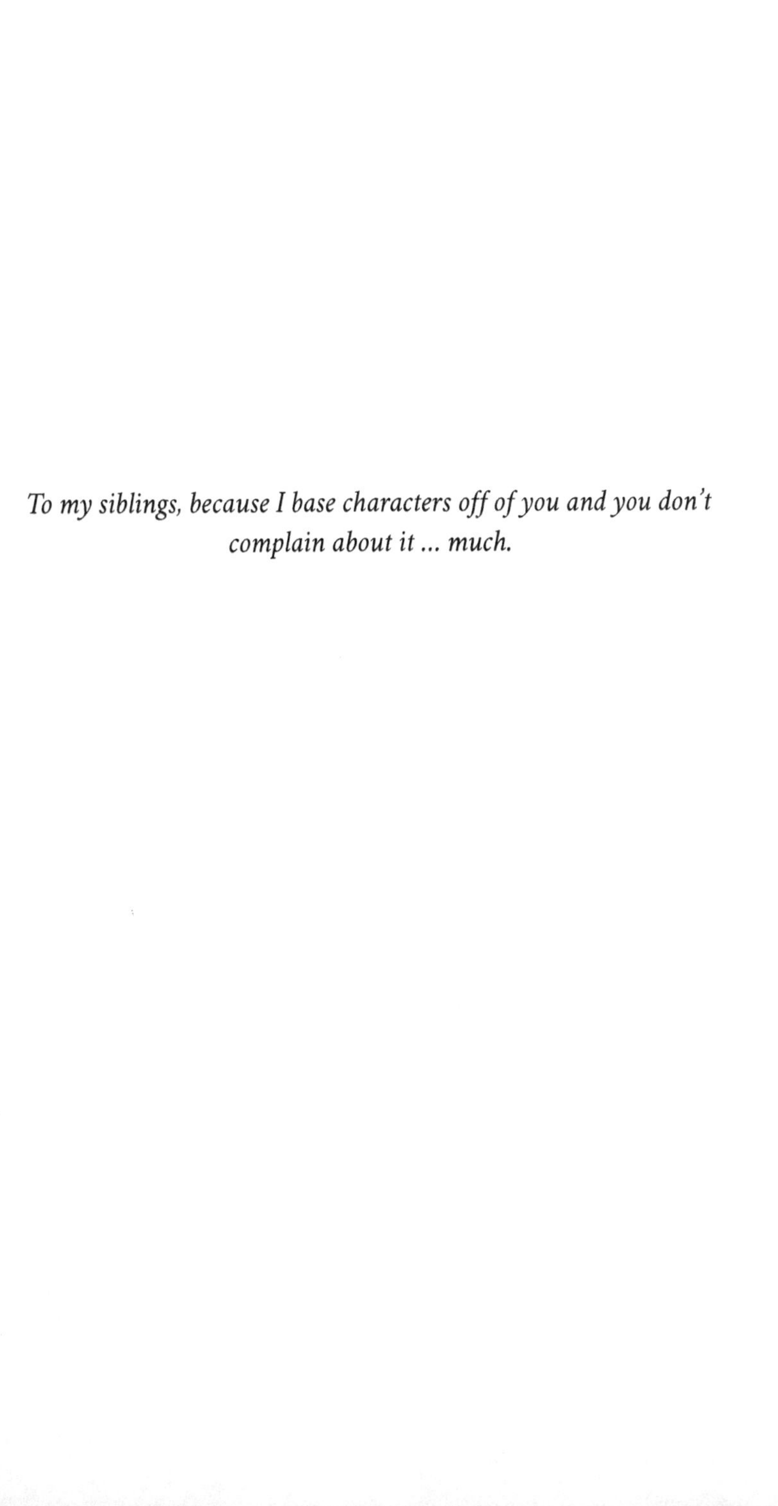

To my siblings, because I base characters off of you and you don't complain about it ... much.

Chapter 1

I t always begins with the same word.

"*Home.*"

The ghost finds me every time I drive this stretch of road curving through rugged hills of oak and juniper to echo his unfulfilled promise.

"*I'll be home.*"

I roll my shoulders, unable to shake off the chill seeping beneath my skin. It used to be I only heard him right as I passed the site of his fatal crash. Today I'm over a mile away when I hear his final words.

"*Be home. Home. I'll be home.*"

I glance at the car radio clock: 17:54. Time of day doesn't seem to have any sway on whether I hear his voice or not. I'll write it down all the same. I need every scrap of data I can get if I'm going to figure out this supernatural sensing.

Not every highway is haunted, and I do my best to avoid certain roads, but there's only one main way connecting Encrucijada to Austin unless I want to add over an hour of travel time, and I'm just as likely to find a lingering spirit on one of those longer routes as this one. It's a rough fact of life—death is unavoidable no matter where you go.

"*Home.*"

Seeing as this Home Ghost haunting is one of those unavoidable instances, it's just gotta be endured.

"See. See you then. Home. I'll be home."

His voice began as a distant whisper. Now he sounds so close he could be sitting in the passenger seat right next to me. I take a steadying breath. Hearing a ghost is nothing to get worked up over. I can handle disembodied voices, and I'll take the dead hassling me any day over the other haunting things I've come across.

"Home."

The car radio lets loose a series of chirps and whistles. That's new. The radio's never gotten excited over this particular ghost before. I slow as I come to the bend in the road, a precaution in case the radio acting up means something stranger than a ghost is heading my way. My knuckles go white as I grip the steering wheel tight and I brace myself for the crescendo in voice and cold I've learned to expect.

"HOME."

My breath would be misting if the prickling chill was natural. I don't know why he keeps reaching out to me. I've pulled over to the roadside a dozen times to try and figure out why he's lingering. There was no body that needed to be found and laid to rest. No cold hands took hold of mine to guide me to some secret surrounding his death or a lost memento he wants returned to a loved one.

"See you soon. HOME."

It could be he doesn't want anything done. Or I'm not the guy to do it. Or maybe, much like living folk, all he wants is for someone to hear him.

"HOME. HOME. I'll be home ... HOME."

The cold running through me brings out a sharp shudder.

Through chattering teeth I tell myself this spectral spell won't last long. Once I'm through this stretch of road, past the tree bearing the little white cross, his voice will roll back and away, leaving me with nothing more than the ever-present murmurings.

"HOME."

Those murmurings have been in a mood today. The insensible whispers from unseen lips have been skittering with all the unpleasantness of spiders' legs at the edge of my senses. And that's put me in a bit of an unpleasant mood as well. When I first started hearing the murmurings, I dismissed them as tinnitus caused by one too many concussive head injuries. Then I assumed they were another set of voices belonging to the not-quite-fully departed. After last summer I don't think they're anything so benign.

Christ, I just want to get home.

"See. HOME. See home."

The radio rattles out a low, warning snarl.

"See you in a bit."

The roar of pounding rain fills my ears. The overcast October sky hanging low above the road I'm driving down flashes away to become a pitch-black night lost behind a thick downpour. The car's headlights barely find the road and the windshield wipers flick in a rapid back-and-forth.

"I'll be home soon. See you in a bit," he said.

I feel how his car lost hold of the rain-slick road. His panic as he fought and failed to regain control. The all-too-familiar sensation of a car going into a wild spin.

Reality snaps back, the vision of the rainy night rips away, and my heart thuds to a hard stop when I see I'm seconds from driving straight off the curving road.

"Shit!" I slam the brake. Rubber screeches and shreds. The car fishtails, threatening to tip and roll, before it lurches back down onto what's left of all four wheels.

My breath comes short and fast as the dust settles. The driver's side door is inches away from having slammed dead on with a fatally thick oak trunk. A white cross surrounded by rotted streamers hangs from the tree. If I roll down my window I could touch the old scar marring the bark where he crashed years ago.

The radio whistles out concern.

"I'm alright." I rest my forehead on the steering wheel. My heart hammers against my constricting chest. That was too close.

"I'll be home."

Chapter 2

If the murmurings were in a mood before, they're throwing a full-on tantrum now. They've refused to simmer down following me nearly smashing into that tree. Their dark hissing crawls over me like a supernatural itch and has me wishing Kitty would stop biting her tongue and say what's on her mind. I'd welcome any noise of the living as distraction from the skin-crawling murmurs. Grim-faced, hands clenched on the steering wheel, her jaw twitches as she chews over what she wants to say to her burden of a younger brother.

I turn on her car's radio to muffle out the murmurings. Kitty turns it right back off. She thinks I have an unhealthy fixation on radios.

"What was it?" she asks after another beat of uncomfortable silence.

"A deer," I say.

It's the same line I used with the tow company. October kicks off deer mating season so it raised no disbelief when I blamed Bambi frolicking out in front of me as to why I was stuck on the side of the road, facing the wrong direction, and sporting two flat tires.

"You're the third call today who's had deer trouble," the tow truck guy said as he hauled me and the car to Encrucijada's mechanic. "You're lucky you didn't hit it. Deer can really mess a car up."

I didn't say much as we drove back. The murmurings felt tangible as they rushed against my mind, looking for the slightest crack to burrow further in and steal my senses away. The tow truck's passenger seat fabric was at the point of tearing I gripped it so hard, holding onto it as if it were a lifeline to sense and safety.

"That stretch of road seems to be bad luck," Tow Trucker said. "You know a guy died about five years ago at that exact same spot?"

I did know.

While my "a deer did it" story worked on the tow company, Kitty proves a harder sell.

"What was it really?" she asks.

"Nothing." I tap out a piano tune on the arm rest to distract from the headache of building pressure behind my eyes, courtesy of the murmurings. "It was just a hiccup."

"You've been having a lot of hiccups lately."

I scowl because she's right. The last two weeks haven't been my best. The thin line I walk between the living world and what lies beyond gets even thinner when I'm ill, so getting walloped by a bad bout of bronchitis in September brought along a whole camp of what Kitty refers to as "hiccups."

"Did you see something?" she asks.

"I saw a deer."

That she keeps shooting sidelong glances at me tells me she wants to talk about it. That I keep staring dead straight out the window tells her I don't want to talk about it.

"Are you going to tell me what really happened?" she asks.

Nope.

I'm not sold that Kitty completely believes my senses have a bad habit of stretching out to pick up the supernatural. Even after everything that happened over summer—including her seeing a hospital room trashed by the rightfully ticked off spirit of the murdered Silvia Lopez—I don't think she's accepted what I've got going on is a bit more complicated than simple psychosis. In all fairness, there are days I'm not sold on it either. It'd be a strange comfort if this all turned out to be nothing more than bad brain chemistry.

"Is it getting worse?" Kitty asks.

I shrug. "It is what it is."

The honest answer is "I don't know." I've spent the last four months working out how to get a handle on this, recording every ghostly voice, dark murmuring, and unnatural chill, compiling a laundry list of things to do and avoid doing to mitigate supernatural interference. But it's difficult to reliably measure forces that don't abide by natural law, and harder still to know if anything I do makes a difference. In the end, all I know for certain is that I don't get a lot of say in when or how the supernatural comes calling.

"You know you can't be driving anymore," Kitty says.

I expected her to come to this conclusion because I spent the whole tow truck ride thinking the exact same thing. That I had to climb out the passenger door to check my car for damage because the driver's side was too close to the tree was sobering evidence that my grip on reality is dangerously unreliable. Too unreliable for me to be driving at this juncture.

I did hope she'd at least wait a day or two before bringing it up, but as any older sister does, she can't let it drop and instinctively knows all the right buttons to push.

"You shouldn't have been driving at all." She sighs and shakes her head. "Not after June."

Instead of voicing my agreement and telling her we're on the shared page of me being absurdly incompetent, I give an irritated huff.

"We'll figure something out once your car is out of the shop," she says. "You don't have anywhere to be the rest of the week, do you?"

I hate that she's right. Most days I'm able to work around the murmuring voices, cold spells, and unseen presences. Other days, it's a victory to make it to noon before I lose all ability to keep reality sorted. So long as I keep having those other days, keeping a car on the road is asking too much.

"Logan, did you hear me?"

"It wasn't that big a deal," I say. Compared to previous misadventures, this one doesn't amount to a hill of beans. I walked away scratch-free and the car only got a couple flats with the alignment needing adjusting. Last time I crashed, both the car and I were totaled, so tonight's tire-screeching scuffle ain't worth any special fanfare.

Kitty doesn't share that opinion.

"You were lucky it wasn't worse," she says. "That it wasn't like what happened over summer."

I squeeze my left wrist as it twinges under the memory. The break it sustained in June has long healed, yet it still feels tender and has a bad habit of getting uncooperative toward the end of the day.

"Logan, are you listening?" Kitty asks.

I'm trying to. I rub the sides of my head as it gives a hearty thrum under the surging murmurs.

"It's getting worse. Isn't it?"

"Come off it, Kit," I say. "It was one time and it ain't that bad. That doesn't—"

"It only takes one time! You can't be driving."

"You've already said that." I'm sick of hearing what I can't do and sicker of only seeing that list grow longer.

"Well, you can't!" Worry has snipped her fuse short and my shifting to stare out the passenger side window does nothing to help.

"You don't have to be like that," she says. "I'm not the enemy here."

I respond by glaring harder out the window.

"Why do you always have to make it a fight?" she asks.

"Because I'm following your lead."

"Are you incapable of being reasonable?"

"I've got a psychological diagnosis that says so."

"I'm not asking much of you."

Just to give up driving and pretty much every other agency of independence. Watching my freedoms disappear because I can't handle life's barest responsibilities is a slow, suffocating frustration. I don't want to surrender anything more to my inability to take care of myself.

"Honestly, what if you'd hit a tree?" she asks. "Or what if the car had flipped?"

I've already flipped a car this year. Kitty should be more appreciative that my keeping all four wheels on the ground is a sign I've grown as a person.

"You could've been hurt," she says.

I shrug. "That's nothing new."

"Yeah? And what if you'd hurt someone else?"

I don't have an answer for that and Kitty lets me stew until we come to the next stoplight.

"I don't like being the bad guy," she says, "and I know it's hard to hear, but you're not able to—"

"I'll stop driving," I say.

"Logan—"

"I said I'll stop. We can stop talking now, too."

She doesn't turn the radio off this time when I put on a news channel. The weather forecast promises a run of muggy, overcast days and the chance of thunderstorms toward the end of the week. That sounds about right.

The weather report changes to stormier affairs as a news host announces the continued rise of violence among Austin's homeless population. The local business owner they interview is furious someone left bits of a dismembered body in his back parking lot dumpster. He complains about the smell and how bad it is for business. If that's all he has to worry about concerning the dead, he's got it pretty good.

The next interview is a woman who runs a charity organization for the homeless in the city. She makes a heartfelt plea for greater compassion to those most in need and says all the right words to make people feel guilty for not caring and then forget about it by the next commercial break.

"You missed the turn." I point down the street that'd take us to my apartment.

"You can spend the night at my place," Kitty says.

"Why?"

"Because you lost your car and I just found out I almost lost my brother," she says and I pretend I don't notice she's close to crying. I didn't tell her how close I got to the tree. Tow Trucker, talkative fellow that he is, must've given her all the dirty details.

Kitty pulls into the driveway of her home. Neither of us

moves after the car engine rumbles off. Her eyes are dry now and she's back to biting the inside of her lip.

"Whatever it is you want to say, it can wait until tomorrow," I say. She's already had enough of me and my inability to pull off the simple task of driving for the day.

"You know you can move back in," she says. "You didn't have to get an apartment."

"Dr. Day thought it was a good idea," I remind her. And I'm really only half moved out. Kitty suggested—and Dr. Day also thought it was a good idea—I spend weekends at her place to retain a "system of support." Which is his diplomatic way of saying I'm a hot mess someone has to mop up after.

Moving into the apartment was supposed to reassert some control and independence. Instead it feels like the adults are letting the kid play out in the backyard so long as he behaves, and I've got a sour feeling that's another freedom that isn't going to last long. My parents in particular are readying the lassos to rope me back in.

"If Dr. Day knew what was really going on with you, do you think he'd have approved of you getting an apartment?" Kitty asks.

Oh, hell no.

"Did your appointment with him go alright?" she asks.

My appointment went fine. Once a month I drive back to my folks' place for a couple days and meet with the good doctor. Seeing as how I drove off multiple therapists before Dr. Day proved the staying power to put up with me, it was agreed the longer drive was better than trying to find a closer replacement. And again, Dr. Day emphasized the importance of retaining a familial "support system," claiming it a good idea to have regular visits with my parents.

"Are things alright between you and Mom and Dad?" Kitty asks, determined to keep fishing until she catches a problem.

"If I can't drive, I'll need to find a closer therapist," I say.

"No, no, we can make it work, we'll figure it out. And don't change the subject. Did something happen while you were visiting Mom and Dad?"

Not yet, but there's a pyre being built on Mom treating me like I'm six and my father acting as though I've reverted back to sixteen and this is all some extreme form of rebellion. Their demands I behave in a more responsible manner always end in gasps of horror when it's discovered I've taken on more responsibility than they deem I can safely handle, such as getting a job, looking for an apartment, or using scissors.

The last couple times I visited them I was surprised they didn't slash my tires to stop me from driving off. They aren't pleased about the mess I got into over the summer, barely a month out of the mental hospital, and that's shaken their faith that I'm as stable as I claim to be. My forgetting to turn off the lights before leaving a room is damnable evidence I'm not mentally competent enough to be unsupervised and that sentiment has only gotten worse as November approaches.

"Logan?"

"It's just been a rough week," I say.

"Well, what—"

"We can talk about it tomorrow," I say, hoping that by tomorrow she'll have forgotten. Or at the very least she won't be so strung out on the thought that she only had to pick up her brother from the mechanic and not identify him at the morgue.

Chapter 3

"Hello?" I keep my voice low as I answer my cellphone before its ringing can give away my position.

My caution is wasted as Glenny's high-energy voice blares through the line. I might as well throw up neon signs as to where I'm hiding.

"Hey, are you busy?" she asks.

"I'm in the middle of something," I whisper, scooting around the kitchen island to keep Deborah and Alicia from seeing me as they race through. "Hold on."

"Mom! Where's Uncle Logan?" Deborah asks.

"Don't know," Kitty says, continuing to chop vegetables on the other side of the island, totally indifferent to her daughters' distress. "Did you check outside?"

"That's out of bounds."

"Did you check upstairs?"

"Twice!"

"Did you check the garage?"

The pitter-patter of retreating bare feet is the signal it's safe to speak. Ranger training has served me well. A nine-year-old and seven-year-old are no match for my superior hide-and-seek cunning.

"Okay, what?" I return to the phone conversation.

"Do you wanna hang out or something?" Glenny blurts the question out so fast it sounds like it was all a single word.

"No. Not really." Socializing requires a bit more energy than I can muster at the moment. I agreed to hide-and-seek out of moral responsibility to promote the innocence of my nieces and on the condition I was the one who got to hide because that means all I need to do is sit and scoot around the kitchen island. That's a level I can safely function at. Aided by Kitty's poker face, I've been able to sit here for nearly half an hour. Kitty tolerates this behavior because, while I am brooding, I am usefully brooding by taking a couple of kids off her hands for a time.

"Oh." Glenny pauses. "Well, will you do it anyway?"

"Yeah. Sure."

The murmurings have simmered down over the last hour, allowing the headache to let up so it no longer feels like ice picks are being driven through my eyes. Besides, Glenny is pretty easy company. Despite being a teen mom toting around a four-month-old baby, she's about as low maintenance as they come. Which balances out perfectly with the high-maintenance, neurotic mess that I am. She's also psychic or something of that sort, which means she can carry most of our conversations by herself.

"Who is that?" Kitty peeks over the edge of the island down at me and I mouth "Glenny" up at her. I don't know why she keeps asking. The answer never changes.

"Have her come over for dinner." Kitty raises her voice so Glenny can hear.

"Are you at your sister's?" Glenny asks. "Did something happen? Oh my God, something happened, I had a feeling something happened, what happened?"

"I almost wrecked my car." The steady chop of Kitty's knife on the cutting board misses a beat.

"Oh, well okay, I guess that's not too bad. I can head over now!" Glenny says, and I can almost hear her bouncing up and down as she grabs her baby and the diaper bag.

I hang up and shift around the kitchen island as Deborah and Alicia come running in again.

"Mom! Have you seen him?"

I scoot around the corner as Alicia stomps over to her mother. In the stove's reflection I see her, hands on hips, lip stuck out in a pout.

"I don't know where he is," Kitty says. "I'm busy making dinner."

Alicia and Deborah are so distracted pressuring their mother to flip on me they don't notice me crawl over to the living room couch and lay back, hands laced behind my head.

"There he is! I found him!" Deborah points and grins wide to show off her missing front teeth.

Her older sister doesn't share her delight.

"Where were you?" Alicia demands as she stalks over, glaring at me in a way that reminds me very much of her mother.

"What do you mean, where was I? I was here the whole time."

***

Alicia continues to deny my "on the couch the whole time" claim and insists I cheated in some way until Glenny arrives. She's brought the baby stroller, which means she wants to talk about something and is going to use the "let's take Titus for a walk" ploy to lower my guard and trap me into conversation.

"I'm trying to get Titus to fall asleep, so let's take him for a walk," Glenny says.

Titus doesn't show any inclination of cooperating with this fall-asleep plan. He's obviously inherited his mother's talkative gene and is in the middle of delivering a baby babble soliloquy. He screams at the top of his tiny lungs and applauds his eloquence by waving chubby hands as Glenny buckles him into the stroller.

"You are the cutest little guy," she coos and earns a giggle from him when she kisses his cheek. With Glenny as his mother, I wouldn't be surprised if Titus starts talking by the time he's six months old. He's probably heard more words per minute than most seven-year-olds.

"Are you two dating?" Alicia asks, hovering on the front porch step.

"Can we come?" Deborah asks.

"No, you can't. Dinner is at seven," Kitty says, pulling both girls back inside and closing the door after us. Alicia and Deborah watch us through the window, pigtail-framed faces mournful at being left out. Well, at least Alicia looks upset at being left behind. Deborah's breath fogs up the glass as she smushes her face against it and returns my wave.

I don't know why Kitty says Deborah reminds her of me.

Kitty is set up in a pretty nice neighborhood of quiet residential streets hosting spacious houses built for upper-middle class families. Manicured yards are heavily shaded by leafy palms and Texas live oak, and high iron fences fortify rose gardens to keep out a deer population utterly lacking in fear of man or God. Streets bearing names like Sundew Trail, Laurel Creek, and Teakwood Lane wind in lazy lines to the neighborhood's center, hosting a grassy park and community clubhouse including a public pool for all the kids to pee in. It's about as safely suburban as you can get with the minivans parked in brick-paved driveways, tricycles left by front doors, and bright blue signs demanding slower speed limits be obeyed for children's safety. The surroundings make even Glenny and me look presentable—a young couple taking their baby for a walk and not a psychic teenager making the mistake of letting a psychiatric patient get within a foot of her kid. It helps that the pink highlights Glenny wore in her hair have grown out. She's abandoned the punk haircut, halved the number of piercings in her ears, and ditched the eyebrow barbell entirely. She claims the change in appearance is because taking care of a baby means most days she doesn't have the energy to put on anything other than sweatpants, let alone manage hair, makeup, and accessorizing. It's a claim I've got some doubts about being entirely true since I've never known Glenny to be short on energy reserves.

"So what's up?" I ask.

Glenny gives a long-suffering sigh. "Oh my gosh, so Josie has been dragging me along to these young mom meetings at church. Which is fine, you know, and it's kind of nice being around other women who have babies and young kids. And super helpful too with advice and all that. I thought it'd be annoying with other moms telling me what to do, but it's been a total lifesaver. Like, I was having this problem with chafing—"

"We can skip this part of the story," I say.

"Oh, yeah, well anyway, the women at the group are actually really nice." She does a little skip as she pushes the stroller. "I thought everyone would be super judgmental because I'm not married and they're all super Christian house moms but no one has said anything—out loud that is—but they keep it to themselves. And I'm getting better at that, being aware that there's a difference between what people think and what they say. Anyway, when I missed one meeting because I was sick, Martina and Kelsey made soup and homemade bread and brought it over for me, isn't that nice? But there's this one woman there, Audrey, who's absolutely awful and I just want to punch her in the face every time she talks. Oh, and I don't know what to do with my life."

I can relate to that. Not the young mom's group drama, the not knowing what to do with my life.

"I know my dad wants me to go to college or something. And Josie wants me to get some sort of stable father figure in my life for Titus' sake. And my mom—actually no—I don't think she wants anything. She's just happy to have another grandson. She's being supportive to the point of making me feel guilty. Like I don't deserve it. And I'm trying to at least get a job but that's been a lot harder than I thought because I have Titus and can only do part-time right now and I'm not really good at anything."

"Mm-hmm," I say.

"You're not supposed to agree that I'm not good at anything."

"Why do you always have to tear me down when I'm being supportive?"

It's not like Glenny needs a job. Turns out surviving to make a tort claim against a millionaire serial killer's estate is a lucrative way to go about things. She's financially set as her tiger shark of a lawyer is eviscerating every account, asset, and royalty down to the pocket lint of the late Carl Burns who made the fatal mistake of abducting an angry pregnant woman unafraid of using a baseball bat to bash his skull in.

"This is serious!" She keeps one hand on the stroller and shakes her other fist against the heavens with a fervor that'd make Charlton Heston proud. "I don't know what to do!"

My wife was also prone to intentionally overdramatic displays. In a way Glenny reminds me of Maria, petite women whose performances were never kosher as they were always served up alongside a huge helping of ham.

"Anyway, what happened with you? Why'd you crash your car?" Glenny asks. "Was it that Home Ghost again?"

I nod. I don't think I ever told Glenny about Home Ghost, so I must've thought about him too loud at some point.

"Is it getting worse?" she asks.

I shrug. I'm not as convinced as Kitty is that it's getting worse. I think it's more likely she's getting better at picking up when it affects me.

"So you can't drive anymore, huh?" Glenny asks.

I nod and shrug.

"So what are you going to do?" she asks.

"Not drive."

"No, I mean what are you going to do about the ghost?"

I wasn't planning on doing anything. It's not a road I can avoid using, but so long as I'm not the one driving, no one's at risk of getting hurt.

"Aren't you going to help him?" she asks. "Like you did Silvia? And Billy?"

I'm not keen on the idea of making reaching out to the dead a habit. Sorting out my life—the dead and other spiritual entities unwilling to mind their own business aside—is difficult enough. I'll deal with ghosts if they come directly knocking at my door, but I'm not going to search out lost souls on the roadside. That's begging for trouble I don't need. Especially as my last supernatural soiree earned me a hospital stay with a broken arm, broken ribs, a concussion, and I forget how many stitches. If that's the price of my amateurish meddlings, then I need to practice more prudence on how far I'm willing to wade into the world beyond the veil of the living. Otherwise, it's going to be a one-way trip in very short order.

"Oh my gosh, you're always so dramatic," Glenny says. "You wouldn't be picking up *everyone*. Just the ones who need your help. Like when the Delaneys were trying to find their aunt's will and you told them to look in the cushion of the living room chair."

Kitty is friends with a Mrs. Delaney who was bemoaning all through August she couldn't find her great-aunt's will. And all through August I kept hearing this weird creaking sound. After a couple weeks of going near mad from the incessant squealing I started seeing a painfully ugly floral pattern chair whenever Mrs. Delaney came around. We all got a happy ending when I suggested Mrs. Delaney see if her aunt Peggy hid the will in an unconventional place like a living room couch, a mattress, or maybe an overstuffed armchair with green and white floral upholstery. Mrs. Delaney found the will and I stopped having my mind assaulted by the groaning creak of worn-out springs and visions of hideous furniture.

Glenny plops herself down on a park bench and rocks the stroller back and forth to keep Titus asleep.

"I mean, I know it's not a whole lot of fun for you," she says, "but you're always going on about what you're, like, morally supposed to do and then getting all frustrated because you don't feel like you have that clear sense of purpose anymore."

"I never said that," I say.

"Yeah, but oh my gosh, you think it all the time. It's like

a neon billboard on your brain. Especially whenever you're getting into a mood, like right now, it's blaring off you."

She checks to make sure Titus is safely asleep before holding the stroller still.

"And you know you're the only one who thinks that. You can't argue with me there, I have insider information," she says, tapping her temple. "So I know things didn't happen at all like you planned or anything, but if you stopped beating yourself up over the fact that life took a different turn from what you expected and stopped thinking of it as if you failed or something, I don't know, maybe you'd be able to see that you can still do what you wanted to, just do it a little different. Yeah?"

"What do you want?" is one of the most common questions I get asked. Dr. Day drops it once a session, hounding me to articulate what I want out of life. I used to dodge around the question to avoid admitting most days I wanted it to end. Now I dodge around it because it's a stupid question. What I want doesn't matter.

I want to be able to drive and not worry about running off the road because some haunted hallucination takes over. I want to be able to go to the grocery store and not leave a jittery mess because I couldn't keep the murmurings separate from the speech of the living. I want to be able to get through a week without turning up the thermostat because I'm freezing from an overly curious, unseen presence hovering too close by. I want to be more than a barely functioning burden.

"I keep telling you, nobody thinks you're a burden," Glenny says.

One third of the people at this park bench strongly disagrees.

"Yeah, well you're wrong and stupid," she says. "You know, I was trying to do the whole 'therapist' thing, where you lead the person to come to the solution instead of telling them what it is because if you straight out tell them what's wrong they'll reject it but if you let them think they came to the conclusion on their own they'll actually act on it."

After being kidnapped by a serial killer and then bashing his head in before birthing her baby a few hours later, Glenny decided to take a page from my book and get some therapy. After being in a therapist's office for all of a hot minute, she's starting to act like one. Or it could be she's acting like a mom. Her wanting to "talk things through" is as much like Kitty as it is Dr. Day. And she's pretty good at it. Both the therapist-ing and the mom-ing.

"Actually, don't laugh, but I was thinking of maybe getting a degree in psychology or something. You know, start at community college and get all the prerequisite credits before going to a university and then maybe become a therapist, yeah?" She looks to me for approval and then glares like I've tricked her. "And don't do that."

"Do what?"

"Misdirect or deflect," she says. "You always try and avoid talking about yourself by turning the conversation back on the other person."

"I didn't say anything," I say.

"Yes, you did. You asked me 'what's up' and then tricked me to go off on a whole ramble about me and my problems."

I don't remember a whole lot of trickery being involved, but you don't have to be a wily mastermind to get Glenny to talk.

"Yeah, I know," she says, "I'm trying to work on—see, you did it again! You keep getting me off topic! Stop it!"

"Okay, I can be quieter."

"Actually I was thinking that you should … what do you call it, 'think out loud' or something?"

I frown. That isn't a phrase I use. It's a phrase Maria did. Early on in the marriage we found it saved us both a lot of headache if when she had a problem she wanted to talk over she clearly stated if it was a "Logan fixes it" talk where I was allowed to offer suggestions on how to solve the problem, or if it was a "Maria thinks out loud" conversation where she talked and I was allowed to nod and listen.

My right hand drifts to my left, feeling for the ring that's no longer there. I had to take it off over the summer because of how swollen my hand got from the abuse it went through. I decided to leave it off, thinking it might help in moving forward in life, but I didn't like not having that part of her with me. I compromised by looping a chain through the ring and wearing it around my neck. I shove my hands into my pockets to stop them from seeking the feel of the silver band beneath my shirt.

"I mean, I know going to therapy is kind of irritating for you because you can't really talk about what's bothering you," she says, "so I thought maybe I could help, yeah? Because you need to work on your communicating and I need to work on my listening so this is good for both of us."

It's a kind gesture and I appreciate it for that, but I'm not dumping my issues onto a nineteen-year-old kid who's got a baby to raise and her own life to get in order. Her hands are full as is.

"It's not dumping your issues on me, it's being friends," she says. "At least think about it because, I don't know, maybe you're supposed to be all spiritually sensitive. That maybe, in a way, it's a good thing."

I shake my head, recalling some of the lower moments "supernatural sensitivity" has brought me to. There ain't a single good thing about it.

Titus stirs, stretching out tiny fists, and Glenny starts rocking the stroller again.

"That's not true," she says. "I mean, I know it may not be good you have to put up with it, but you do good things with it."

"Yeah?"

"Yeah." She sways side to side in rhythm with the stroller, watching her baby drift back into a deeper sleep. "That me and him are here, that's only 'cause of you."

She looks up from Titus and waits until I meet her eye. "Think about it. Okay?"

Chapter 4

I'm the only one who refers to the spare bedroom as the guest room. Everyone else calls it "Logan's room." The reasonable part of me is grateful Kitty has gone all in with support and made it painfully clear she wants me around. The unreasonable part of me likes to grumble that my overbearing older sister is treating me like one of her kids who's going through an independent phase and she'll humor me until I wise up and grow out of it.

While I'm not sure on many of the factors that determine my susceptibility to the supernatural, getting a consistent eight hours of sleep each night is the best defense against it overrunning me. Which has led to the guest room being transformed into a Morphean temple dedicated to falling and staying asleep. My first night here, I stored away the digital clock to remove any possibility of me waking up in the middle of the night to obsess over the glowing numbers' steady march toward morning. The weighted blanket stayed on the bed all through the summer months. Sweaty sleep is better than no sleep and it's a lot harder to toss and turn under an additional fourteen pounds. A ceiling fan, a portable one on the desk, and a white-noise machine for the more desperate hours are the three-man band of background noise. The ever-present murmurings are most noticeable at night and while I can't escape them, I can temporarily lose them in the fans' mechanical whir long enough to find sleep.

The murmurings are proving harder to shake tonight. They pull at me, dividing my attention so I retain nothing from the pages as I force myself to read a chapter of *The Master and Margarita.* Each word reads disconnected from the previous, making for string after string of meaningless sentences. My eyes move over the black, nonsensical shapes until they reach the yawning abyss that is the chapter's end. Going through the motions is nothing new and I tell myself it's better than quitting. Discouragement allies with all that lurks just out of sight to keep me up long after I turn off the reading lamp.

Cold caresses my skin. I tell myself it's from the fans. The murmurings rush against me like wind-blown sand. I tell myself that's the fans too. I shiver and even though I know it won't do anything, I pull the cover tighter around me.

It's just the fans.

***

"Tell me about work," Dr. Day said.

"I quit." The temporary warehouse job I took was ideal on paper and the first month went well, leading me to get overconfident in thinking I'd get through it fine. All I had to do was shove T-shirts into bags for six hours a day, four days a week. I didn't have to talk to anyone and mix up the voices of the living and the dead, I could listen to headphones as I worked to mask the murmurings, and so long as I wasn't late or caught napping under a table, there was no way to make a mess of it. I had all that going for me and still couldn't get through the six-week contract.

"Why did you quit?" Dr. Day asked.

I sorted a couple of navy puzzle pieces into the pile dedicated to the sky. Dr. Day thought our sessions would go better if I had a physical project to work on. He said it would help me see "the progress" and "pieces coming together." I interpreted that as a gussied-up way of saying I needed busy work to distract me from being so damn ornery. A skeletal frame of the puzzle's borders and unconnected islands of stonework and steeples provided a small bit of order to the five thousand pieces of fragmented chaos awaiting assembly. Once completed, the puzzle would show Notre Dame Cathedral beneath a night sky as promised by the box cover propped up beside me for reference.

Maria wanted us to take a trip to Europe. Go see Notre Dame, the Louvre, catch the train to Lourdes, and make fun of me for remembering next to nothing from four years of French class. She went to France on a high school trip and regretted she was too young to properly appreciate it. The shallow cynicism of a sixteen-year-old blinded her to wonder and she wanted a second chance at it.

"Mr. Dalaguerre," Dr. Day prompted, "why did you quit?"

"Bronchitis," I said.

Lacking Mark and Kitty's child-toughened immune system, I caught every cold that came through their house teeming with the five virus factories affectionately known as Mary Katherine, Emmett, Alicia, Deborah, and Luke, culminating in my overtaxed immune system going on strike to lay me out flat. I spent the last week of September and first stretch of October choking on my phlegm-ladened lungs. At least the warehouse manager was understanding when I called to quit. My wheezing through the call might've convinced her it was a good thing I wouldn't be coming in. But it wasn't suffocating under mucus and running a low-grade fever that pushed me to quit the job a week early.

The voices, visions, it all gets worse when my physical health is compromised and those feverish nights were terrible. I couldn't tell if the shivering was from illness, or the dead and damned paying call. Sleepless nights courtesy of unseen voices and invisible hands slowed recovery and reduced me to a useless wreck. Antibiotics got rid of the physical infection. The spiritual infection proved far more reluctant to leave.

"Mr. Dalaguerre, did you hear me?"

I closed my eyes as the murmurings rolled over me and narrowed my focus down to the physical—the wall clock's reliable *tick-tick-tick*, the hush of water flowing in the small office fountain, and the tap of my foot on the floor pushed the voices back to a tolerable distance.

"Mr. Dalaguerre?"

"No, I didn't hear," I say, "but if you asked what do I want or something along those lines, chances are I'm not going to hear it again."

Dr. Day's smile was more patient than I deserved.

"I asked if you were looking for a new job," he said.

"Yeah." The supernatural impingement brought on by illness was finally simmering down to where I could function as a productive member of society again.

"Do you think that's the best choice?" he asked.

"I do, but I'm gonna guess by that question you don't," I said, "and I'm not sure what else you think I'd be better off doing."

"Grieving."

He got my full attention with that one.

"For what?"

"Your wife. And your friend, Alec Rallis."

"I've had well over a year for that," I said. Even longer for Alec.

My fingers found the wedding ring hanging beneath my shirt. How do you grieve the dead when they barely give you space to breathe?

"The last year of your life didn't allow for much more than surviving. There was very little time for grief." Dr. Day leaned forward. "Just consider it."

Chapter 5

The morning alarm is set for 5:10. I wake up at 5:09. Getting up before the alarm goes off is always a good start and I'll take these small victories, especially after admitting defeat and caving to the shameful weakness of relying on an alarm. A consistent sleep schedule was more important than my trampled pride.

Sunrise is a couple hours off when I begin the morning run. Streetlamps and lights behind closed curtain windows provide artificial illumination against the drab, pre-dawn dark. Heavy clouds hang low, perfuming the air with the promise of rain, and thicken the sickly, sweet smell of autumnal decay. Groans of thunder rumble in the distance and there's a sense of anticipation as the world waits with bated breath for the swelling sky to break.

Figuring out how to reliably stave off ghostly visitors and demonic intrusions is a long ways off, but following a schedule—or at the very least having a daily list of things to do—helps keep me from tripping and face-planting over the fine line dividing the world of the living from the supernatural. The forty-five-minute morning run takes the edge off the anxiety I wake up with courtesy of unpleasant dreams, the post-run shower provides the sound of falling water to mask the murmurings, and the list I write the night before of tasks to get done during the day sets a system of order to fall back on when the inevitable chaos of sepia spells, cold presences, or voices come calling.

I don't feel an overwhelming need to hide from the murmurings in the shower an extra couple minutes this morning—another good sign—and I have the coffee started, dishwasher emptied, school lunches packed for Mary Katherine and Emmett—labeled with their names deliberately misspelled—and the first steps of breakfast going before my brother-in-law, Mark, staggers down the stairs carrying Luke in his arms. Though his father is half asleep, eyes mostly shut, Luke is as awake as a four-year-old can be and fully unhappy about it.

"Go play with your toys or go back to bed," Mark says as he plops Luke down in the living room. Luke chooses the third, unspoken option of screaming in a tearful heap where his father abandoned him.

Being a practiced father of five, Mark is so moved by his youngest son's tantrum he spares a single glance over the top of the morning newspaper before turning to the sports section.

"Thanks," he says, one eye almost fully open when I hand him a mug of coffee.

"Rough morning?" I ask.

"For both of us."

"I'll take care of breakfast today," Kitty says. Her hair is sticking up on one side from sleep but the summons of her screaming child is far more pressing than personal appearance.

"It's alright. I got it," I say.

"No, go sit down." Kitty shoos me to the table. She rescues

Luke from his living room exile and sits him down at the table with a bowl of sliced fruit to tide him over until a more substantial meal can be supplied.

My fidgeting rivals Luke's, and Kitty is giving us both the same look, expecting one of us to succumb to a morning meltdown. Kitty taking over the morning prep steals away my means of building momentum to get through the day and the murmurings creep closer without task-based distraction to keep them at bay. Needing something to do, I grab the blender and pile in whatever fruit is on hand.

"Is that all you're having for breakfast?" Kitty eyes my smoothie-making prep with disapproval. She figured out too quickly for my liking that the pulverizing of fruit and yogurt into a sloppy mess is my way of dodging the effort of eating a real meal. And I figured out pretty quick questions like that aren't questions. They're a trap.

"It's an addition, not substitution," I say and she relaxes an inch.

"Did you sleep alright?" she asks.

"Fine," Mark says.

"I was asking Logan," Kitty says. "I heard the lumberjacks working overtime all of last night so I know you slept well."

"You say the sweetest things," Mark says and Kitty kisses him on the top of the head as she serves up a plate of sausage, eggs, and biscuits.

My hopes that this display of affection would make Kitty forget about me dies when she stares at me so long she risks burning the second batch of eggs.

"Did you sleep alright?" she asks again.

"Fine." I turn on the blender to avoid a follow-up question. She waits for the machine to switch off, opens her mouth to speak, and I turn the blender on again. I get away with the tactic four more times before she pulls the plug out of the wall socket.

"Your light was on at three in the morning," she says.

"Was it? I didn't notice, I was asleep."

I don't know what time I woke up in a cold sweat last night. I didn't check my phone for the time. The pitch of black outside the window told me dawn was a long ways off. I turned on one of the bedside lamps before rolling over to reclaim the sleep being held hostage by a dark dream. Leaving the light on was a child's comfort—not even daylight can dissuade the unwanted hauntings—but it was a comfort nonetheless and tricked me back into less disturbed dreams.

"I sleep with the lights on most nights," I say, lowering my voice as I'm not particularly proud of this.

"You weren't for a while," she says.

I push the blender button again, forgetting it's unplugged.

"I thought it was better," she says.

"It was. It is. It's … it's not straightforward."

"Mom, I want smoothie!" Luke says.

"That's nice," Kitty says. "Finish your oatmeal and then maybe."

"I don't want oatmeal!"

"Then you don't want smoothie, Boo-Bug, because you gotta eat all your oatmeal if you want smoothie," she says. "And you better say 'please' next time you ask."

Luke, the world's grumpiest Boo-Bug, stabs his plastic spoon into the cereal bowl in protest against life's difficulties. Enjoy being four, kid. Life never gets any easier.

"Are you going into the office today?" I ask Mark, who is nowhere near awake enough to realize I'm setting him up as a meat-shield to escape his wife's questioning of my mental well-being.

"Mm-hmm."

"Can I catch a ride down to Austin with you?"

"Yep," he says. The look Kitty shoots him bounces off his oblivious head. "Need a ride back? I won't be done until after six tonight."

"Maybe. I'll let you know around noon."

Mark nods. "That'll work."

"Why do you need to go to Austin?" Kitty asks.

"I'm meeting with the job recruiter today."

"I thought that's what you were doing yesterday."

"No, that was for an interview and Krav Maga," I say.

"How did the interview go?" she asks.

"About as well as the drive home."

"Do you want—"

"No, I don't want to talk about it."

"And what time are you meeting the recruiter?"

"Ten."

"How long is the meeting going to last?"

"Probably no more than an hour."

"Well, then I can drive you down and back," Kitty says. "That way you're not waiting around for an hour before and seven hours after."

"Thanks, but you don't need to go out of your way," I say. Kitty homeschools her youngest three kids so she'd either have to find a last-minute sitter or pack them all into the minivan which I witness her struggle to do every Sunday before Mass. It's a nightmare I wouldn't wish on anyone. "I can keep myself entertained."

"That's what I'm afraid of."

"St. Mary's has a daily Mass at noon. There's a Krav class at one—"

"I thought you signed up for the later afternoon classes," she says.

"I signed up for unlimited. I can show up whenever," I say. "And the library is a couple blocks from Mark's office. I'll be okay."

Kitty gives me the "no, try again" look she usually reserves for Mary Katherine when her oldest daughter attempts to exercise a little too much teenage independence.

"I'll take a bus back after Krav," I say. "I'll call you when I'm fifteen minutes away from the station."

"Call me when you get on the bus," she says.

It's been barely over twelve hours and not being able to drive is already getting old. Next time I run into Home Ghost, whether in this life or the next, I'm going to have a few choice words with him.

Chapter 6

"Are you cold?" Mrs. Rodriguez asks, incredulous I'm wearing a jacket too thick for the season over a long-sleeved shirt in her barely air-conditioned office. She's more sensibly dressed in a short-sleeved button-down blouse and skirt.

"I'm fine," I say. I don't think bundling up does anything to ward off supernatural flash freezes besides make me feel proactive about it.

Mark kept asking the same "Are you cold?" question as we drove down to Austin. I kept giving him the same "I'm fine" answer through chattering teeth as we passed by the stretch of road Home Ghost haunts. I didn't get the chance to give my few choice words to Home Ghost because there was no way of swinging it so that Mark wouldn't interpret it as directed at him. Home Ghost won this round, that spectral bastard.

"How did yesterday's interview go?" Mrs. Rodriguez asks.

"I'm not holding my breath on hearing back," I say.

She raises her drawn-on eyebrows over half-moon spectacles, waiting for the details.

I shrug. "It was an off week and it showed."

I went into that interview starch stiff and hit every negative stereotype associated with veterans: too formal, too rigid, unacclimated to the civilian sector, and flashing all the warning signs of being a powder keg waiting to blow.

"You're still looking for temporary part-time?" she asks, manicured fingernails tick-tick-ticking on her keyboard.

"Three to six months preferably."

The air conditioner's soft whir fails to drown out the murmurings rustling against me. This wouldn't be as much a problem if the people in the next office over had some notion of volume control. As they don't, their voices bleed through the wall, same as the murmurings bleed through the veil. It has me anxious, both trying to hear what they're saying and trying to block it out so I don't lose track of Mrs. Rodriguez's competing voice.

"You're moving up the duration," she observes. "Good for you."

As a veteran job recruiter at a company that helps folks with special needs find employment, Mrs. Rodriguez is unfazed by my twitchy fidgeting. I'm one of her easier cases.

"With the holidays coming up I have a number of openings at warehouses, stocking and inventory," she says. "I can send your resume out if you're still interested in that line of work."

"That's fine." I'm not picky. I just need something to do and an income.

One of the caveats to me getting an apartment is I have to earn the money to cover rent. Which is tricky as I'm stuck at part-time to avoid "unnecessary anxiety" as Dr. Day puts it, and there are certain jobs I simply can't do. Specialized lines of work that my skillsets smoothly transfer over to are knocked clean off the table by the Schizoaffective Disorder diagnosis—I wouldn't even get an interview for mall cop security—and unskilled jobs are no guarantee either. Customer service doesn't go so well when I can't hear the living because the dead won't shut up, and I've noticed an inconvenient link between prolonged exposure to screens and my vision picking up things it shouldn't. No talking to customers, limited computer work, nothing where the safety of others is dependent on me staying rooted in reality—all of that severely whittles down the job field. At this point I'm willing to take anything from janitorial work to graveyard shift grocer. Anything to prove paying for an apartment isn't too much to handle.

My last visit with my parents ended in a fight between me and my father over this. Paying rent wouldn't be a problem if I had control over my bank accounts. Maria's more lucrative career, continued royalties, and life insurance more than takes care of finances. That's all inaccessible. My being let out of the mental hospital involved signing financial authority over to my parents and my father has been wielding that like a club of late.

The people in the next office over break out into laughter, the murmurings pound against my skull, and I grip the chair to hold fast to the physical.

"Mr. Dalaguerre?"

"Sorry, what?"

Mrs. Rodriguez's smile, tolerant and used to such episodes, stays in place. "Have you considered looking for employment closer to where you live?"

"That's the end goal." I do plan on finding a permanent job in Encrucijada, but that's a small job pool and I don't want to poison the waters. Austin is the testing grounds for me to learn what types of employment I can reliably do even when supernatural visitors pay call.

"I should start hearing back on interview offers in a couple days," she says. "We're hosting a free seminar on interviewing, including practice sessions later this week if you're interested. A number of veterans have taken it and found it helpful."

"Thanks, I'll check it out," I say, very aware I'm in desperate need of practice in talking to the living.

***

I don't last long at the table inside the café. The chatter of study groups, the coffee grinders' growl, mugs clinking, and the shift of bodies as people come and go feels like fire ants are throwing an orgy beneath my skin. I take my laptop and coffee out to the empty street-side patio offering welcome isolation from the overstimulation. No one else wants to suffer the heavy, humid air hanging over downtown Austin, courtesy of a distant storm teasing along the horizon. Unfortunately, I'm not as alone as I want to be. The murmurings feel more like a physical presence than hissing voices and there's something else on the air besides the humidity. It buzzes in my ears, crawls over my skin, and promises the coming of an unnatural sort of storm.

Or it could be I've just been staring at screens too long.

I close the laptop displaying spreadsheets translating my hauntings into scatterplots and line graphs. Frequency, duration, severity, if it's a ghost, the murmurings, something unknown, or something worse, are cheerfully mapped out in color-coded lines and dots. Updating the data used to serve as a morale booster. That was back in the tail end of summer when the trends all moved in the downward trajectory and I thought I was making progress in sorting things out.

I drag a hand down my face. The prickle of stubble reminds me I forgot to shave this morning. What am I doing wrong that's allowing the supernatural to hang on like a bad cold?

I've followed the rules I've set with religious zealotry, and up until I got sick in September, that kept it manageable. No skipping meals. No skipping showers. Don't wear the same outfit two days in a row. Eight hours of sleep every night—or at least lie in bed for eight hours. No getting up to pace around the room. Definitely no more plugging in headphones to the electronic keyboard to seek solace in Strauss, especially after that one time the headphones weren't fully plugged in at two in the morning. Kitty was a pretty good sport about it though, seeing as it only woke her up and none of the kids.

At least my hauntings have been comparatively tame of late. Ghosts are nothing compared to what I know can come out from behind the veil. The entity hasn't made an appearance since June, a silver lining I'm grateful for and determined to keep. I tap the pen on my notebook, searching for revelation in the untidy scrawl recording the supernatural instances of the last four months. There has to be a way to control this. It's a problem, it can be fixed, I just have to figure out how.

The murmurings crescendo into a chanting roar and that preternatural pressure hanging in the air weighs me down like waterlogged clothes. It muffles the café chatter, the rumble of cars, and in place of earthly sounds comes a stuttering breath broken by desperate sobs.

"Please don't. Please no. No. No. NO!"

It pounds in my ears, swells behind my eyes. The café, patio, and then the street melt away under an acidic sepia haze as the sobbing presence moves closer.

"Don't! No! No!"

"What the hell are you?" I grip the table in a desperate bid to hang onto crumbling reality. This isn't like anything I've come across before. The hopeless sobbing sounds like a ghost, but no ghost has ever had such a corrupting effect on the physical world. That influence belongs to the entity, yet this new presence doesn't feel like that either. The entity inflicts ruin with a scalpel's meticulous precision. This presence has all the subtlety of a sledgehammer.

"PLEASE!"

A hand grasps my shoulder and I near jump out of the chair.

"Can I get you a fresh—Oh, I'm so sorry, I didn't mean to startle you." The waitress' touch rips the sepia curtain away and snaps the world back with dizzying force. I clutch my head to stop the wild spinning of street and patio.

"Are you alright?" the waitress asks. Her hand is out-stretched, uncertainly hovering as she avoids repeating the same mistake of touching my shoulder.

"Please stop! Stop! STOP!"

"Sir? Do you need me to call someone?"

A disturbance like air folding under heat shifts in the corner of my eye and the sobbing manifests as a dark haze churning over the oblivious pedestrians. I have no idea what that thing is and I fight back the panicked urge to pick the waitress up and rush her inside the café. Physical barriers haven't proven to do much good against the incorporeal, but it hurts to see her so exposed on the open patio.

"Stop! No! NO! NO!"

The sobbing isn't interested in the waitress. It's set on different prey, following after her as a wolf does a lost lamb. The woman walks by, cellphone in hand, as ignorant as everyone else to its approach. Unlike everyone else, she's been marked by the strange. An odd vapor hangs off her. Paranormal pheromones for the sobbing to home in on.

"Don't worry about the fresh cup, I was heading out," I say to the waitress and hurdle over the low metal fence separating the patio from the sidewalk. Leaving by the proper exit demands time I don't have.

"*STOP!*"

I don't apologize as I plow through people on the sidewalk, pushing aside tourists, window shoppers, and businessmen wearing Bluetooths wired into their skulls.

"Watch it, asshole!" a man yells as I shove past.

I ignore both him and the sensible part of my mind screaming at me to stop chasing after this abomination and run the opposite way. What I'm doing is about as wise as swimming after a great white shark, but staying on shore means leaving the woman to the mercy of her spiritual stalker, and there's no doubt it intends malice.

"Hey!" I call out and the wrong heads turn back to look. The woman continues on, unaware she's being followed.

"*Please stop ... please ... please ...*"

The haze hangs so low and heavy it's hard to breathe. I shake my head to clear the sepia creep bleeding over my eyes. It feels like an unseen force is dragging me back to stop me from reaching her.

"Hey!" I grab her shoulder. The world jolts back to normal the moment I touch her. The haze lifts, the sobbing stops, and the abrupt change sends a sharp, concussive ringing through my head.

She turns and gives me a reproachful glare. Her hand dips into her purse to ready pepper spray, taser, or with my luck, a handgun.

"Yes?" She takes a couple steps back, appropriately wary of me. Her black hair is pulled back into an immaculate twist away from dark eyes and aquiline features. Her dress suit has the flawless fit of custom tailoring and she's more perfectly put together than a royal flush dealt out by an haute couture. Already naturally tall, her high heels push her a couple inches above me and the faint lines creasing the corners of her narrowed eyes suggest she's closer to Kitty's age than mine.

"Um," I say, impressed I got to that level of eloquence. I didn't prepare anything to say to justify my behavior. I didn't even plan out what I should do—scratch that—what I *could* do, against her stalker. With the sobbing gone and natural world returned to normal, I've lost the sense of peril that sent me racing after her and in its place comes a sense of feeling right stupid.

"Can I help you?" she prompts.

I should apologize. Say I mistook her for someone else. There are a dozen avenues allowing me to bow out. It's tempting to try and convince myself I imagined the whole thing, except that weird, buckling blur continues to linger around her.

"I think you're being followed," I say, as that falls somewhere between honest and believable.

"You mean by someone other than you—"

A shout and crash interrupts her. I yank her behind me as scaffolding knocked loose by the falling wood cracks hard against the unforgiving concrete. That no one was walking underneath the platform when it collapsed keeps the consequences to accusatory shouts and hot-tempered cursing among the construction crew.

Couture stares at the spot on the sidewalk buried beneath broken construction boards and metal rail. It's right where she'd have been if I hadn't run up to hassle her and it doesn't take much imagination to know how differently the scene would've played out if I hadn't stopped her.

"How did you know I was being followed?" she asks. She doesn't pull away or show any offense at being manhandled by a complete stranger. Her eyes stay fixed on the sidewalk buried beneath construction debris.

"I don't know." I keep my hold on her as I check the surroundings for any sign of the haze. The corners of my vision pulse with sepia strands but the swarming haze of despair isn't there anymore. My purposefully seeking out the supernatural invites the murmurings to rise up. They purr with pleasure and anything that makes them happy raises my hackles.

"Don't lie to me," she says.

"No, it was my mistake. I thought I saw something," I say, deciding it's safe to let her go. The construction crew finishes cussing one another out and the site returns to the typical buzzing and clangs. The new wave of pedestrians is clueless as to what transpired. Cars stop slowing as they drive by. The man with the square-shaped face at the bus stop loses interest in us and goes back to his newspaper.

The murmurings are the only ones who grasp what almost happened. What Couture says next is lost under their delighted crooning.

"Sorry, what?" I tap out a ragtime tune on my leg to get my focus back on the physical.

"Why don't we talk somewhere other than the middle of the sidewalk?" she asks.

"No, that's alright. I didn't mean to bother you," I say, and she grabs my arm.

"This isn't my first time being 'followed' as you put it." Her voice is low and rushed as if she's afraid of being overheard. "And I'm going to guess this isn't your first time either."

I almost say, "I don't know what you're talking about." The lie is too big for me to spit out smoothly.

"You can see it, can't you?" she asks.

"See what?" Her reaction to all that's gone down in the last minute catches me off guard as much as that wailing miasma did. I take a step away, thinking I've sorely misjudged this whole situation.

"Fifteen minutes." Her grip on my arm tightens. "That's all I'm asking. I know there's more out there than what your senses would have you believe. You can see it, I can't, I've already needed your help today, and I'm not so arrogant to think I won't need it again."

Cold ripples over me, and while I don't know if it's an aftershock from that haze, a warning, or an unrelated breeze of paranormal chill, I know I can't justify walking away from her. Not yet, and not when she's looking at me like that.

"Please," she says. I nod and she gives a tight smile. "Thanks. And I don't know about you, but I could really go for a drink."

Chapter 7

I don't like bars and it takes nothing short of a woman being in imminent danger to convince me to go to one.

The lunch hour is in full swing and the open-air layout prevents the barely restrained chaos of concentrated noise and movement from reaching overwhelming. Most folks cluster around the horseshoe-shaped bar. Every hand gesture, hair flick, and the constant comings and goings of customers is reflected in the silver chrome and glass wrapping around the lower half of the room. The reflections trip me up, pulling my attention away from watching the street for unfriendly presences. It doesn't help that I'm looking for anything supernatural lurking about and those warped reflections are easy to mistake as people disappearing beneath a shifting haze.

"You could've told me you don't drink." Couture uses a skewered olive to stir the dregs of her martini. She sits on the couch opposite me at the edge of the open-air patio, one leg crossed over the other, flicking her high-heeled foot back and forth.

My foot bounces in tense agitation. I can't see or feel anything out of the ordinary. That doesn't mean nothing's there. The natural world is seldom an accurate reflection of what's there and my definition of what's "ordinary" includes a heaping helping of the strange. While there's no lurking cold, invisible pressure, or anything to warn of a supernatural interloper, the murmurings are unbearable. Tapping out a piano tune on the couch arm fails to push them back. I can almost make sense of what they're saying. They're so close I can almost—

"You're not much of a talker, are you?" Couture nudges her foot against my leg, dragging my attention back to her. My poker face has gotten sloppy because something in my expression earns a frown from her.

"Did you see something?" Her eyes flick side to side and her hand goes to her purse as if to draw out a weapon.

"No."

"Did you *sense* something?" she asks.

I shake my head. She sounds like she's speaking underwater and the murmurings are about to break the surface. I glance down the street, convinced that sobbing miasma will come swooping in at any moment.

"Are you going to tell me what's going on?" Irritation sharpens her tone and she jabs her toe into my leg again.

"I might if I knew." The dull ache settling above my eyes is consequence of me looking for the supernatural while attempting to stay grounded in the physical.

"What did you see at the construction site?"

"I'll tell you my story if you tell me yours." I get the impression she's got the better grasp of the situation and I'm the hapless idiot who stumbled in on it.

"No need to show me your teeth." Her lip curls up to bare hers. "I'm not the one who grabbed you on the street."

Technically she did, but her being a woman, that's a much lesser offense than my doing it to her first.

"And I'm not asking anything personal," she says. "I haven't even asked your name, I don't know anything about you, and I'm giving you a lot of the benefit of the doubt. If you can't grant me the same trust, at least give me the same courtesy. All I'm asking is for you to tell me what you saw."

She stirs her martini, expecting a response. I sit tight and wait. I can't place why she comes across as so strange and off-putting. As far as evidence goes she's the victim here. All the same, there's something about her that's got me on edge and warns me against showing my hand before seeing hers. Minutes tick by and she rolls her eyes.

"Well, now I do know more about you. You're impossible." She leans forward across the low table. "Consider this from my perspective. Here I am minding my own business, and a stranger, looking like his roof isn't nailed on that tight, runs up and grabs me. Turns out it's a good thing he does because if he hadn't they'd still be scraping me up off the sidewalk."

My roof is nice and tight, thank you very much. I have a dozen MRI and CT scans to prove it. It's the inside of the attic that's the problem. It's got an infestation that ain't in any hurry to leave.

"There are a lot of people who'd dismiss that as a freak coincidence," Couture continues, "but I think both you and I know to be suspicious of what people dismiss as coincidence or dumb luck."

I'm suspicious of a great number of things, earning me the prestigious badge of multiple anti-anxiety and antipsychotic prescriptions. Ironically, Dr. Day believes that my reluctance to take the drugs is born out of that same paranoia they're intended to treat, leading to me being prescribed more anti-anxiety medication. It's a vicious, and at times hilarious, cycle.

"I'm not going to ask how you got here as I'll bet you like revisiting that string of events as much as I do mine," she says. "So rather than getting hung up on the past, I think we're both better off focusing on the now, and making sure I have a later."

"Why can't you see it?" I ask.

"Because I can't," she says, looking at me like I'm being deliberately dumb. "You're the strange one here, being able to see what you shouldn't. But I don't need to see something to know it exists."

This time she's quicker to pick up I'm not going to say anything until she does.

"What do I have to do?" she asks.

"What do you mean?"

"Tell me what I have to do to get you to stop snarling at me."

"How'd you get dragged into this?" I ask.

"I don't know what *this* is," she snaps. "I couldn't see it, remember?"

"That ain't what I'm asking about and you know it. I want to know, if you can't see or hear it, how'd you find out it's there?"

She gives her martini one final stir before sighing and sitting back. "Early on in my career I had a client. He came from old money and had all the power and connections to match. I was living hand-to-mouth so was more than willing to overlook his quirks for the opportunities working with him gave me. I learned a little too late it was a mistake to dismiss his hobbies as eccentricities of the rich. His penchant for the paranormal turned out to be more than a whimsy of someone who had too much money and time on his hands." A wry smile twists her lips. "I'm not going to make the same mistake twice. I'm a little wiser now and much more liberal when confronted by the strange and the unexplained."

"You run into this sort of trouble often?" I ask.

"As I told you, this isn't my first rodeo. Far from, actually." She frowns when she rediscovers her martini glass is empty. "Once you get tangled up in the uncanny, it sucks you in and takes over every aspect of your life. It feels like…" She trails off and I fill in the blank.

"You're fighting just to hold your head above water?"

She nods. "You come off as someone who's been pulled under a few times."

Lately I don't feel like I come up for air at all.

"So what did you see?" she asks.

"Something's after you," I say, not sure how to convey what was stalking her. Telling her she's being chased by a crying haze cloud doesn't do it justice.

"Really? That's the best you can describe it? As 'something'?"

"I think I'm a fair bit newer to this than you are. What I hear and see, they're not always 'something' that fits neatly into words."

"They?" she asks.

"Not my first rodeo either."

"Run into this sort of trouble often?" She echoes the question back at me.

"Increasingly so." And I'm not thrilled over it.

She was right about what she said. Now that I've gotten tangled up in the uncanny, all attempts to get free only tangle me up more.

Couture fishes a business card out from her purse and slides it over to me.

"I'm hiring you for the foreseeable future," she says.

"To do what?"

The card lists her name as Salome Trasmoz and vaguely

describes her as a consultant above the requisite contact information. I don't believe for a second that's her real name. It reads like another one of her fashion accessories, picked out for exotic and memorable appeal. Based on that small peek she provided into her past she's probably swapped her name around a couple times.

"Let's call it personal security. How much do you charge?" she asks. "Do you live close by? In Austin? If not I can put you up somewhere around here. I'll need you on hand whenever I'm out and about."

I keep shaking my head until she stops going down the list of qualifications for the job I'm not taking.

"What?" she asks, eyebrows snapping together. I doubt she's used to people telling her no.

"I'm not an exorcist. I'm not a priest. Whatever's after you is way beyond my pay grade." I push the card back at her. "I can't do much more than point at it and scream."

"That's perfect. You don't even need to scream, just point," she says. "All I need is for you to warn me if that 'something' gets near. So long as I know when it comes by, I can avoid whatever it does. At least I hope so."

"I don't know how to stop it," I say.

"That's not your job. That's mine. And it shouldn't take me too long to figure out who's causing all this."

"Who?" I raise an eyebrow.

She waves a dismissive hand. "Like I said, this isn't anything new. The strange needs an entryway into the normal and that takes a who."

"And when you find this 'who,' then what?"

I'm not sure if I should be impressed or disturbed she's handling all this like it's nothing more than a casual setback in day-to-day business. While she claims not to be able to see and hear what lurks behind the veil of the physical, she's definitely wandered much farther through it, and that has suspicion sticking to me like an angry burr.

"Again, we don't need to make this personal," she says, and that answer rings another warning bell, "but I do need your help."

I check the street again for any sign of the supernatural. The family of tourists sitting at the window table of the restaurant across the way talks happily with one another. The biggest hiccup to their day is probably deciding what attractions to see that best fit everyone's interests. Good for them.

The man sitting at the next table over has none of their cheer. He's a throwback to older traditions, reading a newspaper in place of scrolling through a phone. His business casual collared shirt and slacks look deliberately nondescript and his frown could very well be carved onto his face, square jaw set below square furrowed brow—

Holy shit. It's Square-face. The guy at the bus stop near the construction collapse.

The ghost of a shudder rolls beneath my skin and my drumming fingers tighten into a fist. Now what are the chances of that?

Salome was right about coincidences. They ain't something to dismiss.

"Well?" she asks. She's ordered another martini and looks resigned to having to wait on the fact I prefer to wade and not jump into these dark waters.

"I'm thinking," I say. "It's not my strong suit so give me a minute."

Whether she's a luckless wanderer or intentional explorer of paranormal paths, Salome isn't alone on the one she currently walks. Less than an hour of knowing her has shown she has both monster and man on her trail. That could be why she comes off as so strange and has that odd quality to her I can't quite put my finger on—her supernatural scars from past dealings are what's setting me on edge while acting as the beacon leading her stalker right to her.

I know what it's like to be haunted and hunted. By both man and monster. I know what it's like to be made powerless in the face of beings that have no place in the natural world. The terror of them taking an interest in you. It's not something anyone should be abandoned to.

"I don't charge," I say.

"What?"

"The quality of service I offer for this sort of thing is barely pro bono. Don't worry about payment."

***

"I'm not comfortable having you do this for free," Salome says.

Her heels *clack-clack-clack* on the sidewalk as her stylus *tap-tap-taps* on her phone. She must've been lying about not having any paranormal senses because she flawlessly navigates the sidewalk without looking up from the screen.

"Let's have room and board serve as the first payment deposit and then figure out the rest once we get more pressing matters sorted," she says. "The Granduca's convenient. It's on my way driving into downtown. I'll call and make reservations for you."

I let her continue in this vein of throwing out rhetorical suggestions I'm not going to take her up on. She carries on about how she'll pay me, how she'll have to rework her schedule, how she'll need to meet her clients in more public places so I can be unobtrusively present. She probably throws out some ideas on marketing strategies, desired quarterly growth, and maybe the cost-benefit analysis of hiring on a Santería priestess as well. I'm not terribly interested in paying attention to her managerial strategizing. I'm much more interested in paying attention to the surroundings to make sure she gets home alive.

Salome stops so suddenly I have to do a hopping shuffle to avoid running right over her.

"Well?" she asks.

"Well what?"

"I asked you what you think," she repeats, annoyed I'm not as reverent as I should be to her every word.

"I wasn't listening," I say.

"Do you ever?"

If we keep going down this track I might get fired my first day on the job.

"Listening wasn't part of the job description," I say. "Remember, I'm just here to point and scream."

Her reply is lost as the world buckles under the ugly pressure brought by the sobbing presence.

"PLEASE!"

Salome moves to cross the street, walking straight into the dark haze that blooms around her like blood in water, and the wailing swings up to an ear-ringing pitch.

"Salome!" I grab her arm and yank her back into me.

The gunshot bang of an exploding tire summons a chorus of horns, screeching rubber, and terrified screams. The car rams straight into the traffic pole, bringing out a second wave of shrieks as people stumble away.

Salome's face barely moves a few degrees from calm as I feel the rapid rate of her heart beating against me.

"You alright?" I ask. The few feet between us and the collision feels more like inches. Neither of us needs to say it—we both know she'd be pinned between the car and metal pole if I hadn't pulled her away.

"How did you know?" She's clutching on to me so hard that if she doesn't let go soon I'm going to lose feeling in my arm.

"I saw it coming." What *it* is still needs to be determined.

"Never mind the Granduca." The breathiness to her voice belies her collected mask. "This may seem forward, but I think it'd be better if you stayed at my place."

Chapter 8

"Hello?" Kitty picks up on the second ring. Deborah and Alicia continue to fight in the background. The rising shrillness to their screams and Deborah's high-pitched "No, no, no, no!" promise tears are soon to come.

"Hey, it's me. I got a temp job," I say.

"That's great!" she says with sincere enthusiasm before her tone shifts to one of an overly protective older sister. "What is it?"

"Security."

"What? Oh God, no! They didn't give you a gun did they?" She sounds ready to shoot the idiot who gave her mentally disturbed little brother a firearm.

"No. I'm just there to look like dumb muscle."

"What's the security for?"

"Who, not what," I say and slip into the readymade lie. "It's for some celebrity on tour. I can't say for who or much about it, I signed a confidentiality agreement. They wanted a couple extra guys on staff for the rest of the week. That's all."

"You got this through the recruiter?"

"No, a buddy from Krav Maga hooked me up."

"Oh, and who was that?"

"Mike Russo." I give a fake name just in case Kitty tries to contact this mysterious Krav Maga buddy for confirmation. I'll buy more time if she's chasing after a made-up man than if I bribe someone to try and stand against the devastation that is Kitty in mom-mode.

"What're the hours?" she asks, looking to spring the "you can't drive on your own so can't take a job with odd hours" trap.

"It's on call and pretty informal. Mike lives near downtown so I'm crashing on his sofa."

Kitty's silence is steeped in disapproval.

"Are you sure you're up for this?" she asks.

"I already took the job and it's less than a week," I say. "All I'm gonna do is stand around looking stupid and I do that already so I might as well get paid for it."

The second silence drags longer. I wait it out.

"I don't think this is a good idea," she says.

Yeah, I got that impression.

The inevitable waterworks start in the background on Kitty's line. Deborah's crying escalates to shrieks that'd crack a wineglass.

"I gotta go," Kitty says. "I'll call you back. Don't do anything stupid."

She hangs up and I tuck the phone into my back pocket, knowing I'm not gonna answer when she calls. Suffering her wrath when next I see her is worth dodging another round of interrogation.

Salome already has security—a staff of massive men stuffed into suits—stalking around her home. They mad-dog me whenever we bump into one another as I sweep the premises to get a read of the marble tiled, silver polished, ebony accented, aristocratically furnished terrain. I doubt I'm going to find anything and I'm only doing this sweep out of an obligation to at least act like I'm fulfilling some sort of purpose.

Her house is much too big for a single woman, even with her staff living on site. Twelve-foot-high coffered ceilings have fans that rival the chandeliers adorning the foyer and dining room in decadent frill. Mirrors reflect their rooms for an unnecessary illusion of spaciousness and the effect is oddly disorienting. It's hard not to twitch every time I catch my reflection moving in the abundance of glass, or expect to see an unfamiliar face staring back out at me. Hanging lights in ornate cases line the long halls of dark mahogany doors hosting a library, a sitting room with a bar, a sitting room with another library and another bar, a grand piano, a room set up like a movie theater, and a whole bunch of bedrooms that look to get as much use as a meat cleaver in a vegan's kitchen.

"That's private," one of her staffers snarls at me when I try a door and find it locked. I don't tell him I speak Spanish and understand every word he adds to his telling off.

He spends the next quarter hour tailing me and putting on a show of posturing to prove how threatening he is as I snoop around the house and yard. To be fair, his hostility is understandable. Not only am I, a complete stranger, wandering through the home he's supposed to guard, but my being in this house is like a flea being on a French poodle. Also to be fair, he's an obvious asshole with a face that'd get a freight train to take a dirt road, so it makes sense he's going through life pissed off and snarling.

I shake him by staying put too long, browsing through Salome's main library boasting a substantial collection of occult-themed books. Histories of spiritualism in the United

States, biographies of practitioners, and collections of urban legends, parapsychology, Thelema, Kabbalism, and countless more beliefs line the shelves. Glenny would have a field day here as she's fascinated by all things strange and better left alone. While her interest is mostly born from being weird, Salome's interest may be one of survival if she gets entangled in that veil as often as she claims.

On my second sweep of the house I find Salome in one of the sitting rooms. She waves for me to join her on the S-shaped sectional sofa positioned to enjoy the floor to ceiling windows overlooking oak-covered hills sloping down to an offshoot creek from the Colorado River.

"Who was that on the phone?" She sets her tablet down, rolls over to lie on her stomach, and kicks her bare feet up behind her. She's changed into loungewear, a short kaftan that comes up high on the legs and is generously slitted up the sides. Not to be outdone by the short skirt, the neckline takes an equally enthusiastic dive down into immodesty. "Calling your girlfriend to tell her not to worry?"

"You're pretty at ease considering a supernatural something has you in its crosshairs," I say. Tension visibly melted off her the moment we pulled through the automated gates onto her winding driveway.

"It can't touch me here," she says. "Not in my home."

"And tucking your feet beneath the blanket stops the monsters under the bed from getting you."

"Well, did you find any monsters as you were checking under the beds?"

"No, but I haven't checked the closets yet."

"You're not going to find anything," she says. "In my experience, there are certain thresholds that aren't crossed."

"In my experience, experience isn't to be relied on." Not to the extent to justify Salome's confidence, and certainly not over something so far beyond human control. Spirits and all else that infringes on our puny physical plane don't hold much truck for the natural rules that we're subject to. The power she thinks protects her didn't stop the murmurings from crossing her threshold. Though now I think on it, they do sound different, calmer and more muted. That change makes me wary but most everything nowadays does.

"Don't worry. I won't dock your pay if I die in my home," she says.

"You should take this more seriously."

Salome sighs and stretches cat-like out on the couch. "Trust me, I'm taking this very seriously. My hiring you isn't something I'd do lightly. Believe it or not, I'm not one to pick up random men off the street and take them home the same day. If I do, they have to at least buy me dinner first. But if I got hysterical every time I walked down one of these darker stretches of road, I'd be somewhere between insane or interred."

She props her chin on folded hands and slowly kicks her bare legs back and forth. "By the way, are you ever going to give me a name?"

"Austin," I say.

"That's not your real name."

"If you think you're safe in your home, am I even needed here?" I ask.

"I don't know why men get so hung up on this 'being needed' all the time. Yes, you're needed, so stop expecting me to cower beneath my covers, hoping it all goes away. And it's far more convenient having you here instead of picking you up and dropping you off every day. So relax and make yourself at home, *Austin*."

I don't relax and she rolls her eyes.

"It's too bad you don't drink," she says. "A stiff one would do wonders to loosen you up. If sitting still is too difficult for you, there's a saltwater pool out back, an entertainment room, a gym. Take your pick. You being so tightly wound is making me edgy."

"I didn't bring swim trunks." Other than what I was carrying around for Krav Maga, I don't have a change of clothes at all.

"So?" She puts a finger to her lips. "I'm not much for swimsuits myself."

That turn in the conversation signals it's the perfect time for me to be anywhere else in the house. There are plenty of rooms to choose from and Salome needs my immediate company as much as I want to provide it.

"Dinner is at six," she calls after me, and I can hear a teasing smile playing across her lips.

***

I ought to park myself in the library and dive into Salome's collection of the occult. There may be some wheat among the chaff I expect to find in books on ghosts, demons, and the error in thinking living creatures can wield power through them.

I go back to the room where I found the piano instead. It's tucked away from the main area of the home, looking like its only purpose is to fulfill the obligation that big fancy houses require a grand piano stashed about. There's no sheet music in the bench, the instrument's virginal polish perfectly reflects the room, and the keys have a sleek, unloved look.

A couple bars into Schubert's "Ave Maria" push back the

murmurings to clear space for me to think. Salome knows more than she's letting on. A lot more. While my standard procedure for the supernatural is trial and horror, her protocol is far more mature, which means there's reason to trust her more experienced lead on this. On the other hand, her being well-versed with the supernatural is a good reason not to trust her at all. She is far too comfortable in both its presence and interference. I wouldn't be surprised if she deals with the uncanny in a deliberate manner.

A tired grin pulls at my lips. I'd be less suspicious of Salome if she was dead and reaching out to me. That a living soul is the one asking for help has me more wary than if she was another disembodied voice from beyond the grave whispering in my ear. It may not be anything sinister on her part that got Salome involved in the strange. Her participation in paranormal pastimes might stem from necessity and not design. I didn't choose to start hearing the not quite departed or seeing the spiritual entities that haunt this world. She might not have asked for the hand she was dealt either, and instead of running from it, she capitalized on it. That's the American way to go about things.

I switch over to Chopin's Prelude in E Minor, or as Glenny likes to call it, "Logan is in a mood" music. I should give her a call. Her unhealthy interest in the paranormal might include knowing about sobbing haze monsters. I shake my head, shutting down that train of thought before it leaves the station. There's no way I'm letting Glenny come near this.

Natural light dulls as evening settles in. The dimming room persuades me to break from music's orderly refuge to flick on the lights. I don't need light to see the keys—muscle memory carries me through the pieces—but I don't like the dark and reason can't move me to accept that day or night makes no difference for when monsters come out to play.

There's a covered plate of food on the credenza by the door. A note written in a slanting, elegant hand explains I didn't look up when Lena, who I assume to be one of Salome's staff, knocked so she left me alone instead of dragging me away to dinner. The chicken and apricot chutney went cold long ago and the salad has deflated beneath the dressing and my neglect.

I take the plate back to the kitchen, not wanting to waste a good meal when I'm indifferent to the thought of food. Meals are one of the many things I have to schedule. Skipping them is all too easy considering how disinterested in eating I usually am. But much like becoming lax with exercise or sleep, there's a definite link between my not eating right and the intensity with which the supernatural reaches me. I'll stash the fancy plate in the fridge for someone who'll enjoy it and slap together a sandwich.

A middle-aged woman, hair greying in wispy streaks, looks up at me from her cleaning when I enter the kitchen.

"You play too beautifully for me to interrupt," she says. An eastern European accent thickens her speech and she motions to the table. "Sit, eat."

"Thanks," I say, "but I'm not that hungry."

"If you don't like it, I make something else for you. Go sit."

"No, it's fine. I don't want to cause you any trouble." I'll scrounge around the kitchen later when I won't be in her way.

"Bah, it's no trouble." She reaches to take the dinner plate away. "What you like?"

"This is fine," I say, sitting down to commit to chicken and chutney. It seems a sin to waste it on me when I couldn't care less if it was cold soup in a can but I don't want her to make another meal on my account.

"You don't like my cooking?" she asks. While her arms are crossed, there's a teasing glint in her eye.

"I'm not a big eater."

"All young men are big eaters. What wrong? You sick?"

"I'm fine."

"Bah. You are a bad liar. I make you something else." She snatches the plate out from under me and holds up a strict finger to cut off my protest. "When I am in the kitchen, I am queen. You do not argue to me. No, sit, sit, I make you something."

She bustles back to the kitchen, searching the refrigerator and pantry for something to appease a picky palate.

"Ms. Salome says you be staying here a while, yes?" she asks.

"Yeah." Hopefully not for long.

"You don't need worry," she says, rifling through the vegetable drawers. "Ms. Salome will help."

"Help with what?"

She peers over the counter dividing the kitchen and dining room. "Help you. That's why you are here? She brought you here, yes?"

I nod and she breaks from her studying of me to shake her head.

"Ah, I see. You do not trust Ms. Salome, do you?"

"I don't know her well enough to have a personal opinion." Of course I don't trust her.

"You think she hides things from you, no?" she asks as she slices up a tomato. "I thought the same when I first met her."

"She's got a right to privacy." Although inviting a stranger into your home is an odd way to keep things to yourself.

Lena's hand hovers indecisively over the stove before turning on a burner.

"Do you believe in demons?" she asks.

I don't answer.

"For a long time I did not," she says. "I thought my parents silly, superstitious. I married a man who thought same thing. He was a good man who got involved with bad people."

Butter hits a hot frying pan to emit a harsh sizzle.

"I did not trust Ms. Trasmoz at first," she says. "But these bad men, they were not satisfied after killing my husband. I had no one for help and nowhere to go."

"What does that have to do with demons?" I can guess, but I want to hear it in her words.

The sky is dark, allowing her reflection to catch in the sliding glass doors leading out to the deck. Every once in a while she'll look up from her cooking to stare out as if it's a window into her past.

"Bad men keep bad company. Whether they know it or not," she says. "These men knew it. They had, how's it say, 'friends in low places'? Ms. Trasmoz … she made it go away. She helped me disappear, gave me a job. Another chance. I would not be here if not for her."

The sizzle of the frying pan sputters and quiets as she turns off the stove.

"She can do same for you. But if you need her help, she need your trust."

"Actually, Lena, this time I need the help," Salome says. Her wet hair is twisted up in a towel and she is perfectly comfortable joining me at the table wearing only a glossy red bathrobe. At least I think that's all she's wearing. I can't say for certain as I'm making a deliberate point in not looking too hard. A difficult task as her loosely tied belt is all manner of distracting.

Lines of concern crinkle Lena's mouth. "What wrong?"

"It's nothing serious," Salome says. "He's got a unique skillset I'm in need of."

Lena gives me another appraising look, deepening the frown lines around her dark eyes.

"What's your schedule tomorrow?" I ask Salome.

"What, you have other plans or something?"

"My morning beauty routine takes—" I bite back the rest of the sentence. Circling each other with sarcasm up and hackles raised ain't gonna do either of us a damn bit of good. And even if she acts like the threat stalking her isn't serious, that doesn't excuse me to do the same.

"I don't function well without routine," I say. Since Salome is counting on me to help keep her alive she deserves to know there are major chinks in my armor. "Having a schedule, even a vague one, helps keep things straight."

"Keep things straight how?" she asks.

I wish she'd tighten the tie on her robe. It's hard to think about anything else.

"I can't always keep track of what's there and what's not. It helps when there's … sometimes …" I run an irritated hand through my hair. I'm unpracticed in articulating that in the absence of being able to count on my senses there needs to be a safety net. That when my ability to make sense of the world falls out of my control, having a schedule to follow, something as simple as a set shower time or an alarm to remind me to eat, keeps me sane.

"I can't control it," I say. "There's no on-and-off switch to what I hear and see. And that makes things difficult. I can't rely on my senses to be consistent, so I make a point to keep everything else predictable."

Salome leans forward. Yep, she's definitely not wearing anything beneath the bathrobe.

"You've tried to control it?" she asks.

I keep my eyes locked on the minimalist blue gradation painting above Salome's head to stop them from drifting down and then down some more. "I've found a few things that can dim the volume."

"Isn't dimming the volume a form of control?"

"That's not control of it. That's learning how to avoid whatever might set it off." A man hanging to a life ring can save himself from drowning. It doesn't give him control of the tides.

"Have you tried?" she asks.

"Tried what?"

"To control it."

"I've spent the last six months trying to do just that," I say.

"I mean have you ever tried to intentionally develop your abilities? Be proactive in what you hear and see."

"Schizophrenia isn't a muscle you can flex," I say. Even if it was, I don't think it's one you'd want to strengthen. I've read Machen and have no desire to see the great god Pan.

"You're not schizophrenic."

This is true. My official diagnosis is Schizoaffective Disorder.

"You talk about your ability as if it's a condition or a curse," she says. "Ever think it might be a gift?"

No one living with this could mistake it for a gift.

"Long and short of it is, I can't control it, switch it off, or direct it in any meaningful way," I say. "That makes me pretty unreliable for most anything, so if you want to change your mind about having me around, it's not gonna offend me."

In fact, I'd think better of her if she showed the common sense to kick me to the curb.

Salome rolls her eyes. "You do realize I wouldn't be here tonight if it wasn't for you, don't you? Whatever impossible standards you've set for yourself, don't project that on to me."

Lena slides a plate of grilled cheese and a bowl of tomato soup toward me.

"A distinguished palate," Salome says.

"Don't tease the poor boy," Lena says. "He is guest."

Salome smiles, speaking to Lena in a foreign language to which the older woman replies, throwing up her hands as she heads back to the kitchen.

"I'm meeting some clients tomorrow starting late morning through early afternoon," Salome says. "I'm planning to leave a little before nine. If you need more time to work out your own scheduling or whatever you need to function, that's fine. Just let me know by eight."

"Roger that."

"And thank you," she says, her expression softening, "for helping me."

***

The single fan in the bedroom is whisper silent. Too quiet to mask the murmurings serving as paranormal peas that make it impossible for a fussy little princess like me to find sleep. My eyes feel like they've been taped open in their refusal to shut and have long adjusted to discern the room's outline from the dark. My imagination has adjusted as well, filling the unfamiliar corners with menacing shapes, and there are no bedside lamps to flick on to dispel the dark fantasies creeping out from what is promising to be a sleepless night. I flip over, away from the walnut dresser, to stop obsessing over the possibility the drawers will slowly open to set free hidden horrors. I stare at the wooden screen dividing the half bathroom from the rest of the bedroom instead. Any moment, luminous eyes and a leering smile will peer out from behind the lattice divide.

I roll onto my back, headboard moaning under my restless shifting, to glare up at the too-quiet fan. I can't shake the feeling something's approaching, a maddening presentiment that didn't have the decency to hold off until morning. I should give up on sleep, do some research, check the locks on all the doors and windows, and channel this restlessness into something productive. Except that breaks the rule: once in bed, stay in bed. Don't entertain agitated imaginings. And I've already given the research route a go to no success. Punching "Salome Trasmoz" into a search returned nothing of value. She's got no social media profiles, no website for her intentionally vague business, and nothing comes up in public record searches or data brokers. By digital standards, Salome Trasmoz doesn't exist.

A creak outside the door sits me up like an electric shock. Not for the first time, I hear footsteps in the hall—the solid step of the living. Almost a dozen staff live in this house and by the sounds of it, they're all night owls with a nosy need to walk by the guest room.

I wait until the steady tromp of feet disappears down the hall before flopping back down onto the bed. Paranoia tempted me to barricade the bedroom door. I decided against it after imagining scenarios where I do, only to hear Salome scream in the night when her supernatural stalker fails to abide by the "thresholds" she has such faith in. I have to shove the dresser and bedside tables out of the way before running down the too many halls of her gigantic house to find her crushed by one of her stupid chandeliers loosened by a poltergeist, or sliced to ribbons from a demon exploding one of those enormous mirrors hanging about. And then I'm convicted for her murder and spend the rest of my days in a straitjacket while trying to explain a sobbing haze monster did it.

I slide onto my stomach and shove my head beneath the pillows. While the fluffy white fabric does nothing to dampen the murmurings, it does take the edge off the creeping sensation I'm being watched. Which, chances are, I might very well be. Just because I can't see them doesn't mean they don't see me.

My cell phone buzzes from the bedside table.

"Hey, Glenny," I say, rolling over to lie flat on my back.

"Titus is being an absolute bear and refusing to go to sleep and today was super terrible and awful so can we talk? Do you have time to talk? Oh, and also Kitty wanted me to call you because you've been ignoring her phone calls and she thought if I called you might answer. So are you free to talk or no?"

"Yeah, what's up?"

Glenny sucks in a massive breath as if she's fortifying herself to make a shamefully painful confession. "Penn keeps trying to talk to me."

I wait a beat, expecting there to be more to Glenny's terrible day than the father of her baby reaching out to her. For once, she doesn't have a long-winded follow-up story.

"Well, shame on him," I say.

"This is serious! He practically ambushed me at the grocery store today!"

"Point or area ambush?"

"I was buying diapers and he was in the same aisle!"

"Was he lurking or did he leap out from behind the shelves?" I ask. Glenny ignores me. All her attention is devoted to the outrage of running into someone she doesn't like but made the mistake of banging anyway.

"And then he followed me to the checkout counter and tried to pay for the diapers. When I said no—well, I said something else but it was pretty clear I wanted him to go away—he said we needed to talk, and I told him no we don't, and he came after me in the parking lot going on about how it'd just be dinner and he just wanted to talk and he wouldn't leave me alone until I pulled out the taser."

"Did you shoot him with it?"

"No, he hid behind a suburban and kept asking me to talk to him."

She pauses and I hazard she's waiting for me to share in her irritation. She's going to be disappointed.

"You should talk to him," I say and don't let Glenny's indignant squawk stop me. "It sounds like he's trying to do the responsible thing and that's saying something as he's had every opportunity to walk away and wash his hands of it."

"But that's what I want him to do!"

"Give him the chance to do what's right."

"I don't want to!"

"Titus deserves a father."

"Yeah, I know, but it's not going to be him!"

Sobbing sounds out from the night and any chance of sleep is burned to ash and blown away.

"I just need to get through the day ..."

I relax a little. The sobbing sounded a lot like the hazy

entity, but this is different. It doesn't carry that malevolent pulse nor does the dark room flicker and bend from a stronger supernatural incursion.

"Logan? Are you still there?"

"I just need ..."

The man's voice is apologetically desperate, and a creeping chill moves over me—the paranormal handshake of the dead introducing himself.

"... under a lot of stress ..." he says.

"I know," a woman's voice answers. *"I'm not here to judge ... I can't imagine what you're going through."*

"I can stop," the man reasserts himself and it's more intuition than evidence that tells me the male voice is the one that belonged to the ghost in life. The woman is an echo of what he heard near his death. *"I can stop. Can stop. Stop. Stop. STOP!"*

The voice collapses back into the hopeless, miserable sobs.

"Logan?" Glenny asks.

"I'm gonna have to call you back."

"Why?"

"Because you're not the only one calling me right now."

"Who's calling you? It's like, one in the morning and—oh my gosh! Is it a ghost? Is that what you're really doing in Austin? Paranormal investigation or something like that?"

"Something like that." I wince as Misery Ghost wails long and sharp. His voice and the woman's blend together.

"Get through ... here to judge ... know ... stop ... can stop ... you're going ... stop."

"You're not going to tell me what you're doing?" Glenny asks.

"Nope."

"Why not?" she huffs.

"Because you're a blabbity-mouth gossip."

"I can't help it!"

"Bye, Glenny," I say and hang up so I can direct my full attention to the second late night caller.

"Get through ... stop ... here. Stop here."

There's an echoing quality to the sobs as if they're carrying over more than distance. I check the corners of the room, expecting to see the shape of a man huddled there, rocking back and forth on his heels.

"Hello?" I call out to the dark. Fear that isn't mine slams into me. My skin turns to ice, my heart races, and my breathing tightens to short shallow gasps.

"Stop ... please stop ... please ..."

The fearful cold lifts so suddenly it leaves me reeling and I clutch the bedsheets as an anchor against the sensation I've missed a step going down. Certain thresholds aren't crossed my ass. The rule of staying in bed for eight hours is gonna have to be tossed out for now. Sure as I am that this crying presence isn't what's after Salome, it can't be coincidence both this haunting and the haze sound so similar in their hopeless abandonment.

I pull my pants back on because I'm more likely to run into a living soul than a dead one and propriety matters, even in the face of the paranormal. The floor is cold beneath my bare feet as I hurry through the halls. The mirrors flash my shadowed reflection in their silver surfaces, but I don't see any haunting hint in the glass as to why this ghost is calling out.

"... stop ... stop ..."

His voice is distant and growing quieter. I don't know if that means I'm moving farther away from what I'm supposed to do, closer to what he wants me to do, or none of the above. Not knowing where Salome sleeps is a major oversight seeing as how I have no idea where to go to check on her. I'm about to start shouting her name when light slipping out from a door left ajar winks in the glass ornaments lining the hall. The door announces me with a soft sigh as I push it open. Salome sits on that winding S-shaped couch, staring out the windows night has turned into a reflective, black wall.

"Trouble sleeping?" she asks, seeing me in the glass.

A pint of ice cream and half full bottle of wine sit on the crystal coffee table in front of her.

"I promise, this started out as something productive." She waves her hand over the closed laptop, her phone, and pages of increasingly untidy handwriting scrawled across them. Different colors of ink underline names, circle dates, and the notes crammed into the side margins are topped off by question marks or heavily crossed out in red.

"I think your house is haunted," I say and give her a quick rundown of the sobbing ghost, how it might relate to the sobbing haze, and tack on an unconvincing argument that I don't think the ghost is out to get her. Only the haze is.

"Can you hear it now?" she asks.

I listen past the murmurings. He's there in the background, muffled sobs and begging. I nod and Salome shakes her head.

"It's not the house that's haunted," she says. "It's you."

"You alright?" I ask as she noncommittally pokes a spoon into the ice cream before going for the wine bottle.

"You might as well join me." She gestures to the couch. There's a faint droop to her words. The late hour and alcohol are taking their toll. "I don't often have company so it'll be a nice change of pace."

"I got the impression you had a rather full social life." I take a seat on the sofa's bend across from her.

Her laugh has more than a dash of bitters in it. "My work is social and it's my life, but that's a far cry from a social life. Do you know the last time I went out for a drink with friends?"

"No."

"Neither do I. And don't look at me like that. We all cope in our own ways."

My thinking she was unbothered by all the supernatural hauntings swirling about her was premature. She just does a better job at keeping her composure than I do. At least when others are watching and when she isn't more than halfway deep into a bottle of wine.

"I must've moved half a dozen times in the first two years," she says. "Looking for a place where I could pretend the paranormal was nothing more than shaky cameras and tricks of the light. I thought if I closed my eyes tight enough I could pretend I never saw anything. All that did was leave me feeling like I was walking on a cliff's ledge blindfolded." She swaps out the wine for the ice cream. "You never had that blindfold, did you?"

I'd count the first twenty-four years of my life as blindfolded and oblivious to the cliff's ledge. By that understanding I'd think someone like Salome, who knows there's a yawning chasm but can't see it, has it rougher than I do. At least my circumstances allow me to see the edge and work to avoid it.

"I don't know whether to be jealous you never had to stumble around in the dark and try to figure it out, or if I should feel sorry for you that you get to see what's at the bottom of the cliff," she says.

I haven't seen what's at the bottom of the cliff. All I've had to witness is the least and meanest that can reach out above the ledge, and I do my best not to stare into the abyss because I know it gazes back. That's part of the reason I'm gun-shy about this supernatural sleuthing gig. I don't want to lean too far over and fall.

"I guess it doesn't matter in the end," she says. "No matter where you go, what you do, it's there. And once you wake up to it, well, neither of us can sleep now. Can we?"

She picks up the wine bottle and I catch hold to stop her from taking another drink.

"You've had enough."

She raises a challenging eyebrow but doesn't resist when I take the bottle away.

"You should leave. I didn't mean it like that," she says when I stand to go. "I mean, if you want to leave, not get involved, I won't blame you. It'd be better for you if you didn't. This isn't your problem and it doesn't have to be your business."

She pokes the spoon a couple more times into the ice cream before tossing it away. The silverware clangs across the glass table and onto the floor.

"If you're going to leave, do it now," she says. "You wouldn't be the first and I'd prefer you get it over with."

Her legs wobble when she stands and I catch her before she totters into the coffee table.

"Sorry," she says. "I'm not usually this much of a mess, but it's been a hell of a week."

I nod. I've been there.

She takes the arm I offer to keep her on her feet.

"You must think I'm pathetic," she says.

"No." Usually I'm much more of a mess than this so I can't throw any stones.

She leads the way to her bedroom and I let her go at the door.

"You can come in," she says. "I'm a big girl and not embarrassed to have a man in the room."

"No, you were right," I say. "There are certain thresholds that aren't crossed."

"Are you ever going to give me your real name?"

"Goodnight, Salome." I close the door between us.

I don't go back to the guest bedroom. I can't put that much distance between us after hearing the sobbing echo through her home and there's a sitting space hosting a perfectly adequate couch across the hall from her room.

Chapter 9

I rolled over to give Maria the warmed side of the bed.

"How'd it go?" I asked.

"You didn't watch?" she huffed, feigning offense.

"It's not good for my blood pressure." I never watched her interviews, tuned into her debates, or clicked on any links that led to articles or video clips of her. She could take all the slings and arrows that came courtesy of being a political commentator. I couldn't. Every time I got wind of some punk on the internet writing nasty comments about my wife, she had to drag me down from going out to find him.

"It went fine. We're looking to set up a second interview next month," she said. "You know, you get more riled up and worried about me and my work than I do about yours. No one's shooting at me at my job."

"If I die, you should remarry," I say.

Maria sat up. "Where did that come from?"

"Don't mope around or feel like it's disrespecting my memory," I said. "Move on."

"Isn't that my choice?"

"Ah, let's face it, you could've done better, and you might get the chance."

"Don't joke about this."

"Just promise you won't wait around for … Maria?"

She rolled over so her back was toward me.

"Maria, what's wrong?"

"I don't want to talk about it."

"About what? Did something go wrong in the interview?"

"No. I don't want to talk about you dying," she said.

"You know we're gonna have to."

"Haven't we talked about it enough?"

"If you don't want to talk about it now, I'm gonna bring it up later, so I'd prefer we do it now since you're already mad at me."

She rolled back to face me. "Fine. Then just know anything you expect of me goes the same for you. If you say I should move on, so should you. If I die, you remarry, have seven children, and I don't want to see you until you reach ninety-two. Deal?"

I smiled and brushed loose hair from her face. "Deal."

Those were easy demands to agree to. There was no doubt in my mind who'd have to honor them.

***

I fumble for my phone in the dark and curse when I can't find it. I sit up and it takes a few confused blinks for me to remember where I am. The couch wasn't as comfortable as it looked and a stiff back joins the many reasons I carry chronic tension. I press my palms to my eyes in a vain attempt to find the fading fragments of the dream. It'd be easier to hold smoke in hand. This isn't the first time I've had a dream I know has held some greater significance. It's also not the first time I've forgotten most of the damn thing save for the ill-omened feeling the moment I wake up.

The door to Salome's room is closed. The weak light

slipping beneath suggests she survived the night, is awake, and I'm relieved from the graveyard shift. Bleary-eyed and operating on brain-saver mode from broken sleep, I stumble into the kitchen and curse again when I see the time on the stove clock.

6:37.

I overslept by eighty-seven minutes. That means eighty-seven burpees. If you're going to keep a regimen there has to be consequences when you fail to uphold it.

The house is tomb quiet as I grab my workout clothes from the guest room and head out to the backyard. I carry out my penance for oversleeping on the strip of lawn between the pool and the trees sheltering Salome's home from neighbors' eyes. Speeding through the set summons up a sweat sufficient to ward off the cool morning and makes the saltwater pool look mighty tempting.

I don't bother to take off my shirt or shorts as I step in. They're already soaked and salted. The water temperature hovering in the low sixties prickles my skin, reminding me too much of unseen, chilled hands reaching out for me. I cut to the chase and dive under. I joined the swim team in high school because I was too short to play basketball and only a dumbass would go for wrestling to grope sweaty guys on a mat when signing up for swim meant I could spend the majority of practice watching girls in swimsuits do their drills in the next lane over. I never won any meets. My "lack of attention" during practice kept me a solidly mediocre swimmer.

Swimming doesn't provide the same rhythmic retreat that running does, but the disturbed water rushing against the pool's side masks the murmurs. It's easy to pretend they're nothing more than the hush of water lapping against stone.

I figure it's only a matter of time before that sobbing voice comes back. The sense of something waiting nearby hasn't let up. It's burrowed under my skin to wind my nerves tight and agitated.

Movement in the corner of my eye jolts me to a stop in the middle of the pool. I'm both annoyed by the interruption and relieved it's only Salome, not anything more ghoulish.

"What is it?" I ask. The question comes out curt. Unless she needs immediate help I'd rather finish some semblance of a morning workout alone. It's the only time I get anything close to quiet.

"Did you fall in?" she asks, raising a teasing eyebrow down at me. Coffee in one hand, she places the towel I forgot to grab on a lounging chair.

"It was dark," I say.

She walks over to the pool edge and crouches down. Her date with the wine bottle from last night doesn't look like it gave her a hangover to remember it by. If anything, she looks like she got a full night's sleep.

"Aren't you cold?" she asks.

"It's fine as long as you keep moving," I say and shiver.

"I feel like you never say what you mean."

"But I do mean what I say." I push over to the pool's edge. "Do you need something?"

"There's breakfast. Come in and join me when you're finished," she says. "We can go over the day and make sure we're on the same page."

She tosses me the towel as I clamber out from the pool. "What about you, do you need anything? A change of clothes? You never told me how far away you live. If it's not worth the drive I can have something picked up for you."

"Don't worry about it, I'm not …" I trail off. I made a rule about not wearing the same set of clothes two days in a row. While fresh clothes don't do anything directly to keep the supernatural away, not changing clothes is one of the first backward steps into the despondency that lets the darker denizens in.

Whether it's a memory or really there, I hear the entity calling out, waiting for me to slip back into the depression that acts as its best doorway in.

"Actually," I say, "I'd appreciate a change of clothes."

***

I should've known better. Never let a woman pick out your clothes. Maria was terrible at it. Salome is worse. While I applaud the expediency with which she sent someone scurrying out to find a store open at this early hour, I wholly condemn what she chose. The pants are effeminately tight and the button-down shirt is specifically designed not to be tucked in, an abomination that almost convinces me to go back on my rule of not wearing the same outfit two days straight.

"Everything fit alright?" Salome asks as I come down the stairs to join her at the small breakfast nook off from the main dining room.

"The pants are too small," I say as thanks for her going out of her way for me.

She looks me over and shakes her head. "No, they fit right."

That she waits until I finish a cup of coffee before starting in on conversation earns her more than a handful of points in my book.

"I want to apologize," she says.

"For what?" I brace myself for some sinister revelation.

"I was on edge yesterday and I took that out on you. I didn't show the thanks you deserved and should've been more open. You had every right to walk away after how snappish I was, so thank you."

"I'll give you plenty of reason to be snappish at me before the day is done, so there's no need for thanks or apologies." Although I claim her offering an olive branch wasn't necessary, a palpable tension lifts and it's easier to share the same table. "Besides, I wasn't doing anything to earn courtesy. Acting like you not falling into hysterics was the same as you not being bothered by the thing that's after you wasn't fair."

"Well, now that we've made some progress forward, I'm going to risk setting us all back to square one," she says. "Look, I get that you don't like talking about it—or about much anything really, but I need to know what you can do so I can best plan out how to solve this situation I'm in."

I feel Lena's judging glare from the kitchen as I scoot the eggs Florentine she made back and forth over the plate. "Need to know what, exactly?"

"Can you see spirits? Hear the dead? Or is it just a sense? Can you speak to them? If so, is it complete conversations? Are you precognizant? Can you call ghosts to you?"

I stop pushing the English muffin over the thickening yolk trail. Salome vastly overestimates what I bring to the table. Most everything she's asked presupposes a level of control.

"I hear the dead. Sometimes see them," I say. "I'll get visions or have dreams every once in a while and sometimes I hear and see other things."

"What other things?" she asks.

"I don't know what they are." I think they'd be best described as demonic. They're certainly not angels. My left hand taps out a tune against the too-tight pant leg. The thought of admitting such forces prowl this world makes me uneasy. Forget saying it out loud.

Salome doesn't press. She waits for me to continue which I more than appreciate.

"I know when things are wrong. When things are there that shouldn't be," I say.

Salome takes hold of my hand. The gesture catches me off guard as does the warmth of her touch.

"I make it a practice not to pry," she says, "and I know this isn't easy on you, but I need more specifics than that. Not to be overdramatic, but my life does depend on it."

"It's not …" I mean to pull my hand away but rediscovering the simple comfort of living touch is hard to retreat from.

"It's not something you've really ever talked about before?"

Glenny is the only person I've come close to discussing this with and around her I often don't need to say anything. It's left me woefully unprepared to articulate what my relation to the supernatural is in a way a sane person will take seriously and not assume I'm suffering psychosis. Whenever I tried to explain the murmurings and all their malice to the doctors at St. Jude it got written off as bad brain chemistry.

"Start at the beginning if that helps," Salome says.

Yeah, it all started in Afghanistan and that's not a story I'm going to dredge up. That bit of personal history is a little much this early on in our partnership. I give her the story of Billy Davis instead, what it was like to hear him night after night, the cold chills and pulls to go out and find his corpse. I tell her how those sensations are far from uncommon. The rarity is when they're attached to something specific.

"What else?" she asks.

I hesitate, reluctant to go into last summer's events. That's a much more personal and complicated story that I don't want to share with a stranger.

"Take your time," she says, "but I need to know."

Again she waits for me to string it all together. I redact most of it, keeping names and places private, no mention of Silvia Lopez, Glenny, or Burns. The killing of a serial murderer by a pregnant teen and psychiatric patient made national news for a day and stayed in more local cycles for a week. Anything more than vague details would make it easy for Salome to find the story and learn about Glenny, and I don't want her dragged into this. Not even by association.

In place of physical specifics, I describe as much as I can about the dreams and visions, being called to Silvia's corpse, and how she kept after me until I found who murdered her. Saying out loud all that's been haunting me is a massive weight off the chest. It turns it into a problem that can be solved, not a secret that has to be suffered, and my jaw no longer feels like it's wired shut in an effort to keep the truth from slipping out.

"Were any of those 'other things' you mentioned present any of those times?" Salome asks. I'm reminded she's holding my hand when she gives an encouraging squeeze.

"Yes." The thought of the entity gets my skin prickling like the temperature has taken a ten-degree dive.

"Like what?"

I steal Lena's question from the night before. "Do you believe in demons?"

"Of course." She gives her answer more readily than I did.

"You might call it that."

She goes quiet and I'm afraid she doesn't believe me. Which is stupid. Not only in that there's no reason to think she wouldn't, but I shouldn't care for her opinion either way.

"Is one of those 'other things' what you saw yesterday?" she asks.

I shake my head. "No, that was something else."

She sighs in relief, leading me to think she's had more than her fair share of demonic intrusions.

"When you come across those 'other things,' how did you fight them?" she asks.

"You don't. You run, hide, and pray."

Chapter 10

I flip the blood orange slice across the charcuterie board, up the capicola and over the soft cheese log, doing my best to look like I'm not canvassing the room. I saw it on a television show you're not supposed to eat while you're in the field as you never know when you'll have to run, so the platter of fancy cheeses and cured meats remains untouched. Well, more like uneaten. Restless fidgeting has me sorely tempted to see how high of a tower I can stack the cheese into. I'm not too concerned about looking unprofessional as I've already lost eyes on my target and you can't get much more unprofessional than that.

I know Salome purposefully set me up here so she'd be out of my line of sight and that riles me. She's been right ornery about prioritizing the privacy of her clients over her personal safety. The corner table she called ahead to have set aside for me couldn't be more poorly positioned. I can see the front door fine but not the full room. Entire sections of the dining floor are obscured by decorative walls that come up short of reaching the ceiling. Their sole purpose is to hold abstract paintings, modern wall sculptures, and assure patrons they're sitting in a place of money. The opposite side of the restaurant behind the decorative walls is divided into closed-off, private dining rooms, and I bet Salome's meeting her client in one of those.

She's spent the last four hours flitting from posh office building to fancy restaurant to upscale bar. I've spent that time in Art Deco lobbies, waiting rooms where the furniture is more expensive than my car, and tucked away in corners of frilly dining rooms like this one, sitting around with both thumbs up my ass.

This ritzy restaurant attracts a crowd who prefers a later lunch. Men and women in suits talk logistics and negotiate over sea bass and white wine. The intense conversations of attorneys leaning their heads together is contrasted against the high-spirited business representative going the full nines to make a good impression. He jumps up from his leather dining chair to shake hands of arriving party members and encourages the waiters to be generous with the drinks.

I start stacking up the cheese into a tower. If I knew supernatural stakeouts would be this dull I'd have brought a book. So far I haven't seen anything worse than a man in a business suit wearing tennis shoes. Both Kitty and Mark have informed me this is an unforgivable fashion faux pas, and if either of them becomes Pope of the world, such offenses will earn immediate excommunication from civil society. As someone who has put his pants on inside out at least twice in the past month, I don't have a lot of room to judge. Getting dressed in the morning can be a rough affair when the murmurings are having a day.

The one upside to this stakeout is that those murmurings are pretty calm today. They're little more than a background hush that muddles into the conversations of the living buzzing through the crowded dining room. So long as I don't have to pay attention to any particular speaker, living or otherwise, it's tolerable.

My cellphone hums with a text from Salome telling me she's finished and to meet her on the north street corner.

"Well? Did you sense anything?" She spares me a brief glance up from her phone as I walk over to join her.

"Nothing," I say, irritated to see her waiting for me. It means she and her client used a back entrance to keep his identity private as I had eyes on the main entrance the whole time. Which begs the question why I'm here at all if Salome doesn't want me to keep an eye on her.

"Don't look so disappointed," she says. "Nothing is much better than something."

Jorge the driver—Salome's security man who was dogging me around her house yesterday—looks like he wants to smash my head into the side of the Bentley when I open Salome's door before he can. The vein throbbing in his temple thickens as I slide into the back seat beside her. It isn't simply my stepping on his toes when I open the door for Salome that has him apoplectic. He's been radiating hostility since he took the driver's seat this morning and he hasn't missed a chance to send a death glare my way via the rearview mirror.

"The Driskill, Jorge," Salome says, using a thin stylus to jot down a few notes on her phone.

"Yes, Ms. Trasmoz." If Jorge grits his teeth any tighter they're gonna chip.

Salome ignores the radio's hissing as we drive. She didn't so much as raise an eyebrow this morning when the radio broke into its first fit as we pulled out of her driveway, and my admitting the radio talks to me only got a single head nod from her.

"Today's a light day," she says, putting her phone away to change her earrings from the hoop sort to a more dangly sort. "This is my last appointment. Do you want to go back to the house afterward, or get an early dinner at the Driskill?"

She swaps out her shoes next. The high heel black shoe is changed out for a higher heel black shoe.

"That question was directed to you." She pokes her toe into my leg.

"If you think you're safe at home, you should get back there soon as you can," I say. The vulnerability she showed last night is gone. She's back to acting as though this is no more inconvenient than her phone running low on battery.

"True, but hiding at home isn't going to help me figure out who's at the root of all this," she says.

"I'm not going to use you as bait."

"You're not using me at all. It's the other way around." She looks at me for a reaction and rolls her eyes when she doesn't get one. "That was a joke."

"Ha," I say, the sarcasm steamroller flattening my tone.

"This must all seem rather silly to you." She switches out her necklace for a new one.

"I warned you I wasn't going to be much use," I say. The waiting around for some supernatural horror to rear its head is more straining than silly. That nothing wicked this way has come is a stroke of good fortune I should appreciate. Being unable to tolerate good things, I don't appreciate it. I'm getting more and more agitated over nothing happening and that I'm just another accessory Salome has to tote around.

"I meant me changing costumes between meetings." She pulls out a compact to touch up her makeup, thickening the eyeliner and mascara.

"Looks more exhausting than ridiculous."

Maria constantly complained about the image aspect of the business, always having to accessorize and adjust her appearance based on audience. Salome operates in a similar field where image is the first weapon fired.

"Actually, it's one of the more enjoyable parts of the job," she says. "It's a little reset between each meeting. I get a moment to refresh and start again."

"Just give me a heads up if you need to change anything more personal than blazers," I say as she trades out the pale blue blazer for a glossy black one.

"You know people claim the Driskill is haunted," she says as we pull up outside the Romanesque hotel. "Colonel Driskill himself is said to wander the halls."

"I'll let you know if he hollers," I say.

Salome gives me a look I can't read. "There are people I know who'd kill, or worse, to be able to hear and see what you can."

"Yeah, I know stupid people too," I say, and she laughs.

"You can wait in the lobby. I had to twist my client's arm to get him to agree to meet me more publicly, so for the sake of his privacy, I'd appreciate you giving us a bit more space," she says.

She's given me a similar speech at each stop and each time I hear it I get a little closer to refusing to play along.

"We'll be in the bar," she says. "Don't worry, this won't be long."

She exits first. Jorge will drive down a block or so before I'll get out and follow. If a someone in addition to a something is stalking Salome, we shouldn't make it too obvious we're together. That was her idea and one I was reluctant to agree to. If a haze monster comes calling, I'm not sure I can sprint the distance of separation to get to her in time.

A wave of traffic holds Jorge hostage as he moves to merge back onto the street. He swears, having to jerk back toward the sidewalk as a muscle car barrels by, blaring its horn. Jorge responds with top-notch professionalism, flipping the bird and getting more colorful in his curses.

"Wait, wait! Stop!" I say right as Jorge gets the perfect chance to slide back into traffic. If looks could kill, I'd be a smoldering pile of ash ruining Salome's leather seats as he swings the car back to the curb side.

I ignore Jorge's unspoken promise of death and slide over to the passenger side of the backseat for a better view. Square-face is on the move, bulldozing a path down the sidewalk and heading straight for the Driskill. I pull out my phone and snap a couple photos to see if Salome knows him from somewhere. If not, at least she'll have a way to recognize him in the future.

Jorge doesn't say anything when I hop out after Square-face. He waits for another opening in the traffic then drives off.

The Driskill's lobby is a torture chamber of motion and echoing voices battering my senses. People bustle about the columns, pause to take pictures, or hurry by in a mess of frenzied movement. Their chatter bounces off marble floors and high coffered ceilings, shrinking the spacious chamber so it feels claustrophobically small. The crowd's chaos is easy to disappear into and I don't see Square-face lurking around any of the pale pillars or skulking up the sweeping stairs toward the bar on the second floor.

A cold hand clamps on my shoulder and I almost turn until I remember there's a wall right behind me. No one could be there. No one living that is.

"Careful, pal," I mutter to who or whatever is reaching out to me. "You might give people the idea this place is haunted."

That must've been the insensitive thing to say because the sobbing starts up.

"Please. Stop. Going through ... stop."

I take out the notebook, a struggle as the pant pockets are ridiculously tight, and make a mark under the log I'm keeping for this haunting headed "M" for Misery. Tugs join the grip on my shoulder. They pull at my arms and hands, giving no clear direction of which way to go.

"Get through. Going. Get through. Stop, stop!"

The fear Misery felt rushes through me. It's the kind of terror that rends away hope and reason, found in the moment a man understands he's seconds away from death and helpless to stop it. I've been there.

"STOP!"

The chatter of the living collapses away so suddenly it's like a sinkhole's opened beneath to swallow them whole. The floor shudders and I grab the couch for support, feeling the dizzy, spinning rush that follows standing up too quickly. No one in the silenced lobby pauses or gives any indication they've felt the tremor. They can't hear the sick, slithering sound like rotted flesh being dragged across dead leaves. They can't feel this presence, a hungry breath that threatens to blister skin, crack lips, and turn the air unbreathable. I can't see it as I can the entity, but there's no denying it carries the promise of damnation. This isn't a ghost or that sobbing haze. This is something that's never belonged to the world of the living.

The white columns of the lobby warp, the floor tiles crack to let loose veins of sepia, pulsing dark across my vision. The murmurings rise to greet this new terror escaped from the veil and their voices find greater clarity as the physical world crumbles. A dark form trails after a man whose features are washed out by the sepia blur. Another shade drifts behind the woman walking beside him. The murmurings shape themselves into parasitic shadows clinging to the people passing by, and for the first time, I understand them.

He needs to do it, one says. *One lie. A small lie. They'll never have to know. He has a family after all. He can't take the fall.*

The shade drifting behind a woman turns its eyeless face toward me and its mouth splits open into a leer. The final lines of the prayer to St. Michael, "and all the evil spirits who prowl about the world seeking the ruin of souls," takes on a disturbingly immediate reality.

She told them she said no and they locked him away. She took away his future and she'd do it all again.

He's indifferent to their suffering. He takes pride in it.

Her ruin is her pleasure. She lives to see her made small. Tear her down, make her lesser.

I race for the stairs leading up to the bar. Each running step has the sluggish sense of trying to flee a nightmare. I don't have to know who the ringleader of this dark carnival is to know I need to get Salome out of here. The world moans as the slithering presence more intimately invades the physical world. Its rise from the sepia threatens to send all else into oblivion.

A little lie that ruined a thousand lives, a murmuring croons.

The presence manifests itself in a descending, fungal rot. It seeps out from the walls, curdles over the ceiling, and flows in the direction of the Driskill's bar. I bound up the stairs two at a time and collide into someone or something. It's hard to be sure as the whole world is dissolving into shrouds of meaningless shape and motion. I can't tell what's real and what's wretched. I can hardly see the stairs I climb as I chase after the black, fungal entity. I brace myself against the entryway to the bar, overcome by the terrible sense that I'm standing on a narrow ledge and the slightest misstep will send me tumbling down to where the murmurings rise from.

She leads them to us, seeks to bring them down to us. She'll drag them down, and down, and down.

I grip the doorframe tight in hand and will the room to come into focus. The feel of the wood, the blood pounding in my ears, the copper tang as I bite the inside of my mouth provide the sensations to link me back to the physical world lost behind the sepia.

He wants power that he's too weak to hold. It makes him ours. He'll be ours.

Salome sits on a couch beside a fireplace and across from a middle-aged man, their heads close together in deep conversation. Their placement in the eye of the storm gives them surreal clarity among the rotting mass pulsing around them. There's intelligence in the way the blackness moves, a spider-like delicacy to the feelers reaching out, tugging on invisible strands of web to pull snared prey in.

He'll be ours. He'll be ours.

The blackness doesn't have a face but I feel it shift a fraction of its attention to me.

Don't interfere. Its voice blisters cold in my mind and pushes thought and reason to the point of breaking.

I dash over and yank Salome away from the dark strands uncurling inches from her throat.

"What are you doing?" she hisses, staring at me like I'm the monster. "We're in the middle—"

"Time to go," I say. The rot doesn't charge in as I drag her away. It hovers above us as if there's an invisible line it can't cross. Its want for harm has no such restrictions. I feel the hate pouring from the blackness, bringing the burn of bile to the back of my throat.

The murmurings share in its fury at my interference and scream, *He's ours! He's ours!*

"Let go!" Salome digs her high heels in, oblivious to the evil hanging over us. "I'm in the middle of something!"

Damn right she is. That the presence doesn't lash out a slithering feeler to snare us is almost as unsettling as me seeing it at all. It has me second-guessing my plan for immediate extraction, like I'm somehow playing exactly into the hands of harm. I have no confidence getting Salome away from here will do anything, but it's better than staying and letting that thing go through with what it came here to do.

"Goddammit, let go!" Salome hisses.

"If you don't cut that out," I say, tightening my sweat-slick hold on her, "I'm going to sling you over my shoulder and carry you out."

"Ma'am, is he bothering you?" Two men move to intercept us at the bar's entrance. They've mistaken me as the threat and are completely unaware of the black rot they're standing in as it runs decaying feelers over them.

Salome stops wriggling to get free. "No, my brother just doesn't like bars."

She waves the men away, and just like that, the fungal entity folds back into the walls. In the space of a startled breath, it's gone. The murmurings return to muffled obscurity, the sepia veil lifts, and the bar solidifies back to looking like it was ripped straight from a cattle baron's mansion instead of the fifth circle of hell. I'm unfooled by the change—just because I can't see an evil presence doesn't mean it's not there. Salome isn't safe here.

"What is it?" she asks in a hostile whisper as I lead her out of the bar and down the stairs.

"Get Jorge to bring the car around." I scan the walls and ceiling, certain at any moment the blackness is going to lunge out at us. "We're leaving."

"*Stop!*" My new paranormal partner, Misery, gives his two cents. Brushing him off is easy. His screaming is nothing compared to what the murmurings revealed. I can't believe I ever let something as small fry as a crying ghost rattle me.

I keep hold of Salome as I rush her through the lobby and straight past Square-face. I don't glance over or give sign I recognize him but he's not stupid. By the way he openly stares at us, he knows he's been made and has no bones about pretending otherwise. A haze monster appears when Square-face is at the bus stop and a pants-wetting mass of damnation in black fungal form comes calling to the same hotel he's darkening. What are the odds of that?

I expect the pressure that heralds the haze monster to crash down on us the moment we step outside. Nothing comes and the air is so weightless and free of preternatural presence that it tricks me into a spell of lightheadedness like I'm at too high an altitude and can't breathe right. Jorge pulls up to the curb and I spare no delay for dignity, shoving Salome in and myself after her before the car comes to a complete stop.

"Go!" I snap when he doesn't speed off the moment we're in.

Square-face follows us out of the hotel and his narrowed eyes fix on the car. He doesn't turn into a monstrous bat-winged creature to give chase, nor do dark, demonic hands reach out from his torso to drag us back. We turn the corner and he disappears from the rear window like any other flesh and blood creature would.

"You going to tell me what that was about?" While Salome's tone is dangerously tight, it's nowhere near as threatening as the giant black corruption was so I don't know who she's trying to intimidate here.

"Do you recognize this man from anywhere?" I show her the picture of Square-face on my phone.

"No."

"Keep an eye out for him. He's following you."

"And?"

"And that's it." I don't see what's so difficult to grasp about "there's a guy following you, watch out for him."

"That's it? That's why you came barging in and pulled me out? Because you think some nobody is following me?" she asks, voice and temper rising. "Jesus Christ, do you have any idea what you interrupted?"

No, I don't know what was swarming around her and her client other than that it was malignant, so if she wants to go on a tear because I broke up her party before Belphegor could crash it, she's welcome to it. Sure enough, she lays into me, raging on about me ruining a life-changing deal, undoing months of work, risking her relationship with her clients, so on and so forth. I stare out the window, searching for the faintest hint the natural world threatens to yield to an unfriendly visitor.

Her hand snakes up to grab my chin and jerk my head around to face her.

"You look at me when I talk to you," she says.

"And you keep your hands to yourself." I pluck her hand off me. "If you don't like the way I operate, pull over, and I'll leave."

Her face tightens as if she's seriously considering it.

"I already gave you the chance to walk away," she says. "That was a one-time offer."

"Then save the tantrum. You asked me to do something and I don't care how much I gotta upset your cushy little life of fancy cocktails and high-rolling clients to get it done. I'll do as I damn well see fit. Got it?"

Her eyes narrow and lips slightly part. She looks like she's either about to kick me out of a car moving at forty miles per hour or skip the foreplay and dive straight into unnecessarily angry sex.

Her phone pings, a tiny scissor snip cutting the backseat tension. Even Jorge looks relieved when Salome breaks the staring contest to glance down at her phone and sigh.

"Who is it?" I ask. Not that it's any of my business. I'm just looking for any material to build a wall of inane small talk between us.

"Clients." Her thumbs fly furiously over her phone screen. "Angry clients."

I'm not hungry for a fight, so I go back to staring out the window instead of snapping at the bait she's dangling.

"You're a goddamn pain, you know that?" she says.

I do, but we both have more pressing problems than my character flaws.

"So what did you see?" she asks, making an effort at civility.

"Was that a new client at the Driskill's bar?" I ask.

She hesitates a moment before answering, "Relatively. We were finalizing a contract. Why?"

Although my suspicions fall mainly on Square-face, I can't write off the man Salome was meeting as being uninvolved. Was he bait to lure her in? Or is he even more directly involved? I press a couple fingers to my temple, regretting not getting a better look at the client to see if any supernatural stain clung to him. I don't recall what he looked like at all. I was much too distracted by that black entity eroding physical matter and reeking of damnation. Remembering how it welled up from the walls and ceiling like discharge from a wound, how it encouraged the murmurings to greater clarity, and its cold warning for me not to interfere sucks the breath out of my lungs.

"You alright?" Salome asks when I fail to repress a shiver.

"Fine."

For simplicity's sake, I hope the haze monster and black mold monster are in cahoots, different minions serving the same agenda—though their behavior doesn't line up to support them sharing a goal. The haze monster's desire to see Salome dead extended to having a degree of influence over the physical world. I don't know what that rotting fungal entity was aiming to do as it didn't appear to have any real physical influence. It gave the murmurings face and voice, made my entity stalker look like a Chihuahua in comparison, and felt like it could drag the whole world under if it wanted. So why didn't anything more dramatic come from its crawling out of the abyss? The haze monster collapsed a construction site and blew out a car's tire, yet the rotting entity effected no tangible change despite it feeling like the greater evil.

I tap an agitated tune on the car seat. Square-face being at the construction site and hotel leads me to think he's the connection and the best angle to chase. Him being the root cause keeps it simple and is the preferable theory to the possibility Salome's very presence undoes the locks holding back a menagerie of monsters.

Salome rests a hand on my arm. "Hey, are you sure you're alright?"

"Yeah." The disconnect brought up by the rotting entity won't fade. The physical world feels like it's miles away and hollowed out of substance.

She doesn't press for a better response as we turn off the main road over a narrow bridge crossing the Colorado River. Long driveways cutting through thick oak and scrub hide the large houses set deep in sprawling properties. Mailboxes built into white stucco pillars and the occasional glimpse of clay-colored Spanish tile roofs rising above the trees are the only evidence that the winding driveways lead to homes and don't twist endlessly on.

Jorge takes the branched private street, slowing as the way narrows, and follows it to the very end where it thins into Salome's gated driveway.

"Thank you, Jorge," she says when he pulls up to the house and turns off the car engine. "We'll be inside in a moment."

"You sure?" He sounds very reluctant to leave his employer alone with me.

"Go on ahead."

He shoots half a dozen disapproving glances back at the car as he circles around to the staff side of the house.

"What did you see?" she asks again.

Good question. Dark fungal mass sounds more like an uninvited house guest you battle using bleach, not an evil entity that eats away at the fragile divide between the natural world and darker realities.

"You can tell me," she says. Her phone pings. She ignores it.

I don't really want to talk about it, the same way you don't want to open your mouth when you've been dragged underwater. You want to hold your breath as long as you can and hope to kick free before you're too far down.

"Everything seemed normal to you at the Driskill?" I ask.

"I don't know why you don't believe me when I say I don't sense what you do," she says.

Because I don't believe you when you say you believe me.

"How did it start?" she asks.

"What do you mean?"

"What you saw at the Driskill, did it start with a feeling? A vision? Did you hear something like movement or speaking? What got your attention that something was going on?"

"The murmurings got louder. And they said things."

"Aren't they always saying things?"

"This is the first time I've understood them."

Salome puts her finger to pressed lips, looking like she's going to ask how I feel about it or some other stupid therapist-like question that'll do nothing to solve anything.

"What did they say?" she asks.

"I think they were saying people's sins." Either that or I was hearing the evil they encourage people to commit, revealing hidden desires as well as deeds.

"Can you hear what they're saying now?" she asks and I shake my head.

"It wasn't just the murmurings, there was this other presence, I could hear it moving," I say. "Everything started to feel distant, drained of substance, and then it showed up and surrounded you."

"So you could see it?"

I nod.

"Can you describe it?" she asks and I'm grateful that she's being so clinical about this. None of the shit I got asked when I made the mistake of trying to talk to anyone about this sort of thing before. No tired questions like what do I think caused this episode, how did it make me feel, how was I feeling before and after it started, or have I been taking my medication as prescribed.

"It looked like the black mold version of the Blob with …" I wave my hands back and forth, moving my fingers in what I hope conveys how it reached out for Salome and her client.

She doesn't laugh, which is nice of her.

"Are you sure you don't recognize that man from anywhere?" I ask. Square-face is the best lead I have and it'd be very much appreciated if Salome was able to give me a name, address, and phone number to find him by.

She shakes her head. "No. But I doubt he's the one causing this batch of trouble."

"Why?"

"He's not the type."

"You'd bet your life on that?" I ask, thinking she's too quick to brush off him being present at the scene of both incidents. It has me thinking she might be lying, that she does know Square-face from somewhere, and that knowledge turns him into a dismissible annoyance, not a threat.

Salome smiles the way women do when a guy is missing something obvious. "You might be able to see and hear all sorts of things, but you're not very good at seeing people."

Chapter 11

"Are you sure you're safe here?" I ask for the twenty-seventh time, hovering at the entrance to the dining room.

Salome sits at the table, flicking between the screens of her laptop, phone, and tablet, and making notes on an expanding spread of paper.

"I'm sure." She checks the ping from her phone before returning to her laptop. "It's you who needs convincing. You should eat something before you go. Lena's been fretting nonstop over how little you ate at breakfast."

She pushes the platter of cucumber bites and baguette slices topped by cheese and bell pepper Lena prepared toward me.

"So you're really sure you're safe?" I ask. Leaving Salome even for a short while feels wrong, like I'm abandoning my post. But I'm not going to figure anything out playing reactive defense as I tail after her, and I'm already too fed up with haze monsters, black mold demons, and sobbing ghosts to be patient. And who knows, maybe my bumbling around Austin in hopes of picking up a supernatural trail will earn me another run-in with Square-face. Our crossing paths is shaping into a trend and I wouldn't mind a more direct meeting.

"Are you going to tell me where you're going?" she asks.

"I don't know yet," I say.

"This man of mystery thing is getting old, and if you don't give me a real name soon, I'm going to come up with one for you."

"I was being honest. I don't know where I'm going and that annoys me far more than it does you." Other than a chance run-in with Square-face, I don't know what I'm looking for. I just hope I'll recognize it when I see it, and I know I won't see it here.

"Fine, take whatever car you want." She waves her hand in aggravated blessing for my field expedition.

"I'm fine with walking," I say.

"Are you always this goddamn difficult?"

"I can't drive."

"You can't drive? What, are you going to tell me you're actually blind and only have 'spirit vision' or something?"

I count to ten to keep myself from saying something stupid.

"I can drive," I amend, "but I shouldn't."

Salome waits for an explanation.

"I told you I have a bad habit of losing track of what's real and what's not really there. That complicates getting behind the wheel."

Admitting that shortfall was painful, though not as bad as admitting I sleep better with a nightlight.

"See, that wasn't so hard, was it? You give me a straight answer, we make progress, and now we're on the same page," she says. "Jorge can drive you."

***

I'm sure of it now. Jorge doesn't like me. That's not really any loss as the feeling is mutual. In fact, other than Lena, I'd prefer to avoid all of Salome's staff. Something about them

105

rubs me wrong. It could be that they're all inclined to look at me like I'm something unpleasant tracked into the house on the bottom of a shoe. Jorge was about as pleased as I was when Salome insisted he be the one to chauffer me around and neither of us is enjoying the field trip of him driving me back to the construction site collapse, then to the open-air bar where Square-face watched Salome from across the street, then to the Driskill, and when that dredges up neither supernatural haunt nor squarish-shaped human, we drive the loop all over again. I don't count Misery as anything dredged up because he never left. He's been a soundtrack of nonstop sobbing playing in the background interspersed by his occasional pleas to "stop." I'd like him to take his own advice and cut it out. Or at least be more articulate in his wailing.

"Anywhere else?" Jorge asks. After over an hour of us circling around and nothing to show for it, the thick vein pulsing in his forehead is close to bursting. My incompetency when it comes to supernatural sleuthing is going to give him a stroke.

"Try the construction site again," I say and his eyes bug out of his skull there's so much steam he needs to blow. I'm not trying to antagonize him. It's just an unintended benefit.

The car radio flares. Illuminated numbers spin into nonsense symbols as it plunges through the stations. A second vein jumps out from Jorge's forehead. Cursing in Spanish, he jabs his thumb into the volume and station dial, his patience worn too thin to tolerate the electronic whine. The radio refuses to cooperate. It snaps static at him before settling on Roy Orbison's distinctive croon.

Jorge slams his fist down on the dashboard. The radio lets loose a long hiss the way a kid blows a raspberry before going back to a choppy rendition of Orbison's "Blue Angel." Not one to quit, Jorge punches the volume dial a couple more times.

"Don't bother," I say. "It does as it pleases. Just keep driving."

He glares at me through the rearview mirror as if this is my fault—which in a roundabout way I suppose it is—before settling back into sour mutterings beneath his breath. That everyone around Salome is so unperturbed by this sort of thing perturbs me. I consider striking up a conversation with Jorge to get more insight into what the hell Salome actually does, reconsider, and decide to save that chat for Lena. Jorge and I barely tolerate one another's presence in silence. He'd probably get violent if he thought I was using him as the crowbar to pry into his employer's life.

The song nears its end, the radio skips, and Roy Orbison starts again from the beginning. A haunted radio singing "Blue Angel" on repeat wasn't the sign I expected, but beggars can't be choosers and it's clear I'm expected to do something.

"Take a left," I say. Jorge swerves sharp to make the turn that breaks us from our circling route, a car horn blares at him, and a third vein erupts in his temple.

"Pull over, I'll walk," I say. We're either going to get in a wreck from my guesswork navigating or Jorge is going to deliberately crash the car to kill me.

"Call when you're done," he seethes before screeching off.

Being left on the side of the road with only Misery the Sobbing Ghost for company puts a bounce back in my step. This is more my speed—the dead hassling me, the radio egging me on, and the creeping sense of being watched by far darker denizens than the dead. Just another day ending in "y."

"Please. Stop. Stop. Stop ..."

While Misery gets points for persistence, he's far from

helpful. Unlike Billy Davis and Silvia Lopez, he's got no refinement to his haunting. It's a jumble of directionless despair. I breathe deep and attempt to listen beyond him to see if I can pick up anything that can qualify as a lead. The murmurings hiss, Misery's sobs rattle my skull, and my vision falters as the world dips into sepia. It's a lot easier to let myself fall through the veil than it is for me to pull myself out of it.

"I just need ... I ... need ... to get through ..."

Flickers soft as moth wings play across my sight. Hidden shapes blur over the street, hinting at darker truths beneath physical reality, and the worsening distortion makes it difficult to see the sidewalk right in front of me. A white light shines around a corner, appearing almost solid as it pierces through the hazy mess.

"Now that's new," I say. The light doesn't come off as malign. If anything, it appears to exist in opposition to the sepia, as if it's fighting to pierce through the mire. I hesitate a second before committing the rookie mistake of following the light and turn down the street humming from the radiant glow.

"I just need to get through the day ..."

The white silhouette of an angel on a bright blue background reaches its arms out toward the words "Angel of Austin" and throws out a halo of uncanny clarity to lift the yellow brick building from the distorted world. Looks like I found Orbison's blue angel.

"A little on the nose, don't you think?" I ask, suspecting whatever speaks through the radio doesn't need a radio to hear me.

"Get through ..."

The murmurs roar, infuriated by this revelation. Shadows burst, shapes bend, and the physical world dissolves into an impressionistic painting where instead of oils or acrylics, the artist used the gore left on a slaughterhouse floor.

"I can stop. Can stop. Stop ... please."

I press a hand to the wall behind me, seeking a physical anchor to prevent me from sinking further into the sepia, and the woman's voice rises up from Misery's shuddering pleas.

"I'm not here to judge ... what you're going through."

The ground loses substance and I glance down to see soft ripples forming against my shoes. A dark stream rises from the pavement until it laps at my knees. Malformed faces, their eyes hollow and mouths pleading, brush past me in the sluggish current.

"I'm not here ... judge ... you're going ..."

Unlike Misery, I can't hear the distorted faces but their terror is palpable as they're carried off by the dull current. There's the sensation of fingers grasping at my legs to pull themselves free before being swept away. Tearing my eyes away from the tortured faces, I track the stream of souls to the source: an empty abyss yawns in place of where "Angel of Austin" was.

"Not here ... here. Here," Misery sobs.

The world bursts back through the sepia. Color returns in a whirl of disorienting vibrancy. A crosswalk beeps, a car engine starts, and the smell of freshly mowed grass from the nearby park mixes with the fumes of car exhaust to wash away the scent of bloody rot carried on that shallow stream. Senses reeling, I lean against the wall and breathe in Austin's city air with the desperate thirst of a man taking his first drink after days lost in the desert. I miss the simpler times when all I had to worry about was a murdered woman haunting me to go after her killer. There's no doubt I've bit off more than I can chew with this Salome business and I'm liable to choke if I don't take care.

"You okay?"

A middle-aged woman hovers at arm's reach. Compassion wars against common sense for how close she should approach the guy having an episode in the middle of the sidewalk.

"Thank you, ma'am, I'm fine," I say. "It's just allergies."

"Ragweed? It gets me this time of year too."

"Makes me tear up more than a Hallmark movie," I say and she smiles.

"Hang in there." She waves as she continues down the street that was moments before a stream of screaming faces. "It's supposed to rain soon."

The smile I return is genuine. However dark and dismal the forces that creep forth from behind the veil can be, it's got nothing on a moment of uncalculated concern from a stranger.

I look back to where the stream flowed from. The white angel against the blue backdrop is far from the hopeful messenger it pretends to be.

"Stop ... stop ... here."

Chapter 12

Entering through Angel of Austin's glass doors doesn't plunge me into a world of howling faces, writhing shadows, and dark powers. I've got mixed feelings on that. My self-doubt is through the roof and self-assurance through the floor, so I won't say no to continuous validation. On the other hand, I like it when the physical world doesn't remind me how frail it is and stays where it's supposed to.

The smiling faces of the families helped by the charity greet me as I step into the tidy lobby. They beam and wave from pictures hung on sky blue walls, their stories detailed beneath the images. Bulletin boards covered in flyers for upcoming events, community outreach, and job opportunities welcome all who walk in with the hopeful promise of new beginnings. The receptionist at the front desk gives me a smile, points to the phone at his ear, and raises an apologetic finger to let me know he'll be available to help after he finishes the call.

I pick up one of the brochures from the information table beneath the pictures and success stories. The blue and white angel slogan heads the front page above the biblical psalm:

"For the oppressed will not always be forgotten; the hope of the afflicted will not perish forever."

Thumbing through the pamphlet provides the predictable

summary information for an organized charity: Who We Are, What We Do, Get Involved, Locations. Nothing jumps out as sinister or even suspect. There's no hint of Angel of Austin being a cover for a Satanic cult taking advantage of people who've hit rock bottom, offering them access to food pantries and soup kitchens in exchange for their souls. Illegal organ chop shop isn't listed under "What We Do," sandwiched between "job training" and "addict outreach," and the image of the current CEO, Amanda Verkauf, doesn't exactly freeze the blood. She looks to be in her mid-fifties, her hair is most likely dyed the soft auburn shade to cover the grey, and her professional smile brings out the laugh lines framing her bright blue eyes. Her story of rags to riches to philanthropy is detailed below and the biography doesn't hide her less than stellar past with the law. Instead, it's presented as evidence that no matter how far you fall, God can always lift you up.

"Hey! Thanks for waiting, can I help you with anything?" the receptionist calls out as he jogs over to join me. He's about my age, brown hair bleached blond at the tips and cut short on the sides to leave a shaggy, untamed mop on top. He's got a cross tattooed on his neck beneath his ear and a couple more Jesus-themed inks on his arms.

"I'm looking for volunteer opportunities," I say.

"Cool. We've got some training events coming up." He points out a couple of pages on the bulletin board, and his devotion to helpfulness demands he personally hand me the various brochures on the front table.

"You guys offer a lot of services," I say, flipping back to the "What We Do" section.

"Yeah, and it's all thanks to people like you who are willing to volunteer their time, talent, and treasure!"

He oversells the pitch, but eagerness ain't a sin.

"Do you have any events going on right now?" I ask. "If I wouldn't be in the way, I'd like to see you guys in action to figure out where I might be a good fit."

Mop-top frowns. "Shoot. I gotta stay at the front desk and I don't think we got anyone on hand right now for a tour." He sucks his lip between his teeth to do some hard and fast thinking. "But I go on break in ten minutes. I can show you around then if you want."

He looks like a golden retriever desperate to prove what a good boy he is.

"I'd appreciate that." I'm beginning to doubt I interpreted the dark omens swirling around Angel of Austin right. Not if Mop-top is typical of the folks who operate here.

"Alright! There's tea and coffee if you want, make yourself comfortable."

Mop-top jogs back to the front desk to pick up the ringing phone with a cheery "Thanks for calling Angel of Austin, it's a beautiful day, how can I help you?" and I scope out the coffee table. The cheap smell and overabundance of dried creamers and mixers to mask the coffee's taste warn me away. It's for the best I don't make myself a cup as there's no guarantee I won't step in something supernatural while I'm here. When that happens, I'll need both hands free to scream and flail about which is better done unencumbered by a paper cup filled by hot bean water posing as coffee.

***

"This is the community hall." Mop-top opens double doors to show a room about the size of a grade school gym. It looks like one as well. Chairs are stacked along the walls below upbeat motivational posters, circular folding tables are flattened to rest against a low-rise stage, and the floor is the generic hardwood designed for regular abuse.

"We hold our education training in here every evening at seven. We also use the room for addict counseling—that's on the weekends, and donation dinners—the next one is coming up two weeks from now," he says. "So what got you interested in volunteering with Angel of Austin?"

"If it weren't for certain people in my life I'd probably have ended up homeless," I say, which is gospel truth. "It's only right to give back. I was walking by, saw Angel of Austin, and decided now was as good a time as any to check it out."

"Oh, cool. Like a sign from God?"

I think back to the dark stream of souls.

"Yeah, something like that."

The clatter and clank of dishes announce our approach to the kitchen before Mop-top does.

"And this is our soup kitchen." He leads me into a clean cafeteria packed by long white tables. A bald man carrying a rag and spray bottle wipes down the surfaces.

"Hey, Craig!" Mop-top's enthusiastic wave would make a puppy's greeting look cold. "Most volunteers start working in the kitchen. It's got the most flexible hours and opportunities."

Ladies in hairnets scour down the service line to prepare for dinner. The scent of garlic and cooking tomato drift out from the swinging door behind the counter.

"It's spaghetti tonight," Mop-top says. "By the way, I never got your name."

"Logan." I was planning on giving a fake name on the stupid assumption that a supernaturally delivered truth was going to drop neatly in my lap the moment I walked through the doors. That nothing specific has reared its head doesn't mean there isn't anything darker haunting these halls. It means the dead don't hold to the schedule of the living so I might have to volunteer a few shifts to figure out if some of the angels of Austin are the fallen sort.

"I'm Matt. Do you have a food handling permit?"

I shake my head.

"That's okay," he says. I couldn't flatten Matt's optimism if I dropped a piano on it. "It's real easy to get one."

"I'm not here to judge."

The bright fluorescent lights go out. That no one else reacts tells me it's not a physical change.

"I'm not ... not ... judge. Just need to get through."

Skeins of dried blood streak across the room as if a clawed hand ripped through the natural world. I clench my fists and go rigid against the sense I'm being dragged down into that churning stream, past the screaming faces. Down, down—

"Logan?"

"Sorry." I shake my head and can only halfway get my senses back. The kitchen walls groan and the floors buckle against something eagerly pressing through. "I was figuring out my schedule, when I'd be available."

"Not here to judge ..."

"That's cool." Matt's face is distorted as if seen below water clouded by grisly pollution. That's nothing compared to the woman who enters the cafeteria.

As no one screams or flees in terror, I assume she appears normal to them. They can't see the festering corruption hollowing her features. Ruined layers peel off her as if burned away and the air bends around her like I'm seeing her through a scalding heat. The serial killer I met last summer had a similar mark upon him, a dark flickering beneath the normal front he presented to the physical world. This woman's corruption is far worse than the supernatural stain that lay claim to the man who abducted and murdered women.

"Matt," the woman says. The cheer in her voice is jarring coming from decayed lips and her high heels clicking across the linoleum floor is the sharp scrape of blade on bone. "I thought you were at the front desk."

"Kelly's covering for my break and Logan here is thinking of volunteering so I thought I'd show him the basics."

The woman turns to me. I go rigid to stop myself from recoiling.

"It's alright, I don't bite." She offers a corrupted hand to shake.

I take her hand, Misery screams, and the cafeteria disappears. Distant streetlamps light a dark room, slipping in through the plastic tarp covering unfinished windows, and throw cold illumination across the exposed wood and concrete of partially constructed walls. High-heeled shoes click as Amanda Verkauf strides across the dusty floor toward me. She smiles and a sharp prick in my neck plunges me out of the dim room into complete darkness.

I flinch back and the vision drops away. The cafeteria is too bright, the clatter of trays on the food line too loud, and the inescapable murmurings too close. Amanda Verkauf's lips move. I can't hear what she says as she walks off while casting a confused frown over her shoulder at me. If anything important was said I completely missed it, but as I didn't fall into some supernatural seizure and stayed on my feet through the unbidden vision, that's a win in my book.

"Yeah, I was also intimidated the first time I met Ms. Verkauf," Matt says. "But she's really nice. She'll drop in on group meetings, come in to work the line for meals, sit with people and talk to them. She even goes out to some of the rougher neighborhoods to post flyers and get the word out there's a place looking to help people. There was this one guy in the addict program who stopped coming to meetings so she went to his house on her own time and dime to talk to him. She's right in the thick of it."

"Did he come back?" I ask.

"Who?"

"The addict."

"Oh, no." Matt grimaces, a facial expression I didn't think he could make. "Actually, he died. The police found his body in a dumpster, well, what was left of it. We think he got in deep with some drug dealers and it was pretty bad. You might've heard about it, it was on the news."

"So Ms. Verkauf isn't afraid to get her hands dirty," I say and Matt nods, glad to shift the subject back.

"Yeah, she's right in the middle of it."

***

I don't call Jorge for a ride. Walking the two miles to the public library is well worth not having to listen to him grind his teeth.

The computer lab is overcrowded with people and noise. Plastic chairs creak under their occupants, fall allergies have summoned up a dissonant symphony of coughing, sniffling, and throat clearing, and the incessant click and tap of fingers on computer mouses and keyboards sets my teeth on edge.

I didn't have it in me to jog over to the last available computer seat and cut off the little old lady shuffling down the row, so I've spent the last half hour sitting on a slatted bench, waiting for the next opening.

"Stop ... please, stop. Stop. STOP. STOP!"

Waiting would be a hell of a lot easier if Misery had the decency to back off for a minute and give me some peace. It'd also be easier if I didn't get the feeling each minute lost is another minute evil seeps further into the world, flowing in on the slow, steady current of that face-filled stream. Sitting still in absence of proper distraction gives everything witnessed today a chance to settle in—the sight of Ms. Verkauf radiating corruption as she walked by, the putrefied feel of her hand in mine, and the terror-tainted image of the room under construction. The rotted thing at the Driskill, insubstantial, inhuman, and terrifyingly intelligent. The murmurings manifesting as more than senseless chatter to share the dark deeds and desires hidden in the human heart.

Cold fills my chest and my fingers find the wedding ring around my neck. There's a bright side to all of this. I'm gonna be thrilled when I go back to only hearing murmurs and feeling cold hands reaching from beyond the grave. This adventure has been a solid lesson in gratitude, showing me how good I had it before today.

A portly middle-aged man sporting a thoroughly impressive beard braided down to his navel squeezes himself out of the chair. The skinny, chicken-legged college-age kid who's been prowling on the other end of the row for the last ten minutes makes a mad dash to the open chair.

I beat him by a mile.

"Hey, I was waiting for that," Chicken Legs says.

"Then keep waiting," I say.

"My friends are all online," he whines. "I'm going to miss the start of the game!"

That's a "you" problem if I ever heard one. Chicken Legs

gets mouthier when I sit down and log on. I give him a look and he gets the message, skittering back to the sidelines to sulk.

I'm not sure if I'll find anything useful via mundane research, but relying solely on the dead for intel is a risky roll. Ghosts tend to skew information and I have a tendency to interpret it all wrong so it won't hurt to do some unbiased research on Ms. Verkauf.

"Please ... please stop ..." Misery moans.

People's inability to mind their own business works to my advantage. Searching "Amanda Verkauf" provides no shortage of articles running from mainstream publications to tabloid rags. Not even philanthropists these days can escape having their past dug up and brandished about to sell stories. Particularly not absurdly rich philanthropists like Amanda Verkauf and there's plenty of meat on her life's story for journalists to sink their teeth into.

The articles documenting her ascension to one of Texas' most prominent philanthropists after numerous run-ins with the law present her as either a hero overcoming obstacles, or a charlatan who cheated the system. To her credit, Verkauf isn't shy about the immoral escapades of her younger years. Her interviews are blunt and she wastes no words sugarcoating her checkered past. The more I read about her the more I'm convinced her transparency isn't to serve as inspiration. It's a play to get out in front of a story before it becomes a mud-slinging bombshell.

Clicking on the article titled "Why Don't Austin's Wealthy Give More to Charity?" in which Ms. Verkauf is named as being one of the chief offenders, leads to splinter stories on the topic, and each one gives me a better idea of where she lives. An article from a few years back panders to the outraged mob who took up their pitchforks after she purchased a multimillion-dollar estate in the West Lake Hills neighborhood. The egregious offense of a rich woman buying a rich home has carried to present day. A more recent rage piece decries that she found time to remodel her pool patio while her low-income apartment project continues to hit snag after snag.

From what I've read, the blame for the apartment complex scandal shouldn't be pushed onto an innocent pool patio. The endless construction delays stem from conflicts over building codes, local residents complaining they already have more than their fair share of crime without the homeless and drug addicts being moved into the apartments, to a lawyer allegedly banging women in key offices to get corners cut—which a few articles explore in salacious soap-opera level drama.

The author of one fluffy hit piece is terribly offended that Verkauf's estate has a porte-cochere and spends a good paragraph breaking down how this feature epitomizes decadent elitism. The triggering architecture is included in a picture of Verkauf's multimillion-dollar house below the headline of the next puff-piece bemoaning folks who spend their own money. A specific address or street is never provided but with a bit of wandering about the neighborhood it shouldn't be too difficult to find a gated estate that's got big-ass palm trees all over the place and the offending porte-cochere. Particularly if my supernatural senses start tingling.

"PLEASE STOP! STOP! STOP! STOP! STOP!"

Misery swings his undying tantrum up another octave, blasting a cold front over me to chill me to the core. He's not even trying to send a clear message. He's just throwing the ghost equivalent of Luke's outbursts when he can't use his favorite sippy cup because it's in the dishwasher.

I close my eyes as the edges of my vision waver. I'm not convinced "energies" or "spiritual connections" can be picked up by snooping around certain places, much to Glenny's constant annoyance. She's been on this psychometry kick of late and is right huffy I refuse to go to pawn shops with her to handle dead people's old stuff to "read the energy field." But it wouldn't hurt to scope out Verkauf's home. Based on how she appears through the sepia lens I shouldn't have to delve too deep to find the source of her spiritual corruption if there's any to be found there.

A thrum shakes my skull and I pinch the bridge of my nose as images flicker behind my closed eyes—gloomy skeletal halls, plastic sheets hung over exposed wooden beams, unfinished walls lit by streetlights. My free hand clenches into a fist as Misery's sobbing and terror hits a high note.

"Stop, please stop!"

Couldn't this have waited until I wasn't in a public place?

"STOP!"

The vision shivers and reforms into a single light glaring down at me. I get the sensation I'm lying supine. Blurred faces move across the surgical light and Misery shrieks.

"PLEASE!"

I blink and rub my eyes in a vain attempt to get my senses back in order. The library and the visions of gloomy rooms and cold lights flicker, flash, and melt into the other. The lady sitting at the computer to my right glances over. It's only a matter of time before she asks if I'm alright or gets up to escape the guy on the verge of having a breakdown.

"Stop ... please stop ..."

Misery is one of the few souls who needs to get his shit together more than I do.

"Stop ..."

My left hand taps out "Liebestraum," providing a rhythmic order so I can think straight. The unfinished apartment complex caught in a suspicious loop of unending hang-ups—which I bet is the place I'm seeing in those Misery-provided visions—and Verkauf's residence in West Lake Hills are both worth checking out. Reason leads me to think I'm more likely to find damning evidence against Verkauf in her home than at a closed-off construction site. Creepy as it may be, it's too public a place to stash evidence of evil deeds, especially when she's got that private mansion tucked away from prying eyes. A neighborhood being high income doesn't exclude it from being a place of misdeeds. There's no shortage of police raids in well-to-do neighborhoods that turn up meth labs and sex-trafficking rings. Another fun fact I've learned from having barbeques with Sheriff Suarez.

Since I know Verkauf isn't home, or she wasn't an hour ago, I settle on paying a house call first. The creepy, abandoned apartment site can wait.

Chapter 13

Misery continues to be a nuisance. He harrows me down the library steps then mopes around as I wait for the car. I play out "Ave Maria" on my leg to maintain a grip on reality and clench my jaw to keep myself from yelling at Misery to knock it off. Snapping at a ghost stuck in a sobbing fit won't do anything and me being a garbage ghost whisperer ain't his fault. Still, he's driving me into a right foul mood.

Jorge takes his sweet time bringing the car around so I feel justified when I open the driver's door and say, "Move it."

"Come again?" he asks in a tone that tells me he heard clear and proper the first time.

"I'm driving," I say.

"Like hell."

"I'm not in the mood for a pissing contest. I got something that needs doing and where you are right now is in my way. I don't care if you tag along or park your ass here on the roadside, but you're gonna move."

Jorge glares at me like he's about to fall back on a machismo cliché like "make me" or "what're you gonna do about it if I don't?" Sooner or later the two of us are going to come to blows. I'm banking on it not being today because the well-being of Jorge's boss—supplier of his paychecks—is riding on me. He's got the required brain cells to put that much together and realize this ain't the hill to die on. After a half-minute standoff he figures this out, gets out of the driver's seat, slams the door shut so I need to open it again, and clambers into the passenger side, cussing me out the whole time.

"Thank you kindly," I say, sliding into the driver's seat and sending out a quick, quiet prayer that no supernatural impingements cause me to crash, and if I do, nobody dies. I'm okay if Jorge gets banged up, though. Nothing serious. Just him going through the windshield so he's eating through a straw for the next six months.

The radio chirrups in greeting and hisses in warning.

"You gotta turn the key in the ignition to start the car," Jorge says with a smug snake smirk slithering over his face.

I ignore him and listen to see if I can pick up anything more from the sobs echoing in the back of my mind. There's nothing new to hear. It's like Misery's cut a piece of a recording and is playing it over and over on a continuous loop.

"You wanna use your words and tell me what's going on?" I ask.

"What?" Jorge asks and I shush him. Neither he nor Misery listen. Misery doesn't even make an attempt at clarity and Jorge lists all the unpleasant things he's gonna do to me.

Misery's cold fingers pull at me. Problem is, it's from every which way. There's no tug on my hand or cool push to indicate a direction to go. The radio gives an ugly burst of static and like most things otherworldly, I have no idea what it means. So I ignore all of them—Misery, the radio, and Jorge—and drive off to the West Hills neighborhood no matter what anyone dead or alive says.

***

The turtle pace I'm cruising at through West Hills has Jorge at the edge of fatal hypertension. He keeps clenching his fists like he's barely stopping himself from grabbing the steering wheel or my neck.

The neighborhood's layout is similar to Salome's with twisting, convoluted streets. Large homes are pushed far back into the privacy of trees and those perched atop the highest hills have views of the slope down to the water. None of the houses I see at the ends of their long driveways have a porte-cochere and no towering palm trees catch my eye.

I creep up one of the curving roads at a blistering speed of seven miles per hour, causing Jorge to gnash his teeth. Cold plucks at my skin, the murmurings scrape and scratch over my mind, and a sepia skittering fills my vision so the world looks like it's a breath away from disintegrating into a scattering of bloodied sand. I slow the crawl I'm driving at to a molasses drip when Misery lets loose a fiercer round of his screaming pleas. I don't want to risk missing anything and I don't want to drive any faster as I can hardly see over the racket he's making.

"No one's forcing you to be here," I remind Jorge when he hisses through grinding teeth. I'm doing my best not to look over at him. The sepia staining the world has turned him into a flickering figure of rot and black in the corner of my vision. It's nowhere near as bad as Verkauf but it confirms my suspicion he's not a good guy.

"*STOP!*" Misery wails, and the radio lets loose a deafening static roar. Both Jorge and I jump, causing the car to lurch.

"Holy shit." Jorge curls his ham-hands into fists and looks ready to punch the next thing that makes any noise.

"*Stop. Stop! STOP!*" A dozen frozen hands rake over me, but

Misery's theatrics aren't necessary. I know I'm in the right place by the tops of tall palm trees rising over the oaks.

"Where're you going?" Jorge asks.

I slam the car door shut as answer.

"STOP!"

"Simmer down some," I say. Misery screams in agony.

Limestone pillars and iron fencing wrap around Verkauf's home. I hang back in the trees as I circle around the lot. I don't see any cameras or fancier security other than the short fence and seclusion. There isn't even a yappy little lapdog to tell me off. The low fence barely reaches my shoulder and is easy to hurdle over. If there's a security system that I'm missing, and my snooping around trips an alarm that gets me arrested, I'm sure Salome has the money to bail me out.

Palm trees shade the limestone pool patio with white lounge chairs tucked beneath brightly striped umbrellas. The patio's door isn't locked and slides open in ready welcome to a home that's a polished blend of rustic and modern ranch style. Rooms run together for a spacious floor plan that allows natural light to fill the kitchen, dining room, and sitting area where iron chandeliers hang from the exposed red cedar beams. The home is warm, inviting—and my skin won't stop crawling. The open design and large windows leave me ridiculously exposed, begging to be seen.

"Please ..."

"If breaking and entering is gonna become a habit, I really oughta invest in gloves," I tell Misery as I search through the little nook by the kitchen. Either that or I should start carrying around superglue to paint over my fingertips to solve the pesky print problem.

"Just ... get through ... today."

"Now that almost sounded like a sensible response." Looks like Misery and I might be starting to understand each other.

"Stop. Stop. Stop. Stop. STOP. STOP!"

Or maybe not.

Verkauf has kept it old school with a landline phone, physical calendar, and address book. Riffling through the paper, I don't find a receipt of evil to explain how she purchased the corrupted state of her soul I saw earlier today, and the reason that Misery's haunting me isn't included in her phone bill.

"Stop."

A soft thumping comes down the hall and my heart near explodes out of my chest from fear I'm not alone in the house. I calm down when I realize there's no one else here and the knocking is just a ghost. Probably.

"Stop."

It's difficult to tell where the thumping sound is coming from. There's no change in volume as I search the halls for the source, and the more I listen for it, the more unsure I am if it's footsteps, knocks on the wall, or a heartbeat. Movement blurs in the mirror above a hallway cabinet. I check my surroundings this side of the glass to be sure it's not reflecting a physical presence before stepping closer. The figure in the mirror is shrouded behind thick skeins of sepia flowing like rainwater down the surface. His mouth moves in muted screeches and his hands tear at his blurred face. The room behind him isn't the hall I'm in. It looks like a morgue without cold chambers under a bright surgical light gleaming off the chrome walls.

I take another step closer for a better look and the soft thumping goes quiet.

Bang!

The door to the hallway bathroom slams shut. Knickknacks on the shelf shudder from the force and a glass vase tumbles to shatter on the floor.

"I just need ... I just need ... please, stop. Stop. STOP!"

Faces stare out from the fragments of the broken vase. None of them are mine.

Bang!

Bang!

Bang!

A dozen more doors answer the first, slamming shut to shake the whole house. I turn slowly on the spot, unsure if the slamming doors are a sign from the guys on my team that I don't need to check out those rooms, or the opposing team aiming to drive me both out of the house and out of my mind.

"Don't! Please don't!" Misery's cries dissolve into hopeless shrieks. The house gives a groaning lurch and I grab the hallway cabinet to keep my feet. The walls and floor bend like putty that something is seeking to push through.

"Jesus fucking Christ." I skitter up to stand on the cabinet as the floor beneath me ripples from the unseen force. I tell myself it's all in my head, none of this is really there—and fail to either comfort or convince myself.

"Not here to ... get through ... judge ... STOP!"

The floor rises up like water disturbed by a surfacing leviathan, and the wake it leaves in the hardwood reshapes into writhing bodies. Their hands reach up in desperation to be pulled free, their mouths gape as they press through the bending floor in stifled screams, and my stomach heaves from witnessing the physical world so violated. This Misery Ghost really knows how to take the drama up to an eleven.

"STOP!"

The house settles back to obey the laws of physics. The floor and walls smooth like ripples in water dying away, the murmurings go back to their background hush, and Misery's pleading softens from agonized shrieks to a ragged whisper.

"Please ..."

I give the floor a couple testing taps with my toe to be sure it doesn't decide to turn to putty again before putting my full weight on it and heading down the hall to where that lurching leviathan rolled in from. After such a display of supernatural impingement, a sensible person would run as far away as possible from this house that'd make Shirley Jackson swoon. But my senses don't follow logic so why should I? These haunting theatrics mean I'm in the right place.

Misery's pleas are joined by the thump-and-creak cadence of invisible feet on stairs. My own feet are weighed down by the spiritual filth infesting the house. Walking is harder than it has any right to be and my legs burn as if I sprinted a mile through knee deep muck by the time I come to the ceramic tiled foyer overlooked by a wide sweeping staircase and a crystal chandelier.

This is the most expensive haunted house I've ever been in.

I press my ear to the wall panels beneath the stairs—a bold gamble as less than a minute ago there were hands and faces reaching out from the floor—because all evidence points to there being something about this stairwell foyer that's got Misery worked up. I rap on the wall and listen for a hollowness suggesting a hidden place to store away a dark secret. The soft thumping within the wall answers.

"Need to get through the day ... get through the ... get through."

Trusting Misery that there's more to this staircase than meets the eye, I run my hand over the wall paneling, feeling for a catch or hook that'll get it to open. My fumbling takes too long for his liking. Pale hands made of bloody plaster dart out from the wall to grab hold of mine.

"Fuck!" I instinctively jerk back as he yanks me over to the edge of one of the decorative panels and slams me hard against it. The wall swings in and I catch hold of the railing for a hidden staircase at the last second, stopping me from plunging down the stone steps.

"Do you want my help or not?" I snap and an apologetic tone slips into Misery's sobs.

"Stop. Stop."

"Then take it down a notch." I rub my wrists where the phantom hands grabbed me. There's no sign of injury but they feel numb.

I don't recall a hidden stairwell being one of the points of outrage for Verkauf's new home, leading me to suspect this wasn't in the original floor plan. A high water table, a low frost line, and soil that's either clay or a thin topping over limestone make basements a rarity in Texas. That Verkauf took the time to carve this one out is most likely for reasons other than a wine cellar.

Finding the unlit stairway leading down was the easy part. Taking that first step into the dark is proving a bit harder. I've kicked down doors knowing there's a good chance a man holding a gun and complete intent to blow me away is on the other side, I've driven down roads where IEDs were as common as the potholes, but this staircase makes me hesitate. Misery's cries reach from the depths as does something else I don't want to meet. Every instinct and learned discipline of survival is throwing up a fury of red flags to warn me away.

The stone stair makes no sound as I take that first step down.

Chapter 14

Light from the foyer spills down to the stairwell's base. There's no need to click on the light at the top to see the vague shape of the gloomy room below—a perfect square with a small table sitting in the center. I hold my breath as I descend, doing my best not to take in too much of the air down here. The murmurings cheer, drowning out the soft scuff of my shoes on the stairs. A rhythmic chant underlies their ecstatic cries and the chorus sounds an awful lot like my name. I don't listen closer to find out. I have no intention of paying heed to anything they have to say.

"Stop … stop … stop …"

I pull out my cellphone and flick on the flashlight.

"I just need … stop … need … get through …"

The two candles standing on either side of the table were once molded into human shape. The tops are melted beyond recognition, the faces and torsos reduced to lines of wax running down naked bodies to pool at the candles' feet. Sealed jars form a circle on the minimalist altar. The murky liquid and gloom hide the vague shapes pressing against the glass. A warning shiver rolls over my skin and the next step I take toward the altar feels like I've been dunked in ice water.

"Stop …"

Crouching down, I peer into the nearest jar. My insides give a sympathetic squirm when I realize I'm looking at someone else's innards. All the jars share in the macabre trend of sealed and preserved body parts. Teeth mixed in with viscera. Finger bones and flayed skin. Male genitals, a heart, and a severed tongue.

"Well, shit," I say. I'm never going to unsee this. Verkauf has taken her pickling hobby way too far.

Alien scrawl in a wheeling, spoked pattern covers the table beneath the jars. The pale chalk lines, smudged at the edges where a hand must have dragged over them, spiral in toward the table's middle, and in the very center of it all is a photograph of Salome.

Not much surprises me nowadays. Sure, I startle a hell of a lot easier than I used to—getting a jump scare out of me is easier than sliding backward off a greasy log—but it takes a bit more than your average serial killer's trophy collection for me to be taken aback by the shady pastimes folks get up to. The childish crudity of the altar has me teetering dangerously on the edge of not taking it seriously. There's a petulance to it that belongs in the diary of a teenager going through a goth phase, where pentagrams are doodled in the side margin next to incantations wishing harm on the girl who sits next to her in science class.

I don't believe in magic. Not the cottony modern notion of rhyming curses, talking mirrors, or occult rituals that'll make you levitate. But I know the supernatural has sway over us and there are folks who seek to domesticate it in more dangerous ways than trivializing it to pretty pictures on tarot cards or crystals that bring luck and ward away evil. The creator of this altar is seeking to grasp at a power that'll rot first the hand and then the soul. And just because the altar looks like Wednesday Addams' kindergarten arts and craft project doesn't mean it lacks the ability to impact the physical world or anyone who comes into contact with it, so I'm as eager to touch the altar as I'd be to stick my hand into one of the jars adorning it. Note to self, bring latex gloves when supernatural sleuthing.

The murmurings laugh as I raise my phone to take a picture of the altar. Salome might have an idea of what this means, is supposed to accomplish, or know if this is a singular hobby of Verkauf's or part of a larger group. There could be a whole cult of philanthropists by day, Satanic summoners by night, who call up demons to take out their white-collar competition.

The camera click is impossibly loud, especially since my phone is on silent, and it's not a mechanical snap. It's the wet crack of breaking bone.

The murmurings fall back into their rhythmic chant and the phone screen crackles to complement the sepia streaking at the corners of my vision. The image flickering beneath the spotting on the screen is different than the scene before me. The altar is still there, bleak and crude, but the jars are gone. Fresh pieces of a dismembered corpse take their place. The end stump of the hand sticking straight up was sliced off with surgical precision. Its neighbors are parts of a rib cage and vertebrae. Tissue trails off the bones stacked in grisly columns. What couldn't fit on the table spills onto the floor in a charnel heap of discarded body parts. Crimson smears replace the chalk lines beneath the dissembled jigsaw puzzle that was once a man. His head rests in the center, face turned away from the screen, hiding his identity.

Scrick.

Another wet snap in mockery of the camera's click and a

new image flashes onto the screen. It's exactly the same save the head is turned a fraction closer to facing front.

Scrick.

The head turns a little farther.

Scrick.

The edge of a bloodied brow and jawline comes into view.

Scrick. Scrick. Scrick.

With each bone-snap camera click, the head slowly revolves in jarring stop motion to face me, each image replaced faster than the one before. I know who it'll be. I recognized the features the moment I saw the outline of the jaw. Morbid fascination holds me hostage for the rest of the show.

Scrick. Scrick.

I watch my face come into full view. There's a gleam of life lingering in the eyes staring out at me from the flickering screen. I drag my eyes up from the phone to be sure the real altar hasn't descended any further in its gruesome worship than preserved body bits in jars. The altar is unchanged in appearance, but any hint of skepticism I had on its efficacy and the evil brought forth by it is long gone.

"Charming," I tell whatever has crawled out from the abyss to hack my phone. They can flash whatever images they want at me. Doesn't matter if this is a promise of what's to come or the demonic version of a dick pic. All it changes is my being able to call Salome for advice on the abattoir altar since my phone is frozen on that final picture. That's not much of a setback. I don't need a second opinion on the matter anymore.

Wary of any hand that might shoot out of the altar to grab mine, I pluck Salome's picture from the center. I don't know if that'll do anything for the better, but it seems wrong to leave her image there.

Movement darts in the dim light reflected off the jars, inhumanly fast and too large for the small space.

I whip around. There's nothing there, but an empty room is no promise of being alone.

It's here. The lesser denizens surrounding the altar yield to the entity's coming and shrink away from the greater evil. A fresh wave of sweat chills down my neck, my breaths go shallow, and my heart rate rockets in ready anticipation for fight or flight. The stone floor cracks. The ceiling groans down.

Scrick.

I glance back down at the phone and watch the lips on my dead face part into a wide smile.

Logan, the entity croons, directly behind me.

Chapter 15

I'm running before I have time to react, taking the stairs three at a time. I don't look to see what's clawing at my heels to rip me off my feet and pull me back down into the cellar.

The door at the top of the landing slams shut, plunging me into darkness. I don't stop. I race up the stairs and use the little momentum I can build on the small landing to ram right into the wall. The thin plaster caves beneath the impact. Blisteringly cold hands from farther down than the basement tear through my clothes and skin. I feel them ripping chunks from me as I give two hard kicks to force an opening I can shove my way through into the foyer.

There's a tunneling effect where the house is plunged into a writhing mess of dark and rot save for the patio door to the backyard. For the briefest moment a man's shape flickers on the other side of the glass, yelling at me to get out. I can't hear Alec over the entity's roar but I know what he's saying.

"Move it, Doll!"

An unseen hand slides the door open for me, which is good because I'm far more focused on getting the fuck out of Dodge than any of the finer motor skills required to open a door. I got all the speed I need and more to clear the back fence and don't miss a beat when I land and roll straight back into a run. The cold raking claws died off the moment I got outside the house. The entity's voice won't let up. It calls after me.

Logan. Logan. Logan.

I see it from the corner of my eye, keeping easy pace with me as I tear through the trees. I feel it grin, delighting in my terror at this reunion. The winding driveways, red tile roofs, and low oaks erode away to leave me sprinting through dark halls, a skeletal building of exposed woodwork, plastic tarp, and cement floors. I can't tell what's really there from what's not and the entity uses the fracturing of the physical to slip farther through the veil.

Logan.

I slam into Salome's Bentley, fingers slipping on the handle, and nearly sob in relief when I get the door open and throw myself into the backseat.

"What the hell happened to you?" Jorge asks.

I'm too busy willing my stomach not to rise any farther up in my throat to shoot off a witty response. I run shaking hands over my legs and back. I'm in one piece, but I don't feel like it. It's like there are gaping chunks of me missing, torn out by those frozen claws. I lose the fight against my rebelling stomach, throw open the back door, and vomit into the street.

"Jesus Christ," Jorge mutters and pulls out his phone. "Get in the car and stop making a scene."

The murmurings laugh, Misery whimpers, and the radio fusses out a broken jumble of Orbison's "Blue Angel" as flashes of unfinished apartments, plastic tarp, and surgical light flicker outside the car.

"No, he's a mess," Jorge says. "I can bring him back."

At the risk of being rude, I yank the phone from his grip.

"I'm fine," I say.

"I don't believe you," Salome answers.

The radio is gargling static and I cover my ear to hear her better.

"Would you believe me if I told you Amanda Verkauf, the CEO of Angel of Austin, has a dismembered body on a black altar in her basement hidden beneath the stairs?"

"Oh yeah, she's a bitch," Salome says. "What did the altar look like?"

I give her the rundown, ignoring Misery needling me with cold, the murmurings' hunger to be heard, the radio stuttering out nonsense, and Jorge glowering at me like he wants to smash my head through the car window.

"Okay," Salome says, giving no indication this revelation has her fazed in the slightest. "Should I tell Lena to make some dinner for you or are you going to be home later?"

"Later," I say.

"Did you call the police about what you found?"

"No."

"Good, don't. Verkauf has connections. Leave that to me."

I'm well aware Verkauf has connections and they go much further than fallen mortals.

"Keep me posted on what you find, and call if you get into trouble," she says.

I offer Jorge back his phone. He doesn't take it.

"Where to?" he asks, lips skinning back to show his teeth.

"I just need ... just need ... need ... NO! STOP!"

"Verkauf housing project," I say. "Off south highway 183."

Chapter 16

The sun hangs low in the sky, casting long shadows down the last few blocks separating me from the construction site. I had Jorge park half a mile away. He and I spent the drive making unspoken death threats to one another, and every once in a while I saw flickers of black rot creeping over him. I don't like him, I don't trust him, but the car radio jumping from white-noise chatter to broken bits of "Blue Angel" possessed an urgency disallowing the time needed to wrangle up another way for me to get from Verkauf's home to the construction site.

A couple of teenagers hanging around a rickety porch stop chatting to stare as I walk by. They and the home they loiter outside of are in keeping with the neighborhood aesthetic: mean, unkempt, and unwelcoming. Chain-link fences divide unmown yards. Weeds grow up thick to split crooked driveways hosting junker cars. A number of houses have boarded up windows, their residents unable to pay for repairs or landlords unwilling to make them.

I check over my shoulder to be sure those teenagers aren't tailing after me. They're not. If the sun were a little lower it might be a different story.

Beer bottles lay discarded below basketball hoops hanging

lopsided over garage doors. A truck with a bad muffler growls down the road, slowing as it passes me to get a good look at the guy who clearly doesn't belong and is begging for a mugging.

I should have spent more time at the library computer, toggling through street view to familiarize myself with the neighborhood and gotten a better sense of the area. I should have paid more attention to the upcoming events listed at Angel of Austin to see if there was one that'd guarantee I'd know where Verkauf would be. I should have brought gloves, a lock picking kit, a gun, a plucky sidekick.

I add not changing clothes when dropping Salome off at her house after the incident at the Driskill to the list of questionable choices I've made today. These stupid pants are going to rip if I take too long a stride. I'm surprised they haven't already split.

"Need to get through ..."

At least I've got Misery's company, moaning and screaming for mercy he didn't receive.

"Stop ... please ... PLEASE!"

Son of a bitch, it's been a long day.

I cut through the lawn of a graffiti-splattered Baptist church and dash across the arterial before the next wave of traffic comes. A six-foot-tall chain-link fence surrounds the construction site. Green tarp hanging down from the top rail obscures the interior from prying eyes and numerous Keep Out signs are slapped down the line. I find a secluded patch of fence and take a run at it, drive my foot in to get a hold in a link, swing my other leg over the top, and stick the landing on the other side. Alright, I cashed in my one "things that go smoothly" token getting in here. Which means I'm either going to rip my pants or die on my way out.

The apartments' framework is complete, as is most of the exterior of exposed brick and wooden beams atop a concrete foundation. Debris litters the ground and dust is settled thick over the site held in an ever-lengthening limbo.

"STOP!" Misery hits me like a truck and sends me crashing into a stack of orange and white barricades. *"Stop. Stop. STOP."*

"If you don't simmer down, I'm gonna find someone to exorcise you," I hiss. "Got it?"

Misery screams and his theatrics complicate my listening for any noise indicating I'm not alone. The site isn't as abandoned as the articles claim. Scuffs in the dust betray there've been recent guests. I keep to the trail tracked across the floor, hiding my footsteps in those left by previous trespassers.

"Please ..."

Sepia folds over the scene and the floor drifts away. I close my eyes, willing my senses to stay grounded in the physical. This is not the time to lose touch with reality.

The delicate *snick* of heeled shoes on the concrete floor jerks me back to attention. My feet barely touch the ground as I sprint cat-quiet over and drop behind a pile of plywood. Misery wails after me and I can't tell if it's in approval or criticism of my choice of action.

I peek around the wooden boards. Shapes move behind a sheet of shivering plastic. They turn the corner, come into clearer view, and it's a weird relief to see they're all human. The shadows of four large men dwarf the feminine form in their center.

"STOP! STOP! I just need ..."

"Go keep an eye out," the woman says, and two of the men break off.

Ms. Amanda Verkauf, dyed auburn hair pulled back in a high

bun away from her beguiling blue eyes, strolls by and out of sight. The cadence to her step shifts as she ascends the skeleton of a staircase. The heavier trod of her male companions overwhelms hers, the unfinished floors creak overhead as they move directly above me, then all their footsteps dull into uncomforting silence.

I slink out from behind the plywood. As the owner of this construction site, I'm sure Verkauf has every right to be here. That doesn't mean she has good intentions for it.

Lacking high heels, the second set of footsteps is softer, and I don't hear them in time to make it back behind the plywood. I press myself into the shadows, hoping immaterial cover will serve to keep me unseen. The man's shoes scuff up dust as he skulks through the construction. I stay stock-still in case he's as paranoid as I am and quick to jump at the smallest hint of movement masked by the dark.

Turns out he's even jumpier than I am. Wood creaks from the floor above and the man whips around, hands held up in either pathetic defense or to show his ready surrender. Faint light catches his pale face and the wooden slatted walls cast disfiguring shadows across his sunken features. He's younger than I am but won't look it much longer. Drug use is in the early phase of stealing his youth. The bags under his eyes are darker than mine. His skin clings too tight to bone. He's a frail, shivering mess impossible not to feel sorry for.

When nothing from the shadows reaches out for him, he lowers his trembling, insect-thin arms. His build has been so withered by addiction he barely has the weight for the stairs to announce his ascension through their telltale creak.

"Stop! STOP!"

The floor above groans and a dull reddish hue infects my

sight. I swipe at my eyes which does nothing to stop the surroundings from blurring as I tip toward the wrong side of the veil. Sepia swirls, the murmurings hiss, and Misery screams.

"Please! I need ... please ... get through ... STOP! STOP!"

"Shut up." I clench my fists, fighting to hold on to the tenuous strands connecting me to reality.

I didn't see where the two men Verkauf told to keep watch got off to. The construction site gives them a lot of ground to cover, so I'll bet they'll stick to the outside perimeter to ensure no one unwanted comes in rather than checking to see no one's already let themselves in. The other two men are most likely stationed closer to Verkauf. Somewhere they can keep an eye on things while staying at an easy distance to get back to her quickly if anything goes south. It's a safe bet one of the goons is covering the staircase, so I go looking for another route up.

As I don't know the layout of the upstairs—if it's open or if it has a similar amount of cover as the ground floor—I skip the first two gaps in the unfinished ceiling, opting for one a good fifty meters away from the staircase in the opposite direction the footsteps overhead sounded. The narrow opening to the second floor is conveniently close to an exposed wall so climbing up is easy. A jungle-gym enthusiast kid could've done it and had less trouble squeezing through the tight space between the wall and floor.

I stay in a crouch, moving quiet instead of quick. The second floor's internal structure is in a similar state of completion as the floor below. Concrete columns intersperse wooden slat walls and plastic tarps provide a ragbag of cover, glaring exposure, and blind spots for the trouble I'm walking into.

"Please stop," Misery whimpers. *"Stop. Stop. Stop ..."*

The murmurings grow precariously loud and I strain to listen for earthly noises through the supernatural din. If I can keep one foot in the physical senses, I'll be fine.

A floorboard groans from the next hallway over. Hunkering down, I peer around a corner of concrete. One of Verkauf's goons shifts back and forth on his heels. He's got an army man's buzz cut and lean, wolfish features. He turns his head to check the opposite end of the hall and I dart across the opening. That no shout or creak of curious footsteps comes after me means he missed me. I hope.

The murmurings hover at the edge of discernible and are all the more maddening for it. They want to tell all the secrets and unspoken sins carried by Verkauf and her hired thugs. I swipe at my ears as if to bat away swarming mosquitoes. I can't hear properly over the murmurings and the effort to keep supernatural influence separate from my natural senses is stirring up a sick pit of nausea and headache to match.

"I'm really trying."

I pause, unsure if the voice belongs to a living soul or something else.

"I know." Verkauf's voice is soothing and empathetic.

I move toward the speakers, struggling to see through the haze of sepia and shadow, and accept that luck will determine whether or not I run into Verkauf's second goon as I wind my way through the maze of incomplete walls.

"I'm weaning myself off." The man's voice is frail. I bet it belongs to the emaciated Drug-Bug. "Quitting cold ain't working. This is the last time, I swear."

"I understand," Verkauf says. "Don't worry, I got what you need, and I'm not here to judge."

I shudder, having heard this scenario play out before.

"Thanks for helping me out with this."

"Of course ... not here to judge."

It's a different script, but it's all too similar.

"I just need to get through the day."

Misery echoes how it played out for him, drowning out the voices I need to hear. I hold a finger up to my lips, a request for quiet he snubs. His sobbing rolls out from every shadowed corner. His pain soaks into the scene and his terror twists it into shuddering distortion.

"Stop! PLEASE! STOP!"

"Cut it out." Pressing my hands over my ears does nothing to block him out. Each of his pleas severs another fraying string to reality. Panic that isn't mine constricts my chest. I want to scream, I want to run—but I can't get free and they're going to kill me.

"STOP!"

The construction site flashes away as those surgical lights turn on overhead, gleaming off the stainless steel of the morgue-like room where I lie restrained against a cold table.

"DON'T! PLEASE!"

I bite the inside of my mouth hard to stop myself from yelling an echo of Misery's final desperation. The pain and blood's sharp taste sweeps me back to reality in a staggering wave and I realize I'm in a different hallway than the one I was in when Misery started acting up. Fucking shit, I'm lucky no one saw me stumbling around in a drunken trance, especially since Drug-Bug and Verkauf's voices carry clearer now. They sound like they're the next hallway over.

The lower walls in this section are closer to complete and give better cover as I scoot against the boards to peer over into the next room. Dull light from streetlamps clings to the outlines of a woman and a thin man. Verkauf's back is to me, her attention on Drug-Bug. He's a twitching mess, tongue darting nervously over cracked lips, eyes wide and sunken from the hunger that's consuming him.

"Take what you need." Verkauf offers a small kit to him. Drug-Bug's hands shake so bad he has to put the kit on the ground before he can open it. A weak smile trembles over his drawn face as he picks up a small orange bottle and turns it around in his stick-thin fingers. All his joy has been reduced down to whatever those pills provide him.

He's too busy worshiping what's slowly killing him to pay any mind to Verkauf. She pulls a medical needle from her purse and removes the safety cover in a cool, practiced motion. He offers no resistance when she gently tilts his head to the side, and without violence or ceremony, sticks the needle point into his exposed neck. He sways and hits the floor with a hollow thump. Verkauf spares him a glance of casual indifference before pulling out her phone. Booted footsteps announce a goon's arrival. Even in the gloom his fake tan and obsessive devotion to the gym is evident.

"Go get Harris and carry this down." Verkauf nudges Drug-Bug with a high-heeled toe before turning her attention back to the phone. "We got it," she says and pauses to listen to the other end of the line. "Of course. See you there."

Settling herself back on a stack of cinderblocks, she crosses her legs at the ankles and starts texting. Gym Rat slings Drug-Bug over his shoulder like a boneless ragdoll and carries him out. Between the drugging, the employment of goons, an abduction in an abandoned construction site, and the black altar in her cellar decorated by dismembered body parts, I'm pretty damn sure Verkauf's up to no good and I am therefore justified in aggressive intervention.

First things first, get Drug-Bug clear. I'm not putting his life in jeopardy in the hopes leaving him in their clutches will allow me to tail them to their secret Satanic hideout and find out who Verkauf was chatting up on the phone. Life doesn't pan out that neat, and Drug-Bug's life—despite his attempts to prove otherwise—is worth more than that. Based on Verkauf's cellar, I've got a good guess as to what's in store for him. Maybe the act of ritual murder rips a hole in the veil for something specific like the haze monster to come through and be courted to do harm against another. Or maybe they use the victim as the weapon against the target. The haze monster's and Misery's sobbing sounded awful similar. He might've *been* the haze monster before whatever dark power riding him wore off.

I hurry back to the opening in the floor I climbed up through. There are closer gaps in the floorboards, but I don't know where those lead and don't want to risk the time I'd lose taking a wrong turn down an unfamiliar route. I shove myself back between the floorboards and wall, dash over to the staircase, and take an ambush position around the corner. There's a familiarity to this that makes it easy to steady my breathing. A learned readiness gets my blood racing and heart pounding in preparation for conflict.

Gym Rat, carrying Drug-Bug over his shoulder, reaches the ground floor first and heads out the same direction they walked in. Buzz follows, oblivious to me stepping out behind him. I got no chance of keeping this discreet so I put it all on speed.

Knocking someone out is surprisingly easy. A hard strike

to the temple and Buzz is out before he hits the floor. The *thwump* of him falling gets Gym Rat's attention. He's real considerate and turns to perfectly fit his jaw to my fist. He drops Drug-Bug and staggers back. Stunned and doubled over he's easy pickings for my knee to slam against his sternum. He's too busy trying to suck down air to cry out or do anything about the third blow to the side of the head. His heavier build thumps louder against the ground than Buzz did and his head knocks against the floor with a staccato *crack*.

While Buzz and Gym Rat were cooperative in getting knocked out, chances are they won't be down long. Most likely I got half a minute on the short end before Buzz starts stirring and making more noise than I already have. I got even less time if the third and fourth goon were close by and heard the scuffle. As if invited in by the bout of violence, dull red blooms across my sight. I feel myself teetering on the edge, about to lose balance and fall through the veil and out of my senses.

Not now. Not yet.

Drug-Bug is closer to consciousness than Buzz and Gym Rat are. Eyes half shut and unfocused, he groans in protest as I pick him back up. He's lighter than he looks and I'm surprised I don't hear his bones scrape against each other beneath his reed thin skin as I hoist him over my shoulders.

"Please! Stop! STOP!"

I breathe deep, willing sight and sound to stay rooted in the physical—the mental equivalent of pinwheeling my arms to delay the inevitable tumble—and my sympathetic nervous system flooring the "fight" pedal chases away some of the supernatural's sway.

There's no click-and-clack of Verkauf's high heels to suggest she's coming down the stairs or heard our little dust-up, but there's no trusting my unreliable hearing to be sure on that count. I sprint toward the far fence, Drug-Bug bouncing on my shoulders. Thirty seconds is all I'm giving myself to get this poor kid clear before Buzz or Gym Rat wake up.

"Get through. Get. Get. Stop! Stop! Stop!"

It might've been more pragmatic to have killed Buzz and Gym Rat instead of leaving them lying unconscious on the floor, but I haven't quite reached the needed callousness to kill folks based on supernaturally raised suspicions. Besides, bodies complicate things. Dead men do tell tales and worse, they can't lie like living folks can to keep law-abiding authorities away.

Twenty seconds. We're out of the main part of the building and I see the chain-link fence. No sign of goon three or four. I scan the street running opposite us, looking for the light of a bar, a night club, or a gas station open at this later hour. Anywhere to drop Drug-Bug off. All the windows are dark and I find no easy salvation.

I gave myself too wide a time window before discovery. I'm counting down the last ten seconds when I hear the cry of alarm.

Time's up.

I accelerate to a sprint as I come to the fence and leave all chance of stealth behind. Hopping over is a hell of a lot clumsier and louder with Drug-Bug slung over my shoulders. The chain-link fence rings to eagerly announce my location. Angry shouts answer and I don't waste precious time looking back. I swing us over, hit the ground, and the first gunshot roars out. I don't see where it hit and that's good enough because that means it wasn't me or the kid I'm carrying.

Verkauf shouts and a second shot hits brick a couple feet to my left. Being under fire is a great way to get you to push your cardio limits—you realize how much faster you can run with the right incentive. I'm across the arterial, past the graffitied church, and back in the neighborhood of unkempt lawns and cracked windows in less time than it took me to get over the fence.

The roads are empty and most of the streetlights don't work, offering plenty of shadow to duck into. Listening for pursuers coming on foot or by car, I don't hear anything besides the distant rumble of a highway, a muffled stereo's heavy bass, and frogs chirruping from a nearby swale. The shirt I'm wearing is ruined by sweat and I'm pretty sure my pants ripped on the way out. Coming to a four-way intersection, I drop Drug-Bug off by the dumpster behind a coin laundry business. I check his pockets and pump my fist when I find his cellphone still works despite the cracked screen—most likely from one of his many falls this night.

And it's an Android. So God is on my side.

Hanging out with Glenny—and by extension her father—has considerably deepened my knowledge on police operations. Sheriff Suarez always has nuggets of information he's willing to share at backyard barbeques while flipping burgers. Like when he's complaining about how obsolete police technology is, lagging so far behind that most of the time they can't trace location when people call in on cell phones.

Except for Androids which automatically share your location when you dial 911.

I wait until the emergency dispatcher answers before placing the phone back down beside Drug-Bug.

Two blocks to the southeast is a playfield that's got good tree cover and a clear line of sight down the street to this parking lot so I can be sure the right people find Drug-Bug. I run over to the green, settle into a clump of bushes, and wait. Five minutes. Ten. Fifteen. It's closer to twenty minutes when the police finally arrive, blue and red lights flashing in the glass of dark windows. I'm not versed on the legal consequences for being found passed out in a business' parking lot with God knows what coursing through the bloodstream. Whatever it is, it's better than what Verkauf had in store for him.

"Happy now?" I ask Misery.

He sobs, and in the breath between his cries, the brush I'm hiding in melts away. I'm lying flat on cold metal. Harsh, fluorescent lights shine down on me. A dark figure moves against the white to stand over me. The vision fades, the night returns, and I sigh in exasperation, interpreting that vision to mean there's still unfinished business keeping Misery tethered in death.

"What's it take to get rid of you?" I rub my neck to ward away the chill of Misery's presence. I'm hazarding a guess Verkauf's partner in crime, the person she was speaking to on the phone, is the one who butchers the victims, and those surgical lights in the stainless-steel room are the last thing Misery saw.

"Please ... please ..."

"You gonna tell me where that is?" I ask.

Bright lights flash, and again I'm lying supine in the medical room, looking up at a dark figure hidden by the glare. This time the cold white light glints off the bone saw in the figure's hand.

"Do you know who that is?" I ask.

The vision of the dark figure standing over me holding blade in hand plays in a flickering, unhelpful loop. The figure's shape leads me to think it's a man but I can't be sure.

"Please ... please ..."

I send Jorge a text giving my location for him to pick me up. Since Misery either can't or won't provide specifics, I'll go back to the mundane research route and see if I can dig up any connections Verkauf has to hospitals, doctors, or mobile charity clinics. She definitely has the money to buy cooperation. I just need to find the person willing to sell his soul for the price she offered.

Chapter 17

Misery gives me an earful the whole ride back to Salome's. His cries are a broken record of sobbing babble and provide me nothing of value besides a throbbing headache that feels like sledgehammers are going to town against my skull. I don't care how pathetic I look lying in the car's backseat with my palms pressed over burning eyes in a failed attempt to suppress the flashing vision of bright lights and blurred faces he's throwing at me.

"He's not doing well," Jorge says.

"What?" I lift my head up.

Jorge has an earpiece in place and shakes his head. I lay back down. He's talking about me, not at me. None of my business, then.

"Yeah, we're about ten minutes out. I'll call if anything happens." Jorge glances at me through the rearview mirror. "If you're gonna puke again, tough it out."

Salome's waiting for me in her foyer, wrapped in a kimono robe, barefoot, hair pulled back in a messy bun like Maria wore when getting ready for bed. She looks me over, eyebrows arching higher as she takes in the mud covering my shoes and pants, the dust coating the rest of me, my split knuckles, and the red flecks spattered across my shirt around a bloody tear that I don't remember earning. Her eyes fix on a point below the belt and she smirks. I look down to discover I did indeed rip my pants at some point during the night in the most inopportune of places.

"Well. You've had a busy day," she says. "I hope it was fun."

"My working theory is Verkauf lures in drug addicts, kills them, does some over-the-top occult ritual in her basement, and their ghosts get twisted into a crazed homing-missile-poltergeist targeted at you. She's got at least one partner in this, I heard her talking on the phone and—"

Salome puts a finger to my lips. "Let's sit down first."

She invites a bottle of brandy to join us and grabs two glasses.

"No thanks," I say, "I don't—"

"I know you don't drink, but you might want to make an exception for tonight," she says. "Go sit. You look beat."

"I'm fine."

She scoffs. "Who are you trying to convince with that lie? Because it's not me."

"You need to get rid of Jorge."

"Why?"

"He's bad news," I say and describe the black rot I caught flashes of drifting off him.

Salome nods. "I know."

"Then why—"

"Because I'm not paying him to be nice. Quite the opposite. I know that offends your delicate sensibilities, but just because someone isn't a good guy doesn't mean he doesn't do a good job. I hired Jorge because the north star of his moral compass is a dollar sign and he gets the job done."

"Is that wise?"

"It's reliable," she says, "and it's nice you're worried about me. Now sit down, take a breath, and let's start again from the beginning."

Salome settles onto the couch, swirling her brandy. I'm too wired to sit so I pace along the coffee table as I give her the mission report: breaking into Verkauf's home, finding the cellar—I hand Salome the picture I lifted from the altar's center—and my snooping around the construction site. I tell her what Verkauf did to Drug-Bug and how that kicked off the game of hide-and-seek escalating into bullet tag.

"And that was my day," I say. "What about yours?"

I opted for brevity instead of depth in the retelling, leaving out the unnecessary details like the murmurings, Misery, the walls of Verkauf's home collapsing in as reaching hands and faces pressed through, or any of that unimportant chaff.

"You sure you don't want a drink?" Salome nods to the glass she poured for me.

I shake my head and she shrugs, polishing off and refilling her brandy.

"So before you ask, yes, I've got a hunch as to why Verkauf would go after me," she says. "One of my clients is suing her, the lawsuit is dragging her through the mud, and she's got it in her head that I'm in commune with the great beyond and can access information that'd ruin her."

"Are you and can you?" I wouldn't be surprised if Salome's consulting extended beyond the grave.

"I let her think that," she says. "Melodramatic rumors give me a more memorable business reputation than 'really good at research' does. Speaking of which, I'm not letting you off the hook that easy."

"What hook?"

"You're not telling me everything that happened tonight. Don't look at me like that, you didn't say anything about hearing voices or seeing something strange." She gives me pause to deny or defend myself from the accusation. I don't see reason to do either. "I need to know everything that happened. Every detail, however unimportant, from when you and Jorge left, to when you crossed back over my threshold."

I do a quick mental playback of the night. The thought of having to talk that much and that long on a subject I'd rather not talk about at all sounds more exhausting than the actual events.

"That's a much longer story," I say.

"I'm a good listener. Go ahead and get cleaned up first. I'll put on a pot of coffee. Are you hungry?"

"No."

"I'll get you something to eat too."

"I said I'm not—"

"I heard you." She catches my hand and stands up to kiss me on the cheek. "Thank you. You did a lot more than point and scream. I'm going to have to give you a raise."

***

Night ends before the story does. Dawn is peeking above the trees, a second pot of coffee is brewing, and the spread of note paper in front of Salome has entirely overtaken her side of the table.

Caffeine can't cut it anymore. Somewhere between three and four in the morning I hit a wall. The adrenaline rush from the night's fun is long gone and I'm flagging well beyond the aid a third cup of coffee can bring. Salome is unaffected by the lack of sleep and, once again, I'm doubting her claim of no supernatural abilities. Either that or we must be drinking different coffee because she's as alert and relentless now as dawn blooms in the east as she was when we began.

"Tell me more about the murmurings," she says. "You said you could hear them earlier today."

"I always hear them." At first it bothered me, Salome asking questions, pressing for the information hard habit has taught me to keep to myself. Now I'm finding a catharsis in openly talking about what lurks behind the veil as a fact rather than a figment of deep-seated psychosis.

"Earlier today you said you understood what they were saying." She points the pen she's been using to jot down notes at me. "Do you remember what it was?"

I shake my head, turning the coffee mug over in hand. I don't remember any specifics, only the dead certainty they were announcing the dark secrets of those they stalked.

"And that's the first time that's happened?" she asks. "You understanding the murmurings?"

I nod. Tiredness is a coarse sand rubbing behind my eyes.

"And you still think that they were talking about the people you were around? Things they had done or wanted to do?"

Another nod.

"Damn, that's some serious insider trading you got there. Could you understand them when you were at Verkauf's house or at the apartments?"

I shake my head.

"But they were there?"

"They're always there."

"Can you hear them now?"

I nod again. They're quiet though. Barely a distant breath.

"Don't go quiet on me now," Salome says. "We're making great progress with this session."

"Maybe later," I say, unable to rub the latest wave of tingling exhaustion away from my eyes.

She pauses and I figure she's mulling over if pushing is going to cause me to clam up or wear me down.

"I'll get you a fresh cup," she says, grabbing my empty mug. Her hand accidentally brushes my arm as she stands and I sit up straighter to stop slouching into her space.

My mental faculties are going on strike from being denied sleep so long. They refuse to cooperate as I look over the notes she took through the multiple retellings of tonight's escapades. Her neat handwriting is an alien script, reminding me of the spiraling symbols chalked onto the altar.

"Here." Salome holds the fresh mug in front of me.

"Thanks." I place it down on the table without drinking any. She put creamer and, judging by the smell, some sort of syrup sweetener in it. I don't understand what the appeal of complicating coffee like this is.

Misery screams. His voice rips through me like an electric shock and a sharp stab of pain hits my neck, waking me up better than caffeine. I clamp my hand over the burning cold.

"You okay?" she asks.

"Fine," I say through a clenched jaw.

"You're a bad liar."

"I suppose I'll have to practice more."

"You can tell me what's wrong."

"Nothing's wrong."

"You're also a goddamn hypocrite," she says. "You give me endless grief when I don't act like the world's ending because I'm being stalked by a demon—"

"Let's not exaggerate. It wasn't a demon, more like a ghost being enslaved through occult ritual."

"—and then after everything you say happened tonight, which I'm sure is a watered-down version of events, you have the nerve to act like you're not overwhelmed by it all."

"Me getting overwhelmed is not a hard bar to clear. I'm overwhelmed by this atrocity you're claiming to be coffee." I gesture at the offending drink. "More than two people talking at the same time is overwhelming."

"Is that because of the murmurings? You can't tell if what's being said is actually being spoken?" she asks.

Yes. I take a sip of coffee to avoid answering. Her intuition is straddling a fine line between helpful and annoying.

"Because if so, I feel awful for dragging you around to public places where there's a dozen conversations going on at the same time," she says.

"Nah, that's fine. It's only a problem when I'm expected to engage in the conversation."

"So how do you cope?"

Good question. I take a larger sip of coffee in a second obvious dodge around giving an answer. I grip the mug tight as Misery goes off on another tear and sends more needling pain into my neck. Even souped up on sugar, the coffee doesn't make a dent in the exhaustion. I shake my head to knock lethargic thoughts back into focus.

"Sorry, what?" I ask, realizing Salome was speaking to me.

"You sure you're alright?" she asks.

"You keep asking that."

"I'll stop when you give me a straight answer."

"It's been a long night."

Whatever Salome says is lost in the thickening brain fog.

"Yeah, sure. Fine," I say, hoping that's an adequate response and that she didn't notice my words slurring. I'm having a hard time keeping my eyes open and sitting up straight is a lost cause.

She gets up and I take advantage of her abandoning the couch to sprawl out. Drowsiness is an irresistible force, and all of a sudden the distance between the couch and the guest bedroom sounds miserably far.

Chapter 18

Daylight streams in bright through the guest room windows. It has to be close to noon if not past. A dull grogginess keeps my movements sluggish as I sit up. My limbs weigh heavier than they should and that makes getting free of the sheets embarrassingly difficult. My T-shirt clings to my clammy skin, there's a lingering dampness to the bedsheets from a sweat-soaked sleep, and I've got the clutterings of a bad dream rolling around in my brain. None of that is anything new. What is new is my breath scraping rough down my throat. It feels raw, like I've been having coughing fits or talking for hours on end.

I stare around the bedroom, searching the corners and usual places I check for wrongness. Nothing. No voices, creeping chills, shadows threatening to shudder beyond their natural place, or any sign of supernatural impingement. So then why do I feel so off?

I frown at the vague bit of dream coming back. The entity had me pinned down and I was struggling to get free. It didn't speak as it normally did. It stole my speech away to speak through me instead, but I can't remember anything it said. I run a hand over my throat, feeling like someone went at it with a cheese grater. Was I screaming through the nightmare?

The floor is too far away, and I stumble as I slide off the bed, crashing into the closet's mirror doors then the floor.

"What the hell?" I rasp. There's something wrong with me and it ain't bronchitis this time. It could be demonic dengue or a supernatural sickness I picked up from being too near that altar. If that's all this is, there's no need to get strung out over it. I've been dealt worse hands and we all die of something. If I bite it because I was a dumbass fooling around with an ungodly altar and didn't wash my hands afterward, that's nobody's fault but mine.

The kitchen and main living area are empty when I shamble down the stairs, relying heavily on the railing to safely navigate the curve. The dial clock on the kitchen stove reads a little past one in the afternoon. That oversleeping is going to cost me four hundred twenty-three burpees. Another thing to look forward to today.

My hands are shaking so hard I spill most the water out of the mug when I stick it in the microwave. After three failed attempts, I manage to open the paper packet for the tea bag and end up ripping that as well to spill dried leaves over the floor. Jesus Christ, I'm not even sharp enough to slice warmed butter this morning.

"Maybe you should go back to bed," Salome says. She's dressed in a business suit, hair and makeup done, and wearing this half-smile of amused pity.

"Nah, I don't want to break this momentum I'm building," I say in a voice scratchier than an old record.

"What's wrong with your voice?"

I consider saying "I went all out in shower karaoke last night," but I can't handle any follow-up banter.

"Was I … did you hear anything last night?" I ask.

"Like what?"

"Like me screaming," I say, hoping I come off as carelessly casual.

"Um, no. You feeling okay?" She asks her go-to question.

I feel like I'm hungover, got hit by a car, and am having an allergic reaction to life.

"Fine," I cough. "Did you go out?"

As much as I doubt Amanda Verkauf was able to summon up another sacrifice between last night and now—unless one of her goons was unexpectedly and violently terminated from her employment—I'm not crazy about the idea of Salome running around without me.

"One of us has to work around here," she says.

"Don't do that if I'm not there," I say, sounding as fierce as they come when the strain of talking cracks my voice. What a crap paranormal bodyguard I am.

"Yeah, I know it was a risk, but I didn't want to wake you and I needed to talk with some people. Conversations that couldn't be had over the phone," she says. "It's going to take more than a concerned citizen leaving an anonymous tip to take Verkauf down, so I've got some work to do."

"You should've woken me up."

"Are you kidding? You were dead to the world. I couldn't even wake you to get you to bed. Jorge had to carry you."

Glad I was passed out for that.

"So really, what's wrong with your voice?" she asks.

I shrug. "Allergies?"

She shakes her head. "I'm not buying that. Unless it turns out you're allergic to cocaine because it looks like you went on a binge last night."

I wink in response because talking hurts too much.

"Has this ever happened to you before?" she asks.

"Yes. I admit it. I have botched tea prep operations before." I open a new bag and this time I succeed in getting the mug into the microwave free of spills.

"Don't start. It doesn't take a psychiatrist to figure out you being flip is a coping mechanism, and I'm far from the saint it takes to put up with it. So, has this happened before?"

"No." I wish I remembered more of the dream to give me a better idea if this is a natural cold or the first sign of possession and speaking in tongues. My head hurts when I think back. I can't remember much of last night. There's a black hole swallowing up the memory between me sitting down to talk with Salome and waking up this morning.

"What're you doing?" I lean away as Salome presses her hand against my forehead.

"You don't have a fever," she says. "If I told you I know a doctor who is a lot more open-minded about what can cause illness, would you let me take you to him?"

"No." I don't even like going to orthodox doctors. Forget witch doctors.

"Yeah, I thought that's what you were going to say," she sighs. "If you start vomiting ectoplasmic goo or crab-walking down the stairs, I'm taking you to him whether you like it or not."

"I think you're overreacting." The odd heaviness to my limbs is fading and my throat has stopped rasping so it's not as painful to speak. If this weirdness clears up by the hour, I'll sweep it under the rug to deal with later. I've got enough on my plate as is without worrying over this latest hiccup.

Salome crosses her arms. "You're not getting it. We couldn't wake you. At all. I was about to call an ambulance."

"It's not the strangest thing to happen." I say with another shrug, grateful she decided not to. I'd feel less off-balance if I knew what caused this flu-like awakening. Until yesterday I thought I had a sense of what the unknown could do in this world. The last twenty-four hours has thrown open too many unpleasant doors.

Salome opens her mouth to speak and I shake my head.

"One supernatural mystery at a time," I say. "We have to solve your case before I'll let you get on mine."

***

"Are you feeling better?" Salome pokes her head over the deck's edge to look down at me, lying flat on the lawn.

"Fine," I say.

Waking up six hours outside of a respectable time doesn't excuse the rest of the day being wasted. I've knocked out two hundred of the four hundred and twenty-three burpees I owe as penance for oversleeping. I'll save the rest for tomorrow. Last night was sufficiently weird to grant a reprieve.

"You sound better," she says, coming down the stairs.

Shaking off the morning malediction didn't take long. An hour after waking up I felt reasonably normal, which if I'm being honest, isn't saying much. The goalposts I use for scoring what counts as normal move about twice a day.

She drags over a pool chair to where I'm sprawled out on the grass. She has a large box perched on her lap and a look in her eye that turns me mighty suspicious.

"What is that?" I sit up to better glare at the box.

"It's for you." She holds it out to me.

"Thanks, but no thanks. I didn't get you anything so it wouldn't be right."

"You'll pay me back in some other way I'm sure."

"What's in the box?" I ask, not moving to open it.

"It's a dressier occasion."

"What is?"

"The dinner party."

"What dinner party?"

"The dinner party you're my plus one for."

"I'm not going to a dinner party."

"Yes, we are," she says. "It's a private event for the more eccentric sort."

And by eccentric she means wealthy, well-connected people who have an unhealthy interest or involvement in the paranormal.

"Chances are Verkauf will be there," she adds.

"Good for her. All that means is you won't be going either," I say. When someone has you in their crosshairs, you don't stand up to make yourself a bigger target.

"She won't try anything. Not there."

"You're sure on that?"

"Sure enough to bet my life."

"Don't ever go to Vegas. You'll come away broke."

"No, I wouldn't. I'd cheat. Just like I'm cheating now by bringing you as my date," she says. "Don't look at me in that tone of voice. We're going to have to confront this sooner or later. She won't try anything with so many witnesses, and if she does, you'll be there to give a heads up."

"We're not going."

"Would you stop being so damn ornery for five minutes?" Salome's glare would set fire beneath most folks' feet.

"Just 'cause you say jump doesn't mean I'm going to ask how high," I say. This is a terrible idea even by my low standards and I'm not going to needlessly place her in danger.

"Trust me on this," she says. "I trusted you to run around

and do whatever you do. Now it's time to swap places on that score. I know what I'm doing."

My fingers play out a ragtime tune on the grass. It's not Salome's plan to charge in guns akimbo and a-blazing that's got my hair up. Frankly, I'm leaning toward that tactic as well. It's that Salome's insisting she lead the charge that I don't like. Throwing caution to the wind and running straight into the firestorm is a lot easier when no one else's neck is on the line.

"You're sure?" I ask, leaving it open ended as to what she's sure about.

She nods. "As long as you're there."

Chapter 19

"Give me a minute," I said, pulling the bottle of bourbon out from beneath the car seat.

Maria rolled her eyes in half-hearted admonishment. She had long accepted this ritual preceding the obligatory formal dinners, fundraisers, and private parties she attended for work.

My strategy for her dragging me to these sorts of events was to get pleasantly buzzed in the first ten minutes and do my best to maintain that cruise control level of inebriation. For the social gatherings hosting a more intolerable crowd, such as this one, I'd crack open a bourbon in the car and sit out there until sufficiently drunk to handle people as shallow as their pockets were deep.

"No one can deal with the Huffs sober," I said, offering her the bourbon. Not that I ever tried.

"I do," she said.

"Well, you're just better than me." I gave it ten minutes before I found Maria taking advantage of the work party's open bar.

"I'm not in college anymore. My pre-funking days are over."

"Oh, so that's what you do in college. Is that why you dropped out?"

"What are you doing?" she asked the obvious when I started filling up a hip flask.

"Preparing for the journey. We still gotta make it across the street and look at that driveway, it goes on for miles. Why didn't you park closer?" I asked from the driver's seat.

She shook her head, working hard not to smile. "You're being excessive."

"No, this is excessive," I said, pulling out a second flask.

"Okay, I draw the line there. There's going to be better drinks than car-stashed bourbon and you don't need to be walking in wearing an alcoholic arsenal. Pick one."

"Settle down, woman, one flask is for you. Did you think I was gonna let you walk into enemy territory unarmed?"

"Well, that was very thoughtful, but like most things you think, you didn't think it all the way through. Where am I supposed to carry that?" She waved a hand at her slinky black cocktail dress and held up her uselessly tiny clutch.

"Don't underestimate me." I held up a flask leg holster. "I prepare for this sort of thing."

"I am not wearing that," she said in a tone that invited me to try and make her.

"Why? Because you'll look badass and sexy?"

"Because I'm not reaching under my dress to pull out a flask of bourbon."

"Ah, I see the confusion. See, this was going to be a team bonding experience. I was going to carry yours"—I pulled aside my dinner jacket to show the holster strapped above the pants' line—"and you were going to carry mine. So don't worry, you won't be the one reaching up under the dress."

"Oh yeah?"

"Yeah. It'll go a little something like this."

I leaned over, running my hand along her leg and pushing her dress up.

"And then like this." I kissed her.

"I can't take you anywhere, can I?" she asked and kissed me right back.

Chapter 20

Teetotalism doesn't allow for my traditional tactic of handling large social gatherings. So I adopt a new strategy: find a garden bench toward the back of the lawn that has a clear view of all the revelries. The dinner party is the rich people version of a backyard barbeque where instead of jeans and T-shirts, folks stand outside in party dresses and designer jackets. It's not a scene completely unfamiliar to me thanks to Maria, but it brings back her absence in a way that hurts.

I'm at the right distance that I don't look like I'm trying to make a statement of how much I don't want to be there, all the while ensuring only the most intrepid social explorers will venture out to my bench. Unfortunately, Salome was right in describing these people as eccentric. There are many intrepid personalities who have no reverence for basic social convention.

One woman sends her sixth glance over my way. She wears her late fifties well, has prominent cheekbones, wide brown eyes, light brown hair softly curled at the ends and the blonde highlights distract from the grey creeping in at the roots. The dress she's wearing looks like formal wear for hippies, a tie-dye pattern of pinks, purples, and whites dripping down to the ankle length hem above bare feet. Excusing herself from her current group of companions she glides over the lawn toward me, her step airy and light, and I stand to meet her.

"You have a dark, psychic energy around you," she says, giving me a cheerful smile.

"Thank you, ma'am, I dressed to match it," I say.

"Don't worry, most people can't sense it. You don't have to sit so far away."

"But you can sense it." I play along because she comes off as a nice sort of lady who means well despite her head being lost in a cuckoolander cloud. "So out of courtesy for people like you who can, I'll hang back a bit."

"Oh no, you don't have to do that." She sounds sincerely distraught her claimed sensitivities keep me socially isolated. "It isn't harmful and even if it was, I'm protected."

She holds up her necklace of a carved black stone.

"It's black tourmaline," she says. "It keeps away negative energy. I was attending a conference with my husband years ago and there was this one woman there, very toxic energy, you could feel it coming off her. Well, it's a good thing I had my black tourmaline with me—I kept it in my purse back then—because after talking to her at dinner, I got out my wallet and saw that the stone had snapped clean in two."

She pauses to give me the chance to respond to the telling of this world-shaking event. I oblige with a nod.

"Her toxicity was so strong it broke the stone!" she says to be sure I understood the point of the story. "Imagine what would've happened if I didn't have the black tourmaline to take in her dark energy. That could've been my psyche that snapped in two."

I'm pretty sure her psyche is a bit more fragmented than

just two pieces. I nod again because it's the polite thing to do and her sincerity turns the kookiness charming. Wearing a rock around your neck provides the same level of protection as chucking it at an incorporeal entity—which is to say, none at all.

She leans closer and lowers her voice to a conspiratorial whisper. "I always wear it, especially to events like this. You never know what energy people are going to bring."

"How do you know the Jacksons?" I ask.

"Through experience. I'm Mrs. Jackson."

"And I'm a plus one not worth being introduced to the host." I offer my hand for proper introduction. "Pleasure to meet you, Mrs. Jackson."

"Call me Dana." She sits down on the bench and motions for me to join her. "So who's your date? Must be a brave woman to let you off her arm."

Either that's a nice way of striking up a conversation with the awkward, loner guest or a very smooth way of making sure I'm not gatecrashing.

"Ms. Trasmoz. She's an independent sort, so I gotta keep a healthy distance to not come off as clingy."

"Oh." Dana nods as if that explains why I'm sitting a good bit removed from the other guests more than my negative psychic energy. "She also has a dark energy."

"Maybe it's contagious," I say.

"Oh, it is! It is! Stay right here." She springs to her feet. "I'll be right back."

She dashes across the lawn into the house, waving away a man who calls out to her.

It's easy to pick Salome out from the crowd milling about on the patio. Her red dress is designed to beg for attention and she's finding the men generous. There's a distracting amount of slink to the way she walks and that gets the notice of anyone she wants without her having to say a word.

I lean back against the stone bench. It's too early in the evening to call coming here a bust, but that looks to be the promising forecast. There's no sign of Amanda Verkauf, and while Mrs. Dana Jackson is able to sense the dark energies plaguing her guests, I'm not getting anything out of the norm. There's the usual low hush of the murmurings and an occasional word from Misery interrupts his incessant sobbing. Beyond that, I'm sensing nothing.

Movement out of step from the casual ease of the other guests catches my eye. Square-face walks with the same unyielding stiffness by a backyard pool as he does stalking people through downtown Austin. I don't know how he wrangled up an invite to this exclusive shindig of eccentric spiritualists. He's dressed the part of a guest even though his trousers, button-down, and sport coat are of a lesser quality than the other attendees.

His eyes fix on me and I don't break his stare. I expect him to retreat into the crowd to continue his previous standard operation of being a lurking creep. Instead, he makes a beeline toward me, parting the guests like the Red Sea.

"Samuel Campbell." He offers a thick, unfriendly hand to shake. "Do you have a minute? I'd like to speak with you. I'll grab you a drink."

I keep my hands laced together. There's a bullying tone to him. He spat out the words like any pretense of cordiality caused him physical pain.

"I don't drink," I say.

"I'll get you a cranberry juice."

"If you wanna talk, right here is as good a place as any," I say. Besides, Mrs. Jackson asked I stay put, and far be it from me to go against the host's request.

"What's your relation to Salome Trasmoz?"

"What's your interest?"

"I'm a private investigator," he says.

"Investigating what?"

"Private matters." He hands me a card. Much like Salome's business card, there's no address, company, or specifics to his trade provided. All that's listed is his name and contact information.

"Anyone who wants to talk with you is going to be over that way." I point to the gaggle of people and do a quick check to be sure Salome is still there and safe. She's chatting with a grey-haired man sporting an outdoor tan. I shudder, not sure what brought that chill about.

"I'm where I need to be and I'll be here as long as it takes no matter how much shit you give me," Square-face says.

Pleasantries done, I can tell talking to this guy is going to be akin to slamming my head against concrete, but I'm willing to sacrifice my skull for the chance of more information. Even though Verkauf has taken his place as prime suspect for calling up hazy ghost monsters, I wouldn't mind figuring out what his role in all of this is. Alright, Samuel Square-face Campbell, we can chat over drinks.

"I like my cranberry juice served with an orange wedge and pink umbrella."

***

Square-face smirks when he brings me over the tall glass of cranberry juice garnished with an orange slice and topped off by a pink Hawaiian umbrella. The smirk shifts to scowl when I dump the drink into the grass so it splatters his shoes, one-upping him in the petty jab department.

"So, what did you want to talk to me about?" I cross my arms and don't hide an ounce of my dislike for him.

"Salome Trasmoz," he says, "what's your relation to her?"

Good question. I don't really know myself.

"She's my sister." It's not an unbelievable claim. Salome and I are both ambiguously brown and we look more alike than Kitty and I do.

His bushy square eyebrows knit together. "Sister?"

"It means a female sibling."

"Stop selling me bullshit, kid."

"No, honest to God, that's what it means. A female relation through shared parents."

"She hire you for something? Security? Bodyguard? Or was it something more intimate?"

"I don't hire on for sex," I say. "I do that for free."

"I can make sense as to why she'd pick you out. What doesn't make sense is why you'd be running with her. Sergeant Remington Dalaguerre. Silver Star, Purple Heart, honorably discharged."

He left out a couple ribbons they slapped on me as apology for my getting left on an Afghanistan mountain and having to hike out on my own with a bullet in my side.

"Diagnosed with Schizoaffective Disorder," Square-face plows on, "but that didn't stop you from going after a serial killer who'd been hunting through Hill Country."

I'm not going to demand how he knows all this. Most is public record and he's an alleged private investigator. But him knowing who I am when I haven't even told Salome my name drives a couple barbs under my skin. My life would be a lot simpler if everyone, both the dead and the living, minded their own business.

"What does she have on you that's got you tailing after her like a whipped dog?" he asks. "Or is it that you couldn't adjust to civilian life and needed a livelier job than warehouse work?"

He did his research, I'll give him that.

"Is Trasmoz your employer?" he asks.

"We don't have a working contract," I say.

"Then what do you have?"

"What business we had is none of yours."

"So you've terminated whatever *relations*"—he puts an eye-rollingly lewd emphasis on the word—"you had between the two of you?"

"Can't really terminate something that was never there. Like I said, no contract."

"How did you first meet Ms. Trasmoz?"

"I don't know. I wasn't there."

"You're acting awful loyal to a woman you don't have any relationship with."

"You're confused. I'm not acting loyal to her. I'm acting antagonistically toward you."

Square-face gives me a look as if he's trying to figure out if I'm playing stupid or really am stupid. Little does he know I can do both at the same time.

"Do you know what she is?" he asks.

That he says "what" instead of "who" catches me up for a second. I figured from the start Salome Trasmoz wasn't her birth name and Square-face's question has me considering the hidden depths of Salome go far deeper than I originally guessed. It also confirms that Salome was lying when she said she didn't recognize Square-face. These two have a history.

"I don't care what she is," I say. She's probably a lot of things that trespass into an area of very grey morality. At the very least, she doesn't abide by traditional conventions, particularly the legal ones. "And whatever business I have with her is mine and not yours."

I stand to leave. Square-face steps in front to cut me off. He's a lot bigger than I am, both vertically and horizontally, and he thinks this gives him an edge. I roll my eyes. There's nothing more embarrassing than a guy thinking he's more intimidating than he really is.

"You think she's done with you?" he asks. "That she's going to let you walk away?"

"What're you talking about?"

"She's never let anyone go once they get involved with her."

"Then maybe you should stay away from her," I say and he doesn't miss the threat edging into my tone.

"Sorry I took so long." Mrs. Jackson, the charming cuckoo of impeccable timing, comes prancing back across the grass. "I knew I had an extra tourmaline somewhere."

She breezes right past Square-face to place a smooth black stone in my hand. "I think you'll need it," she says with as much gravity as an airy personality like hers can manage. "You know about the law of attraction, right?"

I've got a response for that I don't share as it's entirely inappropriate to say in front of a lady.

"It's the effect our energy has on our experiences. If you carry around negativity, you'll attract negative energy. If you carry and do positive things"—she pats my hand holding the stone—"you'll attract positive energy."

God bless her, she's sweet as pecan pie and just as nutty.

"Oh, how wonderful!" She claps her hands together, only

now noticing Square-face scowling a foot away. "You've met Sammy!"

She takes hold of Square-face's arm and beams. "Sammy is an old friend. He's been such a blessing to my family."

"Really?" I lean forward in rapt interest. "Mr. Campbell was just telling me he's a private investigator."

Square-face's stony façade is crumbling. I suppose the positive energy that is Mrs. Jackson can erode even him.

"Yes! That's how we met," Mrs. Jackson says, not letting go of Square-face's arm, oblivious to how difficult it is for him to endure this. "Arnold—my husband—and I had been cursed if you can believe that! A business competitor hired on a black magic practitioner to give us a string of bad luck. We tried the police, we tried ethics boards, called up a dozen private investigators, no one would take our case."

I wonder why.

"That is until Sammy came to us. Arnold was skeptical at first. He wanted to reach out to a shaman in New York to do a spiritual cleansing, especially after"—again her voice drops into a whisper like we're all sharing in on an inside joke—"he learned more about Sammy's reputation. But I was so desperate I agreed to let him take the case. Less than a week later, all the bad luck stopped, and Arnold and I now refuse to even consider hiring anyone else. I can't sing Sammy's praises enough."

"Is that so? Good thing the bad luck couldn't keep the good fortune of Sammy away," I say. So not only is Square-face a stalker and a thug but a con artist as well. He takes advantage of credulous people like the Jacksons who have thick wallets and no skepticism filter, sets up scenarios so they think they're haunted or cursed, then "solves" the mystery for a nice fee.

"So you investigate supernatural mysteries," I say to Square-face. Mrs. Jackson doesn't pick up on the knives being drawn beneath my smile. Square-face does and bristles. "How very niche."

"I investigate what my clients want investigated and go wherever that leads," he says.

"And that's what makes him so good," Mrs. Jackson says. "He isn't bound up by narrow-minded convention. You'd never think that by looking at him, would you? And he's on a case right now, did you know?"

Square-face opens his mouth but there's no rescuing this conversation from racing down the tracks it's headed with Mrs. Jackson as the conductor.

"He wouldn't tell me who or what, confidentiality and all, he is a professional, but when he told me it looked like there were paranormal aspects to a case and that he has to be able to talk to certain people"—she does a double wink so I don't miss that talking to "certain people" meant investigating someone here at this prestigious gathering—"I told him he just had to come to our little party tonight. You never know what energy people are going to bring and this may be the only time Sammy would be able to get all these energies in the same place."

Square-face's jaw is going to crack he's clenching it so tight. "Dana, if you don't mind, I—"

"Oh, I didn't interrupt anything, did I?" She finally lets go of Square-face's arm so her hands can flutter to her mouth. "I'm so sorry, I'll let you two talk."

To her, all of this is a funny game, and her grave offense is that she skipped someone's turn.

"Oh, we already talked," I say and wink. Mrs. Jackson claps her hands together, delighted to have more company to share in her game of paranormal mystery, protective stone charms, and letting astrology columns dictate her day. "Thank you for the tourmaline. If it keeps away negative energy, I don't have any more excuse not to mingle."

I offer her my arm. She gives a beaming smile and takes it.

"Oh my, what a gentleman," she says. "You don't find many of those these days. I might not give you back to Salome."

Square-face doesn't say anything as we walk back to the throng of people hanging closer to the house and Mrs. Jackson misses my flipping him the bird behind her back. There's not much he can say or do right now if he wants to stay in Mrs. Jackson's good graces which he is clearly dependent on.

I safely situate Mrs. Jackson in some lively gossip about how astrological retrogrades or similar nonsense have affected sex lives when I make my excuses to go find Salome. My patience with this whole affair is worn thin and it's a slow torture to wait for her to finish speaking to the grey-haired man with the sun-weathered face.

"Stop ..."

Up close, there's something about the Grey Man that gets me to do a double take. A strange feeling like I've seen him before.

"Please ... stop ..."

Visions of the dark construction site and the bright room flicker across my sight. I shake my head to clear it away. It's not Grey Man or any other guest that's putting me off. It's just Misery's nagging.

Salome nods, Grey Man leaves, and I slide into the space he vacated.

"Whatever you want, I'll give it to you," I say. "My only condition is that we leave right now."

"I don't think we should go just yet," she says. "How are the murmurings?"

"Present."

"Can you understand them?"

"No, and if Verkauf was going to show up she'd already be here."

"She's not going to show up." Salome hands me her phone. "Lena sent me an update on the evening news."

The article on the screen reads a big, bold, blood-chilling headline: Breaking News: Philanthropist Amanda Verkauf Found Murdered at Angel of Austin Charity.

Chapter 21

The radio won't stop sputtering as we drive back from the Jacksons'. We didn't stick around for much longer after seeing the news report. The article went into sensational detail, delighting in the drama of the night janitor coming in to find Verkauf's mutilated body splattered across her office.

Salome wasted no time reaching out to her "inside connections" as she called them to get details inaccessible to the public and her phone has been buzzing nonstop through the entire car ride. Forensic reports have yet to be finalized, but the trauma inflicted on Verkauf far exceeded what's possible to be done by human hands. No sign of forced entry, nothing stolen, no murder weapon, and the building had no camera security system to catch the intruder.

"Any mention of there being signs of a break-in at her house?" I ask.

Salome shakes her head. "And if there is, I'll take care of it."

"What about her partner?" I ask. "She was talking to someone on the phone when—"

"Taken care of."

"Taken care of how?"

"That's my end of the business," she says, checking her phone as it buzzes. "You just got to talk to the right people. That's why I dragged you to this party."

"How was she—"

"Black market organ trade. You can buy a butcher cheap who won't care if you're using an occult spice on the meat. Like I said, you just got to talk to the right people."

"That's it, then?" I ask. If Verkauf is dead, then this latest supernatural soiree is all wrapped up, I'm not needed anymore, and Salome doesn't have to keep dragging me around as an impending doom receptor.

"Kind of anticlimactic, isn't it?"

"You don't sound happy about it being over," I say.

She shrugs. "It doesn't feel neat. It feels like it's lacking proper closure."

I agree. There's a gaping hole in this mess and I can't help but feel something worse is due to crawl out.

"Do you think you're still in danger?" I ask, unable to shake the feeling this ain't done.

Salome laughs. "If I ever stopped thinking I was in danger I'd be dead. But if you mean from this, what you got tangled up in, no. That's done."

I'm not convinced on that score. Misery hasn't moved on. He continues to wail and beg in the background. That might not mean much. He hasn't proven to be a reliable haunt.

"What do you think happened to Verkauf?" I ask.

"Certainly wasn't natural causes," she says. "I'd like to think she tried to swim alongside too-big of sharks and one of them got her."

I wouldn't. I'd much prefer to think that someone rather than something got her. That altar she built certainly chummed the waters, but the idea that an incorporeal power has such reach into the physical world to rip Verkauf apart disturbs me. I'm unconvinced her death resulted from the evil she summoned turning around to bite the hand that fed it, and I can't shake the misgiving I'm missing a necessary ingredient in all this, leaving me stewing in blind vulnerability.

The black tourmaline stone is warm in my hand. I understand why Mrs. Jackson swears by its protective power. That a little charm can ward away the evil haunting this world is a comforting superstition and I'm not going to fault anyone for clinging to that.

Salome touches my hand fisted around the stone.

"Did you hear me?" she asks.

"I'll pack up my stuff and call a car," I say.

"To go where?"

"Home."

"Easy there, cowboy, you don't need to ride off," she says. "It's almost midnight. You can at least wait until morning."

I don't think it's a good idea to hang around much longer. There's this slow, sinking feeling that if I don't kick hard and swim back to shore, I'm going to lose sight of it entirely. I'm uncomfortable with the idea of leaving Salome as I think she's still at risk, but she's always going to be at risk. This is the life she's chosen, me sticking around will only follow her down roads I think wiser to leave unwalked, and I'm tempted to disregard that bit of wisdom telling me to turn back. There's a sense of purpose in this strange war of haunting entities and their earthly actors. A sense of meaning I've been missing. I'm willing to suffer a hell of a lot more than the murmurings of the damned, the shrieking of the dead, and all that moves in the dark to hold onto that.

"Or is it that you couldn't adjust to civilian life, and needed a

livelier job than warehouse work?" Square-face hit a little too close to home when he threw that line out. I'm so desperate for something to fight against I'm willing to enter into a ring where I'm suicidally out of my weight class.

"What's that?" Salome nods to the small black stone I'm rolling between my fingers

"Black tourmaline. Mrs. Jackson thinks I need protection from negative energy."

"And you believe that?"

"Oh, absolutely. I most certainly need protection from dark psychic forces."

"I mean do you believe it will actually work."

"I know what you meant. And no, I don't." I don't think physical objects have magical or holy powers. The black tourmaline will do nothing to ward away dark energies, just as my wearing a crucifix won't give me access to divine privilege and liberation from suffering.

"Then why did you keep it?"

"Because it was a gift and well-intended," I say.

The car follows the twisting road to Salome's driveway.

"You sure you won't wait until morning to leave?" she asks.

"I need to get back," I say.

"To what?"

Getting my life back together. These last couple days have broken all my defensive routines and it's high time I start the necessary repairs.

"Do you have a job? A girlfriend?" she asks.

Nope. Nope.

Jorge doesn't come around to open the door for Salome. He throws the car into park, shuts off the engine, and stomps off to leave us sitting in the back alone.

"Do you want a job?" she asks.

I don't answer.

"Look, I don't know what you've got going on in your life right now," she says, "but I do know you're a hot mess and while I've seen similar situations to yours before, never has it been as bad as what you have. A few of those folks have tried to do what I think you're planning on doing—"

"That's cute you think I have a plan," I say.

"That's cute you think I haven't caught on to this little game of yours yet. Tell me if I'm wrong, you're going to go home and try to ignore all this. You want to live as if none of what you see and hear is there, and you're going to waste a lot of time and energy acting as though it isn't."

She's not wrong so I don't tell her anything.

"It's never worked," she says. "For any of them."

I follow as she exits the car. Neither of us speaks until she pauses at the foyer's curving staircase.

"I can drive you home," she says, "but I'm gonna change first. If you change your mind during that time, let me know. If you change your mind any time after, let me know. You have my number and there's a place for you here."

***

If Salome was disappointed I didn't change my mind, she didn't show it when she came back down the stairs to find me waiting by the front door. She swapped out the red dress for loose, silken lounge wear that contrasts against the formal makeup she skipped washing away.

I keep quiet for most of the drive, taking my cue from the radio: no static or station to be found when Salome turned the dial. She looked to me for explanation for the silence and all I had to offer was a shrug. Home Ghost gave an enthusiastic

187

"hello" as we drove by and I pretended it didn't bother me. No one was fooled and Salome kept throwing me prompting glances which I kept pretending not to notice.

"Take this turn." I point down the street for my apartment complex when we cross over into Encrucijada's limits.

"Do you live alone?" she asks.

I shoot her a suspicious stare.

"I'm asking in a roundabout way if someone is looking after you," she says. "I didn't mean it like that."

"I have a roommate."

"That doesn't answer my question."

"Yes it does. It's this complex right here," I say.

"Not what I meant by it," she says, pulling into a parking space and shutting off the engine.

"Then you should've asked that."

I reach for the handle and she locks the doors.

"Is someone looking after you?" she asks.

"I'm fine." I don't look at her and keep my hand on the door.

"Just answer the question."

"It's not your business." It ain't distrust that's got me stonewalling her. It's shame. Not of the modest apartment life I live, but that I can barely manage that. It irritates me that Salome's not only seen enough in less than a week to figure me out, but she's decided it's bad enough to merit her interference.

I flip the lock up. It doesn't budge. She must have an override on the driver's side and her holding me hostage gets me to turn around and glare at her.

"You don't go until I say so," she says. "And actually, it is my business. This is what I do, so forgive me for feeling responsible to offer you help. Especially after all you've done."

"Thanks, but I don't need help. I already have too much."

"Let me guess, your parents or an older sibling act as legal guardians, using finance as the means to keep a hold on you. They're genuinely concerned, even loving, but they don't know what's really going on and so all that support and constant attention is suffocating. You see a therapist to keep your family happy but you don't take the medication prescribed because you know it doesn't help."

I try the door again and get the expected result.

"Your family is still hoping it's not really a neurological disorder," she continues, "that it'll all turn out to be posttraumatic stress from your time in the military—no, don't look at me like that. I know you served, that one was the most obvious."

"Yeah?"

"Your posture, your scars, the way you check a room screams 'uniform,'" she says.

"Alright, you got me." I throw my hands up in mock surrender. "Now open the door."

She's not done. "You have at least one confidant, friend or family, who has an idea of what's going on. It doesn't help much as you put more effort into keeping them in the dark than trusting in them because you don't want to be a burden or let them know how bad it really is."

I push the button to roll down the window. It won't budge.

"Is there a point to all this?" I ask.

"The point is you're fighting a battle on multiple fronts, it's killing you more than you're letting on, and a lot of the hurt you're taking on is from friendly fire."

She unlocks the door. I don't move. Hearing it out loud brings home how tiring it all is.

"It's okay to need help," she says.

"Thanks for the ride." I throw open the door. The claustrophobic feel isn't shaken by stepping out of the car into the night.

Salome gets out and follows after me.

"It's alright, I know where I live," I say. "You don't need to help me find the front door."

"That eager to be rid of me?" She links her arm in mine as she accompanies me across the parking lot. "After all you've done, this is the least I can do."

I slip my arm out from hers as we reach the front door to my apartment and she tries to press an envelope into my hand.

"That better not be payment," I say.

"For once, don't be difficult. Just take it."

"I told you. My fee is the pro bono sort," I say, fishing around for my keys lost in the sports bag's folds.

She moves to shove the envelope into the open bag. I yank it away and she jams herself between me and the door, wedging herself into the frame so there's no way for me to get the keys in the lock in a gentlemanly fashion.

"Don't make this harder than it has to be," she says.

"You really think you're gonna win this?" I arch an eyebrow.

"I always win." She smiles, expecting me to rise to the bait she's dangling. Her expression sours when I sit down against the opposite wall instead of playing by her rules.

"Your time is worth more than mine." I cross my arms. "You've got more to lose dragging this out, so you might as well save your time and money and call it."

"You always have to make things difficult?" She gives a pointless go at squeezing the overstuffed envelope under the door. "Don't you?"

I stand as she stalks over toward me. My grin is a hot poker prodding her temper and she's too slow to snatch the sports bag away.

"Stay still." Her hiss doesn't hide the start of a mischievous grin of her own.

Her hand misses my arm and when she lunges again I skip around to reach the unguarded door. Holding one foot up and out, I pivot to use my leg to block her from getting closer as she tries different angles of attack.

"If you don't stop fooling around, I'm gonna get mean," she says.

I unlock the door and am about to shoot off a suave, witty remark when she grabs hold of my foot and pulls hard. It doesn't move me much but the small stagger allows for her to spring through my compromised defense. Zeal carries her too far forward and we both trip. I twist so she falls on me instead of me on her and we hit the landing in a tangled heap.

"Are you—" I don't finish asking if she's alright. She sits down to pin my legs, takes hold of my pants' waist, and shoves both the envelope and her hand down.

Her lips against my ear are as soft as her whisper. "Gotcha."

Then she kisses me.

My brain does this weird thing where I think, "Where did that come from?" and "You've got hands, dumbass, use them!" and "Eh, whatever. This might as well happen" and "Stop this and stop it right now" and "Hot damn! She's definitely a top!" all at the same time, and that is too many thoughts for me to handle. In the absence of a working central nervous system, the endocrine system steps up to bat and hits a line drive to second base.

I didn't realize how cold I was. How numb. Her skin is warm and her mouth on mine is a resuscitating breath. I sit up and she slides her hips up to meet me, the motion seamless as we find easy rhythm with each other. I wrap an arm around her waist and she coils her legs around me. The feel of her calls back to a long-forgotten sense of life and feeds a neglected hunger. I can't remember the last time something more than terror got my heart pounding. The last time I felt connected to anything. Or anyone.

She's not wearing anything beneath her tank top and I'm seconds away from getting her out of that. I don't care we're in plain view of anyone on the street or looking out from their apartment. None of that matters. All that matters is not letting her go. It's been too long since I held her close. Felt her heart beating against mine. I tilt her back, gently shifting my hold to better pick her up so I can stand. Maria sighs and—

"What's wrong?" Salome asks when I stop. Her hand catches on the wedding ring necklace. I feel her fingers on it, turning it over, and realization dawns behind her eyes.

"It's alright," she says, "I get it."

She stands up, brushes off her pants, and tucks loose strands of hair back.

"Take care of yourself," she says and heads down the stairs to the parking lot. I stay seated on the landing until I hear her car door close and the engine rumble. It took a massive effort to hold onto common sense and not call her back and invite her in. It wouldn't go anywhere good. Not in the long run. And I know better than to put myself in that situation. Neither of us needs the mess that'd follow.

Breaking this off before it becomes anything is the right decision. That doesn't mean I don't slam a fist against the door, furious at myself for letting her go. The silence that follows her departure is fertile grounds for the murmurings.

They find the cracks and take ready root in the growing void I've been pretending isn't there.

Fine. Better that than using Salome to fill that space, because this way all I got to deal with is the hollowness. The other way, I'd have to deal with the hollowness and knowing I deserve it for cheapening someone as a means to be used for empty ends.

Blue light glows beneath Tyler's door and I hear the incessant *click-click-click* of him furiously abusing mouse and keyboard for the game he's dedicating all hours of his night to. I doubt he heard me come in. He's probably wearing headphones blaring either music or audio feed from teammates. His increasingly desperate demands for help followed by a string of cussing ending in a drawn out "Noooooooooo" is good indication he's talking to virtual friends.

Closing the door to my room fails to fully block out his mounting frustration. Flicking on the white-noise machine and the fans helps mask his cursing. The murmurings are harder to shake. They feel physical, brushing over me, reminding me of how exposed and alone I am.

They want to be heard.

I throw off the formal wear, leaving it and the envelope of payment abandoned on the floor. I don't have the energy to pull on a heavier shirt and sweatpants in false hope of warding off the metaphysical chill.

As I lie flat on the bed, my hand clutches the ring around my neck. It feels warm.

The only thing that does.

Chapter 22

"Logan!" Kitty's voice is as sharp as her pounding on the bedroom door.

I consider ignoring her like I've been trying to do the murmurings and Misery. He refuses to leave and has been a damn nuisance, sobbing up a storm all morning. I gave up scrolling back and forth through temporary job listings in the Austin area—the cold, the crying, and building pressure behind my eyes rendered the simple task impossible. The abandoned laptop lies open beside me as I stare at the wall, watching it change from the white paint it's supposed to be, to the stainless steel of the morgue-like room, to the abandoned construction site, and back again.

"Logan?" The knocking and her tone soften. "Could you open the door, please?"

I do and belatedly remember I should put on pants.

"Hold on," I say, close the door, pull on pants, reopen the door, and pretend I got it right the first time. "Who let you in?"

"The front door was unlocked." She pushes her way into my room to scan for signs of despondency and other red flags. The job site up on the laptop screen buys me some good grace in her book. It's a good thing I closed out the tabs of me looking into Square-face, aka Samuel Campbell, an ex-cop who resigned under suspicious circumstances concerning a questionable shooting of a suspect. There was nothing to be dug up about his private investigator gig besides plugging in his name for a license search showing him as certified.

"Are you packed?" she asks. Her eyes lock on the formal wear tossed on the floor and she gives me the "what the hell have you been up to?" look.

"Packed for what?" I ask.

"Mom and Dad are coming by tonight for dinner and picking you up for the week," she says.

"What? Why?"

"Because that's been the plan for the last two weeks."

"No one told me that," I say and she points to the calendar on the wall where the exact same thing is written on today's date and my appointment with Dr. Day is scrawled in for Tuesday. I forgot that under my parents' unyielding insistence my therapy appointments uptick to twice a month as November comes closer.

"So are you packed?" Kitty asks again.

"No." While it's lucky I can hitch a ride with the folks back to their place to avoid explaining why I can't drive myself, I'm not looking forward to any of this. "I have to do laundry first."

"You can bring your clothes over to my place," she says. "You were supposed to come by last night."

"Yeah, about that," I say. I'd rather skip staying at my sister's for the weekend as I need time to sort through the mess I've let infest my life. Kitty is having none of it. She doesn't even let me finish some lame-brained excuse to bail out of dinner.

"Unless you're gonna tell me who Mike Russo is—because no one at your Krav Maga place could when I called—and what you were really doing in Austin, if that is where you were, then I don't want to hear it," she says. "Grab your stuff and get in the car."

***

Everyone in Kitty's house knew I was in trouble so they all fled to avoid getting caught in her wrathful crossfire. Mary Katherine and Emmett are at friends' and Mark took the three youngest to a birthday party up around Burnet, a safe distance away to ensure all his wife's ire stays focused on me. Anyone who has a lick of common sense is avoiding Kitty's home like the plague, which means Glenny arrives an hour after I do. I suspect Kitty invited her over to figure out what the hell is going on with me.

"So are you going to tell me about it?" Glenny asks, dumping diced tomato into the pan. This has to be a coordinated effort between the two of them because after Kitty extended an invitation for Glenny to stay for dinner, she didn't miss a beat in offering to make enchiladas and lo and behold, all the ingredients were freshly bought at the store the previous day.

"Tell you about what?" I ask. I offered to make dinner but Glenny demanded I watch her child instead. She'll be looking to switch roles soon as I'm keeping Titus entertained by doing clapping pushups over him. He thinks it's a riot. Glenny not so much.

"About your job." She throws up scare quotes around "job."

"Wasn't planning on it."

"Why not?"

"It's over and done," I say. "No need to drag it back up."

The feeling that loose ends are left open and are about to be turned into lit fuses nags at me. I teeter back and forth between calling Salome to check if all is clear on her end or

196

washing my hands of her business entirely. I figure if she was in trouble she'd call me. I'm not disappointed when I realize I'll have to call her anyway to give back that suit sitting on my bedroom floor.

"Who's Salome?" Glenny asks.

"What?"

"Salome." She draws out the name. "Who is she?"

"That's my business, not yours."

Different ways last night could've gone play out through my mind. None of them involve Salome leaving and all of them involve a lot less clothing.

Pots clatter as Glenny rifles through the cabinets in a sudden fit of violent fury.

"Do you need help?" I pick up Titus, who is letting loose a monsoon of drool as he tries to eat his fist, and offer to trade the baby for the spatula.

"No." She bangs the glass baking pan down on the stove top.

"Alright, knock it off, you're gonna break something," I say, getting her to switch so she can let this bad mood of hers burn instead of burning dinner.

She sulks at the dining room table, bouncing Titus up and down as she glowers. When Maria got moody like this I learned the hard way she was waiting for me to ask what was wrong. It's a dangerous can of worms to open but a man's gotta do what a man's gotta do.

"Are you really going to throw a fit over me not telling you about Austin?" I ask.

"I'm not mad about that."

"Did you already put the cumin in?"

"She's just using you!" Glenny blurts out.

"Who?"

"That woman you keep thinking about! The one you were playing tonsil hockey with outside your apartment last night. Salome." She spits out the name like venom.

I stop grating the cheese.

"You were there?" I ask and once it's out of my mouth I realize how stupid the question was. Of course she wasn't there.

"Of course I wasn't there!" she says, wet-cat mad. "You just keep thinking about it!"

I go back to grating the cheese. "Is that why you're all bothered? 'Cause if that's the case, that's your fault for snooping around my head."

"It's not my fault you're thinking about it so loud!"

Titus fusses, upset by his mom's yelling, and Glenny glares at me like that's my fault too.

"Alright, I'll stop thinking about it," I say, and I really do try to think about something else. Unfortunately, all roads lead to Salome and they are very dirty roads.

"Well, you should stop seeing her too. Is that what you were really doing in Austin? Banging some creepy witch chick?"

"She's not a creepy witch chick."

"You're being deliberately obtuse!" she says, an accusation she took straight out of Kitty's playbook.

"And you're being nosy."

"Can't you see she's just using you?"

"How would you know?"

"Because you do! You know she's using you and you don't want to admit it! I know what you found in her basement—"

"That wasn't her basement."

"—and you're letting how lonely you are make you stupid!"

"You really want to be casting stones about making stupid

choices?" I ask. South of twenty, with no ring on the finger and a baby on her hip, Glenny doesn't have a lot of weight to be throwing around in this arena.

"So you are having sex with her!"

"I never said that."

"Well you're thinking it!"

"That's none of your damn business."

"I mean, I knew you were looking for a replacement," she says, "or like, someone to fill in for her, but are you really that desperate?"

I'm going to bite through my tongue chewing back words I know I'll regret. Glenny throwing a fit over what doesn't concern her in the slightest is getting under my skin, and she's either clueless that she's got the water boiling or doesn't care 'cause she turns up the burner.

"And don't pretend you don't know what I'm talking about 'cause all that time you were thinking about Salome"—again she says the name like it leaves a bad taste in her mouth—"you kept putting Maria in there instead."

"You need to stop," I say.

She doesn't stop. She goes on about how she knows I've been trying to find a replacement for Maria, comparing everyone and everything to her, how she went about things, how she spoke, what she would do. That I've been doing it more as November rolls around. How I'm willing to let someone who doesn't care about me walk all over me while I ignore everyone who does care. That I'm only making it worse. I'm looking for someone who isn't there and it's making me blind.

"Get out," I say, too quiet to hear, anger strangling off the words.

She says I need to get over it. That Maria's gone and—

"GET OUT!" My fist slamming the cutting board sends shredded chicken and sauce splattering to the floor. Glenny stares at me in a way that makes my stomach hurt but I've had my fill of her rooting around my head.

"Get out, Glenny," I say again, leaving no room for argument.

She doesn't say anything. She grabs the baby bag and makes it to the hallway before she can't keep her tears quiet. Each sob feels like a gut punch. My legs are lead and I don't go after her.

Kitty rushes down the stairs as the front door slams shut.

"What happened?" she asks, seeing the kitchen floor littered in chicken and sauce.

"I don't know," I say and she whirls to chase after Glenny.

I catch a glimpse of them through the kitchen window as I toss the fallen food into the garbage disposal. Kitty talks to Glenny as she packs Titus up in the car seat. Glenny keeps shaking her head, eyes red from crying, and Kitty's face is strained by an expression I can't read. She stands in the driveway for a couple minutes after Glenny drives off, arms crossed and lips pressed tight. I'm ready for a chewing out when she comes back into the kitchen.

"What's going on with you?" she asks. Her weariness is worse than anger.

"Nothing."

"Is this about—"

"It's not about Maria!" I'm tired of people talking about her as if she's just a problem I have.

"Who's Salome?"

"No one."

"Glenny says you've been seeing her. That's what you've been doing down in Austin."

"Glenny says a lot of stupid shit." I refuse to budge when she moves to herd me away from dinner prep.

She also refuses to budge. "What were you doing in Austin?"

I consider saying "Just ask Glenny" or "None of your damn business" or "Could everyone leave me alone for five fucking minutes?"

"I thought someone needed help," I say. And true to form, whenever I try to fix anything, it only makes matters worst. Glenny was right on that score.

I scoot over to make room for Kitty to help finish the enchiladas once I'm sure she's done asking questions for the time being. The quiet isn't a calm one. It's the empty space between the ticks of a time bomb that I'm not gonna be able to defuse.

"I wish you'd tell me what's going on," she says when I slide the baking dish into the oven.

The uncomfortable tension swells as we set the table, clean up the kitchen, and wait for the other to say anything. I should tell her. She deserves to know what was going on. She won't approve, but she'll understand, and then she'll know it's got nothing to do with November.

The doorbell rings and the confession on the tip of my tongue retreats back into silence. Kitty gives me a look that's equal parts plea and warning to keep it together for our parents. That she even bothered shooting me that backward glance speaks how much more of an optimist she is than I am.

Chapter 23

An ominous four minutes of intense whispering pass between Kitty opening the front door to let our parents in and them coming down the hall. Mom's face is pinched in worry as she looks me over, my father's mouth is a thin line of disapproval, and Kitty pretends that she didn't spend that four minute delay updating them on how much trouble I've been.

"Remington." Mom hugs me and I'm slow to return the gesture. It feels awkward, done out of habit and lacking sincerity. Aside from the dark hair, Kitty is our father's carbon copy and I'm our mother's.

"What's this about you not being able to drive anymore?" my father asks.

I shoot Kitty a "you told them?" glare. It's an expression I mastered in childhood and should've outgrown. Looking like an indignant six-year-old being ratted out by his oldest sister doesn't earn me any points.

"Can't this wait until after dinner?" Mom asks.

"We decided it'd be better if he didn't drive for a while. Just as a precaution," Kitty says.

"Are you hallucinating again?" my father asks.

"Chase, this can wait," Mom says. "We just got here."

"Katherine told us—"

"Told you what?" I give Kitty an uglier glare and she gives one back without any quarter.

"Remington, if the medication isn't working you need to tell the doctors," my father plows on, undeterred. Despite using my name, he addresses this to Kitty. It was her job to make sure I didn't fall off the prescription wagon.

"This can wait," Mom says.

The oven beeps and I take that as an opening to escape this fun family talk.

"I got it." Kitty pushes me out of the way to get to the oven first. "Go sit at the table."

"What did you tell them?" I hiss. She ignores me, overcomplicating the enchilada extraction from the oven so she doesn't have to answer.

I grab a wine bottle to bring over to the table as a peace offering for the parents.

"So you're drinking now," my father says, using his courtroom voice like he's setting a witness up for a perjury trap.

"No," I say.

Mom stands up to take the wine bottle away. "I'll take care of that, go ahead and sit."

She uses pouring my father a glass of wine as a chance to whisper to him, "He's looking thin."

"Dr. Day said the days leading up to anniversaries are harder than the actual day itself," my father replies.

"Kitty said he's dating someone."

"She said 'seeing' someone. That's not the same as dating."

Not wanting to burst their bubble, I act like I can't hear them whispering two feet away about their mounting skepticism concerning my mental stability as November approaches.

"How have you been?" Mom sits back down beside me. "Are you doing okay with everything going on?"

"Fine, how about you guys?"

"Don't change the subject," my father says.

"I wasn't changing the subject, I was being civil."

"Just answer the question, Remington."

"How's the garden?" I ask, changing the subject. "Pumpkins growing alright?"

"Oh, the garden's doing well," Mom says. "The deer are giving us a run for our money."

I make it a good fifteen minutes sticking to unswerving garden talk, refusing to follow my father's line of questioning about how I'm handling Maria and my anniversary coming up, or if I'm suicidal and looking to repeat how I celebrated last year's anniversary.

Kitty looks like she's holding a baking pan filled with lit firecrackers as she delivers the food to the table, but as we all make it through grace, I chance the hope we might make it through dinner. Mom tries to hold off my father by talking to Kitty about the kids and Mark. My father keeps trying to get me to make eye contact with him across the table. I'm too busy watching the great enchilada migration as I push it back and forth across my plate.

"You're not eating much," Mom says.

I'm not hungry. There's this hollowness that's been eating at me since last night.

"Kitty says you've been moody lately," Mom continues.

She's not wrong.

"So what's going on?"

"Nothing," I say.

"Aren't you warm wearing that?" Mom plucks at my shirt.

"No."

"It's eighty degrees, why are you wearing long sleeves?" my father asks.

Because I'm cold all the fucking time.

I shrug. "No reason."

My father is unimpressed by my lackluster responses. "Are you hiding self-injury?"

"What? No."

Mom rolls up my sleeve to check.

"Mom, stop." I jerk my arm away.

"What happened to your hands?" she asks.

I tuck them beneath the table to hide the scabbing knuckles from the construction site scuffle.

"Krav," I say.

"Don't you wrap your hands for that?" Kitty asks.

"Not for knuckle pushups."

"Did you get into a fight?" She narrows her eyes at me and I know I've lost any hope of having her as an ally.

"No," I lie, accepting I'm about to get into another one.

My father sighs and folds his hands on the table. He's finished with this farce of a family dinner. "Remington, your mother and I have been talking."

Oh shit, here it comes.

"We think it'd be best if you stayed with us for the month of November."

"Why?"

"You don't have a job anymore and—"

"I'm applying," I say.

"We just think it might be better for a little while," Mom says, resting a hand on my arm.

"Why?"

"Well, we're worried November might be difficult for you."

"And your behavior this last month has been concerning," my father says.

"According to who?" I ask.

"So you haven't been acting strangely?"

"No."

"Has he been acting strangely?" my father turns to Kitty.

"Yes," she says.

"Like what?" he asks, and my snitching sister rats me out. She tells them all about me disappearing down to Austin, lying about where I was, not returning her calls. That she didn't know where I was, what I was doing, only vaguely with whom and it turns out I lied about that. Mom's face goes white and she grabs hold of my arm as if she's afraid I'll scamper off to find the nearest roof to jump from. My father's lips disappear he presses them so tight as Kitty ties it all up with the Glenny-inspired rumor that I've been sleeping around with a strange woman.

Alright, I admit it sounds pretty bad when she lays it out like that.

"Remington, is this true?" my father asks. His courtroom voice is gone and there's anger snapping behind each word.

"No," I say and no one believes me which begs the question why he asked in the first place.

"Katherine, why didn't you tell us earlier?"

"Because it's only you who thinks I should operate on a short lead," I say.

"And you ignoring your sister's phone calls, running off to Austin, failing to keep a job, refusing to take your medication, lying about it, and sleeping around with strangers contradicts this thinking how?"

The murmurings rise up from the hollowness to claw at the edge of all my senses. It's getting hard to breathe, let alone think. I don't want to be here. A hand grabs my shoulder. The flash of panic turns to relief when I see it's only my father come around the table to pull me back to attention.

"Answer me when I talk to you," he says.

"I didn't hear," I say and the last shred of his patience goes out the window.

"Are you hallucinating again?" he asks.

I've never hallucinated but that's not what he wants to hear.

"You are taking the medication, right?" Mom asks.

"Yes," I say.

"How often?"

"Whatever the prescription says," I say.

"Are you taking the medication?" Mom presses. Judging by their expressions, both she and my father already know the answer.

"It doesn't help," I say and my father slams his fist down on the table.

"When are you going to start taking responsibility for yourself?!"

"Chase, don't yell at him. He's not well," Mom says.

"He can yell all he wants, Mom," I say. It might be for the best to let him blow off the steam that's been building ever since he found out his son is mentally disturbed. Being faced with problems that can't be fixed isn't something either of us is good at. "Go ahead and let it out, that's what the therapists always say."

"Don't take that tone with me," my father snaps.

Good start, but he can keep going.

"Let's not pretend you haven't been waiting to tear into me

for months now," I say. "Might as well get it over with." Go through your laundry list of grievances with me. Let it all out.

"You don't talk—"

"But you do. You talk nonstop about how I'm such a goddamn problem. How I don't take responsibility for myself, how I'm a fucking embarrassment to you."

Everybody's staring at me like this is the looniest thing they've ever heard.

"What, you think I didn't hear you guys talking about me? That I couldn't hear what you've been saying every time you drag me to that fucking therapist? That I can't hear what you're saying when you're just down the hall or when I'm in the same goddamn room?"

"Remington, calm down, please," Mom says.

"No one is saying that."

"And now you're using my anniversary to send me back off to St. Jude's!"

"Sweetheart, you're not well." Mom tries to appeal to the reason she doesn't believe I have. "I know this is a hard time of year for you, but we can only help if you let us."

"I don't need help! I'm fine! I'm just sick of all y'all acting like I can't take care of myself and then trying to lock me back up when I do!"

I stand and everyone else rises to meet me.

"You're projecting," my father says.

"This is the paranoia talking," Mom says.

"I'm not paranoid!" I yell, furious everyone is being so dismissive.

"We know you miss her—"

"This isn't about Maria," I snap.

"If you need to talk about—"

"This isn't about Maria!"

"You need to calm down," my father warns, taking hold of my shoulder.

I shove him off. "If you want me gone just say it and I'll go. Don't waste the money on commitment."

"No one wants you gone—"

"Then why did you send me away in June?!"

"Sweetheart, we talked about this," Mom says. "Remember? With Dr. Day? When you feel abandoned you have—"

"I don't have abandonment anxiety!" This has been a sticking point of late. Between being left for dead and losing Maria, Mom thinks I'm going to break down into a rocking mess if no one is around to hold my hand.

"You wouldn't if you were on your medication."

"I don't need the medicine!"

"You need to settle down."

"We're only trying to help."

"I don't need help!" I need everyone to stop talking. My chest is too tight and my hands won't stop shaking.

"Alright, that's enough," my father says. "We'll talk with the landlord, see if we can end your lease early or find a sublet. You're obviously not able to take care of yourself. Go pack up, we'll take you back tonight, see if we can get an earlier appointment in with Dr. Day."

"No."

"Excuse me?" he asks.

"I said no."

"You don't get a say in this."

"And you don't get to ship me off whenever you get tired of putting up with me and then expect me to come back when you feel bad about it."

"Don't take that tone with me."

"You've already said that," I say, "and if you got nothing new to say, we're done here."

"We're only trying to help." Mom reaches out to take my hand and I jerk away.

"You either move back with us and prove you can get your act together, or we're going to have to file for a ninety-day hold," my father says, wielding commitment like some casual punishment waiting for a misbehaving toddler.

"That's not your call," I say.

"Yes it is! You signed the same contract!"

"I don't—"

"We're not going to stand by and wait for you to try and kill yourself again!"

"Well, let's face it, if I hadn't fucked that up we'd all be better off—"

I don't think my father meant to hit me so hard. I don't think he meant to hit me at all. He'd never done it before. I just pushed the right button at the right time and he knocks my head back against the cabinet behind me.

No one speaks, no one moves. There aren't even the murmurings.

"You don't say that," my father says, and only in that silence am I able to hear how terrified he is of what his son has become.

"Thanks for dinner, Kitty," I say, avoiding all the eyes on me as I walk out to the foyer.

"Remington, get back here," he calls after me as I pull on my coat. It's getting colder by the second and I can't hold back the shivering.

"You running away isn't gonna solve anything."

He chases me out the front door. I keep walking.

"I didn't raise a coward," he says.

He gets half a heartbeat's pause with that one. While there's no shortage to my vices and failings, cowardice is not one of them. Knowing that should be an armor against such a stupid attack. If anyone else had said it I would've laughed in their face. That it's my father leveling that accusation flays away the thickest skin, leaving a raw, ugly wound.

I go back to walking. Family fun is done for the evening. There isn't anything left to be said.

"Remington!"

His hand snags my arm to turn me around to face him. I easily shrug him off and just as easily block out everything he says. I've got too much practice building up walls against unwanted clamor for him to make a dent. He follows after me longer than I expect, gives up a little past the driveway, and drops away. The relief at being left alone sours when I hear a car engine turn.

He swings the car up in front of me to block the way.

"You really want to play this game of chicken?" I ask as he rolls down the window. "Because I'm not worried about going under the tires if push comes to shove."

"That's not funny," he says.

It wasn't a joke.

He moves the car forward when I go to walk around and back when I try to go the other way. I vault over the hood. My father doesn't give up. He keeps the car at a creeping pace to drive beside me. After nearly half a mile of this stupid stunt I stop and he brings the car to idle on the road beside me.

"You're really going to do this the whole way?" I ask. It's a dumb question. Of course my father is stubborn enough to drive at a crawl after me for the five miles between Kitty's house and my apartment.

He doesn't say anything. I recognize his expression. It's the one he wore for nearly the whole month after I was released from St. Jude's. Somewhere along the way his son became a stranger and he can't figure out how to fix it.

He doesn't know what to do with me.

Neither do I.

I turn away from the road to walk into the trees. My father's voice chases after me. The murmurings join in, thick as the brush I push through. They snag and pull at me same as the low branches, cling to me like the prickling burrs I pick up as I move farther from the road. I can't tell my father's voice apart from the murmurs. It all sounds the same, chastising, gloating, a reminder of everything I've failed to be. A cold grip accompanies a stubborn branch tearing my shirt and the murmurings laugh, repeating everything I yelled over the dinner table.

I break into a run. A hammering heart and the angry thud of my footfall masks the murmurings. It's not running that has my breathing coming hard and the red I'm seeing isn't from the sepia curtain.

Going as the crow flies shaves off over a mile between Kitty's place and mine. I see my father's car in the apartment parking lot through the last of the trees. He's most likely waiting to ambush me at the door. Or Tyler might've let him in if he was able to hear the knocking through his headphones.

I cut around the back way to clamber in through my bedroom window. I always leave it unlocked. It's not like being more diligent with security keeps out any trespassers I'm worried about.

The moment I pull myself through the window a knock sounds at the bedroom door.

"What?" I throw the door open and Tyler staggers back against the hallway wall.

"Uh, did you know your dad's outside?" he asks.

I close the door on him.

"Does that mean you do?" he asks. "Do you want me to let him in?"

The clock radio on my desk clicks and whirs.

"Good morning … kshhk … kshk … this is Mar … shhhhhkkk …"

I find it in me to ask what I've long suspected.

"You're not really Maria. Are you?"

The radio sighs.

"Are you?"

"No," it says in her voice.

I hurl it against the wall and it breaks into a dozen pieces. That's not enough to get it quiet. It strums out the opening notes of "Can't Help Falling in Love."

"Shut up! Shut up! Shut up!" I snarl and for once it listens.

I drag the desk over to serve as a wedge between the door and wall. The barricade barely allows the door to open an inch when I give it a hard test. A few more tugs chip the door's wood and convince me no matter how much he huffs and puffs, my father won't get in.

Hiding in my bedroom. Looks like my father raised a coward after all.

Red burns hot over my sight and my arm makes a violent sweep over the dresser knocking off books, the rock Deborah painted for me, and the lamp, which shatters against the wall. The dresser is light and too easy to shove over, giving no satisfaction as it slams to the floor. I put a fist shaped dent in the cheap drywall and quick as it came, the flash of temper grows cold, leaving an empty pit in my gut and the sensation of abandoned free fall.

I really do only make things worse.

"Yeah, he's here," Tyler says and two sets of footsteps come down the hall. Tyler's heavy plod is almost a run as he hurries away and shuts the door to his room. If he didn't want the fireworks he shouldn't have opened the front door.

"Remington." My father's knock on the door is soft.

Much as I do for every other voice that needs blocking out, I turn on the fans. It's second nature to hitch onto their whir and let everything else fade away. The door bounces off the desk as my father tries to force his way in.

"Open the door!" He pounds on the thin wood.

I sit down at the keyboard. The fan's mechanical whir acts as metronome to match a tune to. The volume is set to barely audible, allowing only the ghost of Schubert's "Ave Maria" to answer the keys.

A loud crack gets me to turn my head. The murmurings muffle my father's anger as he struggles to get in. The door doesn't budge, chipping on the desk's edge under each shove.

"Remington, please!" The whole door shudders as my father throws his weight against it. All that does is get the desk to dent both the wall and the door. "I'm sorry."

I was doing a pretty good job of tuning it all out until that point. There's something crushing about your father apologizing through a closed door and it hurts to hear.

Going over to open the door never makes it beyond a thought. A chasm has replaced the bedroom floor and I can't find the energy to cross it. I can't see the point of it either. Of anything, really.

I throw the keyboard's volume all the way up. The piano plays mechanical. All rote and no soul.

"Please, I didn't mean it."

I fish around for the industrial headphones beneath the bed and shove them on. The fans, the insects humming outside the window, the soulless plunk of piano keys, my father's pleas all disappear and the murmurings rise up to take the vacated space.

Chapter 24

It's dark by the time I slip off the headphones. All is quiet on the western front. Except for the murmurings. And Misery screaming. And that hollow feel that's taken on a life of its own, whistling cold and empty like wind out from an abyss.

But there's no disappointed father at the door. No click of keyboards and squeak of an overtaxed computer chair from Tyler's room. No static from the broken radio.

The clock on my phone reads a little past eleven at night and there's a throng of missed messages from Kitty, Mom, my father, and Glenny. I run a hand over my face. The slow creep of guilt replaces that cold hollowness and kicks me out of my wallowing.

I'll call them back in the morning. They're not right about the source of the problem, but they're not wrong about my behavior in handling it. Most of all this could've been avoided if I'd been up-front with Kitty. Lying wasn't fair to her. Not after all she's done. Since I stirred up this shitstorm, if the demanded penance for my selfishness is surrendering to the authority of a family who gives a damn and are more invested in my well-being than I am, then the only thing to do is to suck it up and say "thank you."

It's tempting to skip brushing teeth and all those hygienic hang-ups of being a functioning person and just flop down on the bed. Too bad that's against the rules, and the impressive score of failures I've racked up in the last week doesn't excuse my continuing the trend. My phone hums with another message from Glenny asking me to call her if I'm still awake. I'm reaching for the phone when a soft *thump* sounds in the dark.

Did my father camp out on the couch? I wouldn't put it past him.

I leave the lights off as I step out into the apartment's living room and kitchen space. No dark form lays sprawled across the beige sofa or sits in the mismatched sand-colored armchair, both of them rescued from the roadside.

Thump.

I step to the side. Instinct moves me to take up position behind a wall away from the windows. The same instinct tells me the noise isn't from the neighbors or the pipes.

Thump. Thump.

It sounds like it's coming from the front door.

Thump.

I don't walk over to look through the spyhole. It's not really at the door—that's just how my senses are translating the fact that something is trying to get in.

Thump. Thump. Thump.

A static-chopped voice hisses from my bedroom. Not taking my eyes off the front door, I slowly back down the hall into my room.

Thump. Thump.

A panicked whirl of numbers flicker over the smashed radio's digital face despite it being unplugged and the screen hanging by a thin sliver of plastic. The flurry of light casts an eerie glow over the bedroom's ceiling and walls.

"Kssh—it's coming—kshkkk—go—ksshkk ..." The crackling warning can't come through and sounds as though it's muffled by an unseen hand.

Thump.

It's coming from the walls of my bedroom now. Sepia skeins pollute the air, cracking the walls and floor into spiderweb patterns.

Thump. Thump.

The spare car keys I didn't surrender to Kitty are in my coat pocket and she agreed to let the car stay at the apartment in case of emergencies. This is an emergency.

The bedroom light flicks on without me touching the switch, a mocking concession that this coming presence doesn't need the dark. I hear the car keys jingle as I snatch my coat off the floor and rush out to drive to Our Lady of Sorrows. I don't know if holy ground has staying power in a fallen world but it's the only option I got.

Thump. Thump.

The hallway wall shudders as I sprint to the front door.

Logan, the entity calls.

Thump.

The broken radio roars, sepia runs like rot down the walls, and the coat I'm holding shifts of its own accord. The cloth shivers and the sleeve reaches up toward me as if guided by an invisible arm.

"Holy shit!" I throw the coat away. It clings on by a hand coming out of the other sleeve. The flesh is mottled, inhuman, and decaying into me.

Logan, it croons.

The coat hits the floor, the hand holds on, blackening and curling up my arm like a living fungus. Tendrils dart out, snagging my chest to spread the infection.

"Shit! Shit!" I tear at it and bits crumble away like ash as it digs in to spread polluting veins beneath my skin. I feel it rotting my flesh as it slithers up my arm.

I stumble back into the kitchen counter, ripping at my arm to escape the growing black. For every piece I tear away another three tendrils form and burrow deeper into me. I feel it growing inside me, spreading in those sick veins to devour me from within.

"No! NO! Get off!"

The entity laughs, reminding me I once asked for oblivion, and here it is. It delves beneath my ribs toward my lungs and heart.

I grab a knife from the butcher's block and jam it beneath my skin, desperate to cut the darkness out. Blackened blood wells up as I carve and claw to pull out the roots. Broken prayers and pleas hiss between my clenched teeth. My hands are slick and my skin burns despite the cold worming its way in.

"GET OUT!"

The entity laughs and swarms deeper. I chase after it with hands and knife, cutting chunks of it out from me and losing the fight to stop its spread.

Logan ...

A dark hand closes over my heart. Cold fingers puncture my lungs.

"Logan!"

I need to get it out. Get it out. Get it—

"Logan!"

Tyler wrenches my hand back and rips the knife from my grip.

"What the hell are you doing?" His hands are covered in blood and for a panicked moment I think the entity's burrowed into him too.

The sepia evaporates under the kitchen's light and the entity's laughter disappears.

"Jesus Christ," Tyler breathes.

I follow his gaze. My chest, abdomen, and arm are a red smear of slashes and gouging cuts. It's my blood on his hands. On the cabinets. Splattered on the counters and dripping onto the floor. There's no black in the weeping red. My skin isn't rotting, the muscle beneath is no longer withered. I don't feel the skin-crawling presence of the entity and even the murmurings are little more than a hush. My hammering heart slows, no longer clutched in that piercing grip, and if not for the blood, I'd think it was all a nightmare.

"Alright just … just stay there." Tyler slowly backs away. "I'm gonna call someone. You'll be okay, just don't move."

"No, don't! Don't call!"

With the entity gone I'm able to see how this must look to Tyler and my chest goes right back to being cold and rigid.

"It's not what it looks like," I say which is what everyone says when it is exactly what it looks like.

Tyler keeps backing away like I'm going to attack him next.

"Just stay there," he says. "I'm gonna call someone for you."

He's going to call an ambulance. They're going to drag me off to a hospital and then back to a psych ward. There's no way I'm going to be able to convince anyone this wasn't self-harm and telling the truth—that I was trying to cut a demonic entity out from inside me—is the worse explanation. So I do the sensible thing. I grab my coat, car keys, and book it out of there.

"Logan, wait!" Tyler yells. I give him points for coming after me a couple steps before remembering I'm batshit crazy and common sense overrides courage.

The radio is on before I turn the car's ignition and throws a diatribe of static at me. Blood has soaked into my pants and wet, red lines crisscross over my bare feet as I slam down on the gas and roar out of the parking lot.

Chapter 25

The gate opens the moment I press the buzzer. Salome stands in the doorway at the end of the long driveway, silhouetted by the hallway lights behind her.

"So you can drive," she says as I get out of the car.

"I said I shouldn't drive, not couldn't," I say.

It was a harrowing trip down to Austin where Home Ghost was the least of my hiccups. The radio shrieked and sputtered the whole time, never able to break into clarity as it wrestled to be heard against a strangling force. The numbers of the display fizzled into broken lights and whenever I manually turned the dial in hopes of getting a signal, a cold numbing pulse shot up my arm and the murmurings snarled.

"STOP. STOP. STOP!" Misery made an appearance a few miles into the drive and he hasn't let up.

"So what has you rolling up to my door unannounced to make a social call this late …" Salome stops when I step into the light flowing off the porch. Her eyes jump from my chest to my arms, back to my chest and follow the blood trails soaking my shirt, pants, and trickling down to my feet. "Oh my God. Who did that?"

"I did."

"You what? What happened?"

"You said you had contacts in the medical field who don't ask questions?"

"I'll call him." She beckons me inside and shows me to the breakfast nook. "Sit there, don't move, and for God's sake don't touch anything sharp."

She steps away to make the call. Her voice is a soft murmur that joins in with the ones that never leave.

Now that I'm no longer ripping demon fungi out from me and fleeing the scene to avoid being carted off in a straitjacket, I have time to assess the damage. I've skinned a fair chunk of dermal tissue off my arm and scored deeper cuts crisscrossing all over my chest. I don't think I hit anything vital. Blind panic saved me from being too efficient in digging out a demon and kept the damage superficial.

"He's on his way." Salome comes back, carrying a first aid kit in hand. She doesn't ask permission before using small scissors to cut off what's left of my shirt.

"At this hour?" I ask, soaking a cloth in disinfectant and enjoying the sharp sting of dabbing alcohol on an open wound. Most of the cuts have begun to coagulate; a few still ooze lazy, red rivulets.

"He's used to odd calls," she says and hisses when she uncovers a deeper gash in my side right over the gunshot scar.

"DON'T!"

I flinch under Misery's shriek. It's easy to pass it off as me recoiling from the disinfectant burn on the cuts.

"Let me know how much it costs, I'll pay," I say. In my hurried departure I didn't even remember to grab my wallet. Or that formal suit I've been meaning to get back to Salome that's sitting rumpled on the floor.

"You don't pay for favors—and no, don't try and convince me this is unrelated to you helping me out," she says.

"I don't think it is." I'm more inclined to believe it's a consequence of me flirting with the supernatural in general, not anything specifically related to Salome's mess of monsters. I opened the door and as expected, the entity waltzed right in.

"I thought I'd be seeing you soon," she says, "but not like this."

Her first aid kit is impressively prepared. She's got surgical adhesive tape, combat gauze dressing, elastic bandages, a nasopharyngeal airway kit, sharp tubes, syringes—and that's just the first layer.

She puts on surgical gloves before pressing a cloth over one of my lazily weeping gashes.

"You want to tell me what happened?" she asks.

She doesn't say anything as I tell the story. When I get to the demon hand coming out of the coat I feel her hands holding the cloth in place tighten.

"Is this another new one for you?" she asks.

"Yeah."

"But you've seen this entity before?"

"Not since summer. And that blackness crawling over me was more like what I saw at the Driskill," I say.

Salome frowns. "Don't take this the wrong way, but have you considered it might've all been in your head?"

I nod. I know I didn't imagine the entity. Its presence was very real. That doesn't mean it was physically there. I could've been carving away at nothing, my mind translating the spiritual threat into a physical one, resulting in me doing more damage to myself than the entity did. And maybe that's exactly what it means to do, herd me down a path of self-destruction. If so, I'm doing a bang-up job of playing right along.

"What about the murmurings, could you hear them?" she asks.

"Yeah, but it was the usual nonsense," I say. "No real clarity."

Salome shakes her head. "You're one of the strangest cases I've ever come across and that's saying a lot."

"I was wondering if … uh …" I don't like asking for help and can't spit it out.

"You need a place to stay and lie low because your roommate caught you carving into yourself and whoever your legal guardian is doesn't understand what's really going on?" she guesses.

"Something like that."

"I told you before, there's a place for you here, and that hasn't changed." She takes off one of her gloves to rest her hand on my cheek. "Let me help you."

***

The buzzer rings and Salome is not subtle about sliding the surgical scissors out of my reach.

"I'll be right back," she says, disappearing around the corner to greet the new arrival. "Don't touch anything."

"Ms. Trasmoz," the newcomer says. "Always a pleasure to see you are well."

"I've got an odd one for you, Dr. Raim."

"You always do."

I'm certain I've seen the man following after Salome before and look him over for any sign of supernatural corruption—a darkness flickering beneath his features or a haze hanging over him. He's about sixty, face lined from both age and activity. He's got a healthy tan that speaks to large chunks of time dedicated to the outdoors and has a physically fit build to match. Grey eyes peer at me from behind flat top eyeglasses and beneath greyer eyebrows.

The murmurings laugh, soft and dark. They tempt me to listen and invite them closer.

"This is—" Salome gives me the chance to fill my name in.

"Austin," I say.

Misery screams, hands drag at me, and cold pricks my neck.

"What's the trouble? Beyond looking like you got the surgeon who was ten shots deep in tequila," Grey Man says. "Don't sugarcoat it, I guarantee you I've seen worse and stranger things."

"NO! Please don't! Don't, don't, don't!"

On a surface level Grey Man looks normal. But there's a wrongness about him. It comes clearer each time Misery pleads, only to fade away before I can make it out.

"His trouble is that he got dragged into mine," Salome says.

The murmurings march forward, refusing to be ignored.

She trusted him. They all did. He knew it and he used it.

"I can't help you, son, if you're gonna raise your hackles like that at me," Grey Man says.

The murmurings whisper Raim's sins with ecstatic glee.

She led him on, he said. No one would believe her. She believed him.

"How much is this costing?" I ask.

"Don't worry about it," Salome says.

"But it's costing something?"

"I'm not a charity worker." Raim sets his bag on the table.

He craves the power. Lords it over them.

"What's your practice?" I ask.

"General," he says.

"Have any of them come forward?" I ask.

"Any of who?"

"The women you assault."

Dr. Raim stiffens and turns to Salome.

"I didn't say anything," she says, an odd smile curving at her lips.

The murmurings sing a litany of the doctor's sins. The physical, sexual, and mental abuse of his patients, practiced with a methodical discipline that keeps the suffering silent, ashamed, and afraid. The murmurings aren't whispering this to warn me. They celebrate his depravity.

Coming to Salome's was a mistake. All it did was dig me deeper into the hole I'm long overdue to crawl out from. I stand to leave, brushing by Salome to avoid getting any nearer Dr. Raim.

"Where do you think you're going?" She grabs hold of my wrist and a sharp sting hits my arm. At first I think it's Misery until I see the needle held in her hand.

"You need to settle down," she says and the murmurings burst free in a delighted roar.

Sight blurs, my knees buckle, Misery shrieks, and Raim's is the face staring down at me, illuminated by the cold halo of surgical light.

Chapter 26

The moving car toes a fine line between lulling and nauseating. The drug-induced disassociation isn't helping matters. My arms are too heavy to lift and my mouth feels like it's stuffed full of cotton. At least my head isn't too heavy for me to turn toward Salome sitting next to me in the backseat. She catches me looking at her and smiles. Putting down her phone, she takes my hand in hers, thumb brushing back and forth.

"How're you feeling?"

Shitty.

"I said no," I mutter.

"Yes, we heard you," Salome says. "Do you remember?"

"Remember what?" There's a massive gap between me arriving at Salome's and waking up here. Through the fog of drugs and mire of murmurs, faint memories can be salvaged from the wreck. There was Raim—creepy even by my standards—and there were voices.

"You had a fit," she says. "We had to sedate you to get you to calm down."

"What?"

"You were screaming about something stalking you."

"I was?"

"Yep."

"When?"

"You came stumbling into my house, screaming about an entity. The sedative was the only thing that brought you down."

I don't remember any of that. I certainly believe I was screaming. My throat feels raw, supporting the broken and blurred memory of a confrontation.

Whatever drugs the doctor used has walloped me good. I know what it's like to wake up from anesthesia, be knocked out on morphine and most every other FDA-approved painkiller. This ain't that. Mobility slowly trickles back into my arms and I check beneath my shirt. A large, white patch is taped over my side. Smaller bandages are slapped next to black sutures poking out from my skin.

"This isn't mine." I tug at the medical scrub shirt. The matching pants aren't mine either and I look around the car for my clothes.

Salome's hand guides mine away before I can unbuckle to better search.

"You're alright," she soothes. "We're almost home."

"From where?"

"I took you to Dr. Raim's. Remember?"

No, I don't remember a damn thing.

The car's motion has teetered away from lulling and straight into nauseating. I close my eyes to block out the overwhelming world.

"You're alright," Salome says from a great distance. "I've got you."

I open an eye when we pull to a stop in her driveway.

"I'll wait," I say.

"Wait for what?"

I flop my hand about in a limp wave, hoping that explains I don't want to make the trip to the door and back while Salome changes outfits or whatever she has to do before driving up to Encrucijada. Everything is moving too fast and my drugged-up brain can't keep up. The radio is hissing a sad streak of static. It's trying to tell me something. Something important.

Salome catches my hand as I reach for the dials. "It can wait. Can you walk?"

"I'll stay in the car," I say.

"No, you need to lie down."

"I'll do that when I get home." I need to get back. There was something I needed to do. Someone I needed to talk to. I think Glenny called. She'll be expecting a call back.

"We decided you're going to stay at my place for a while," she says.

"We did?" Another thing I don't remember.

"Yeah, come on." She guides me like I'm some grandma who forgot her walker at bingo night.

The ground won't stay put. The thin oak branches overhead reach down to snatch me up into a churning sky. Red rolls rough across my vision and the murmurings are a storm battering against me.

"I'm fine," I say, unable to escape Salome's supporting hold.

"Don't be difficult." She drags me through the front door.

Lena waits in the foyer, hands wringing her apron. Worry deepens the wrinkles in her face and there's something wrong about her. The lines around her eyes and mouth don't end. They wriggle and snake over her like dark, living veins.

"Is he alright?" she asks.

"He'll be fine," Salome says. "He's just a little woozy."

I'm going to have to get used to people talking about me like I'm not in the same room. Salome's moving too fast for my liking so I grab the foyer credenza. My short-circuiting to a sudden stop catches her off guard, we both stumble, and are rescued by Lena who somehow manages to hold us both up.

"Can I get a ride to the bus stop, please?" I ask. I need to get home and I should've asked for the ride while we were still in the car.

"He's on a sedative," Salome explains when Lena's frown deepens at my slurring. "He shouldn't even be up. Raim said he gave him enough to keep him out for the next couple hours."

Sitting down here is as good a place as any to wait for the bus to come. I flop to the floor.

"I'll get Jorge," Lena says.

Not Jorge. I hate that guy.

Salome joins me on the floor. Crouching beside me, she runs a hand through my hair. "Why do you always have to be so difficult?"

"I don't try," I say.

A dark shape that sounds like Jorge stands behind Salome. There's a blackness bending around him. Fungal and writhing. I miss what he says, words lost to the murmurings.

He did it just to see if he could. It was easier than he thought.

"No, give it a minute," Salome says. "He's fading."

Bags of meat, skin, and bone. That's all he thinks of them.

The blackness blooms out from Jorge and the murmurings pull me back into the dark.

***

It takes a minute to figure out where I am. It takes a couple more to sit up. The guest room's high windows show morning rising over the dark rolling hills. The murmurings are insect wings beating against my skull, Misery sobs and pleads in the background, and my skin is raised from an unnatural cold. A glass of water and bottle of pain killers sits on the nightstand beside a note in Salome's tidy handwriting stating to press the white buzzer if I need anything.

I ignore the buzzer and the pain killers. I'm done having drugs in my system.

Not having a plan of action but feeling an aggressive need to act, I shuffle out of the guest room and keep both hands firmly on the banister down the curving staircase. Sepia whispers over the walls and an odd haze trails through the halls.

I'm unsurprised to see Salome is already awake and sitting at the dining room table holding a mug of coffee in hand. Thinking back, I don't know if I've ever seen her asleep. Or even tired. She takes a sip as she scrolls through her phone. The dark hair tumbling over her shoulders frames the deep cut to her loose silk robe and the hazy stain shivering through the halls swirls around her in blurred eddies.

"Morning, Remington," she says. "How are you feeling?"

I stop cold. There's no way, not even drugged up and out of my mind, I would've given her that name.

"How did—"

"There's an APB out for you." She holds up her phone to show a picture of me above bright red text which she reads. "Remington Dalaguerre, twenty-six years old—you're younger than I thought—was last seen late Saturday, at his apartment in Encrucijada, Texas."

That's awkward. In all the fun that was yesterday, I forgot to send out cover stories to stop people from nosing around. That is assuming only a day has passed.

"What day is it?" I ask.

"Tuesday," she says. "You were out for most of yesterday. Don't worry, I had Dr. Raim make a house call."

The name brings back fuzzy images of a face I wanted to punch for reasons I can't remember.

Salome returns to the APB. "It says you're mentally disturbed and were released from St. Jude's Mental Hospital about six months back, and anyone who sees you should call the provided number or the police. That's one hell of a dating profile."

"I gotta go," I say. This one is gonna take a lot of explaining.

"You need to sit down. You're not going anywhere until we figure out what's going on."

"Then I need to make a call." I motion for her phone. At the very least I should let my family know I'm not dead. Considering where we left off they might be thinking that's a real possibility.

"Why?"

"Because I think I left the front door open when I left. Jesus Christ, why do you think I need to make a call?"

"With you, it could be anything," she says, handing me her phone.

I punch in Kitty's number then delete it. Apologies can wait, I should contact Sheriff Suarez first. Helping his daughter narrowly dodge being another page in a serial killer's scrapbook over the summer ought to give me the grace to cash in a favor of this size. With him being one of the few people who knows the truth about my condition he can spin the story and smooth it out so I have the breathing room to sort it out on my end.

The moment I hit "call" for Sheriff Suarez's number the screen flickers and dies. While I don't expect anything to go right anymore, it takes heroic self-control not to hurl the phone into the wall.

"Where's your charger?" I ask.

"I just charged it." Salome snatches her phone back and tries to turn it back on. Her sigh is one of resignation. "I hope you didn't kill it. I have a lot of important information on here—"

Frustration boils over and I slam my fist into the wall.

"That's not going to solve anything," she says.

"Don't patronize me!" I'm sick and tired of people talking down to me. I don't need it from her.

Salome's frown softens. Her pity combined with my hissy fit makes me want to walk under an eighteen-wheeler.

"Sorry," I say. Marriage taught me that doubling down on being an asshole doesn't help. It's better to own up to it and move on. "I'm not trying to make your life difficult. It just comes naturally."

"Lena started breakfast a little while ago. You up for food?" she asks.

"No."

"You should try to eat something. Sit down."

"You're taking this all in stride," I say.

"That's the only way to take this sort of thing, and this is what I do," she says. "Come on, join me for breakfast. All things considered, it's for the best you can't contact anyone. Not if something is after you."

Her chipper tone takes away the solemnity the situation calls for. If anything, she sounds pleased by this turn of events, acting like my showing up is an unexpected treat and not a hot mess dropped on her doorstep.

"Not here to judge. Not here. Stop. Please stop."

Misery finds me before I'm ready to deal with anything. I

slump into the breakfast nook, accepting that it's going to be one of those rougher days.

"What is it?" Salome asks.

"Remember how I told you it's worse when I'm out of sorts?"

"Oh, yeah. You are rather out of sorts right now and—aha!" Her phone beeps back to life and she hurriedly starts typing out messages. "I'm canceling all my appointments today."

"Why?"

"Because I'm not going to leave you when you're like this."

"You didn't cancel your appointments when you were being stalked by a murderous demon, so don't—"

"You're right. I didn't," she says. "But it'd be pretty low of me to be as dismissive about this as you want me to be. Especially since I'm convinced your helping me resulted in this."

"That's not your fault," I say.

"Doesn't mean I don't have a responsibility, and as much as I enjoy our bantering, let's not argue today, please. Why are you smiling?"

"Because I'm giving you an hour tops before you get fed up with what terrible company I am."

"I'm a big girl. I can keep myself busy."

Salome stays true to her word, flitting about, phone never far from ear or hand as she reaches out to her numerous contacts. I spend the morning on a scavenger hunt, collecting books on the supernatural, the esoteric, and urban legends. It's not reading material I've ever gravitated toward, a change I'm gonna have to make considering the direction my life is falling.

Histories of occultism in the United States, Santería, Palo Mayombe, recorded exorcisms, biographies on Aleister Crowley, and any title suggesting supernatural or spiritual subject matter gets stacked into a multitower fortress on the coffee table. I skip over the ones that look like self-help books of a paranormal bent. I'm not interested in wasting time reading pop metaphysics, ten ways to get a wicked wiccan sex life, or paranormal pablum for the masses. I figure the older and closer to the original philosophy the work is, the more likely it'll hold kernels of truth.

I pick out a doorstopper of a book wrapped in a dramatic black cover with a white hermetic-looking symbol embossed in the center. Each page I read sinks me further into skepticism of finding anything useful. Instructions for summoning spirits and communing with demons are listed in a cookbook format and it's difficult to read from all my eye rolling at the supernatural being treated as if it's a science that can be controlled like a child's chemistry kit. Misery, the murmurings, and the cold nausea they bring distract me as much as skepticism. My attention drifts away from the pages to try and plug the holes in my memory, and it doesn't take long for the book to lie ignored beside me as I mentally retrace my footsteps. I remember Raim and how the man was bad news from front page to the op-eds. I can't remember exactly why. I think the murmurings had something to say about him. What it was is lost, as is most everything since Saturday night.

The image of a morgue-like room flickers through my mind and possesses a familiarity that's closer to memory than one of the visions Misery's been pitching. I press my palms against my eyes to block out Misery's pestering sobs and the sepia distortion so I can think.

Sam Square-face was a different sort of bad news than Dr. Raim. What did he say to me at the dinner party? I remember it wasn't friendly and I dismissed it for melodrama. He doesn't seem the type to sew little voodoo dolls of his enemies or summon demons to use folks he's not fond of as scratching posts, but if ever a man had skeletons in the closet it'd be him. He's been turning up like a bad penny and he's gotta be tied up in all of this.

I lift my head from my hands. His card is in the jacket pocket of the suit lying on my apartment floor. I'm confident if I call him and demand a meet he won't say no.

I close the tome on demonic summoning. I'll go back to my apartment, find a way to sneak in, grab the card, and see if I pick up anything via spooky sense before anyone comes for me with a straitjacket.

"Please don't ... stop ... stop ..."

Misery and the murmurings chase after me as I leave the sitting room. I don't care what they have to say. I'm more concerned about sorting out the mess I've made with the living than anything the dead and damned throw at me. I should've come clean to my parents about what was really going on after June, not roped Kitty into lying about what happened. I should've asked Sheriff Suarez to help convince my family of the truth and not deluded myself into thinking I could handle it as it was.

Salome intercepts me in the hall.

"There you are." She takes my hand to lead me back to the sofa in the sitting room. "I've been looking for you. A few people have seen something like what you have going on. I've got a contact in New Orleans who's agreed to come out and see you, and I'm waiting to hear back from a parapsychologist in Houston."

Salome is overcomplicating this. There's no reason to network with folks who are meddling in things better left alone. All I gotta do is go back to my apartment, pick up a supernatural something lurking around that'll tip me off, and I can go from there.

"That's alright," I say. "I appreciate all you're doing, but you don't need to call anyone in. I'll handle this."

"Because you're doing such a great job of it so far," she says and rests her hand on my cheek. "You doing alright?"

"I'm fine." I mean to move away. I shift closer to her instead and her fingers play through my hair. The simple physical contact is a surge of life pushing the murmurs and sepia creep back to a tolerable level.

"I don't believe you." She smiles as she leans in.

A knock sounds at the door.

"Come in," Salome says, irritated by the interruption.

Lena doesn't look at me as she sets two steaming mugs on the coffee table and leaves without a word. She's been acting oddly today. She goes stiff and silent whenever she sees me and last time her eyes got watery before she turned away.

A cold jab pinches the back of my neck and I clamp my hand down over the sharp pang.

"What is it?" Salome asks.

"Nothing," I say and shiver when Misery's voice breathes a sinister life into the room's shadows.

"Stop ..."

"Here." She offers me a mug. "It'll warm you up."

Chapter 27

Fear flushes through me before I realize the room is dark for natural reasons. The swan song of twilight has turned the sky navy and trees black outside the floor to ceiling windows. I don't remember falling asleep and I certainly don't feel like I slept at all.

"What the hell is going on?" It hurts to ask the question aloud. My throat is raw as if I've been talking for hours and breathing sucks more embers than air down my throat. Fragments of the dream linger. I was split down the middle like an animal being bled and blackness was seeping in. I couldn't scream; something was already using my mouth, speaking through my stolen voice to someone lost in the dream's fading.

I slam my fist on the couch, fuming that I'm staring down another gap of lost time and memory. Is Misery sending me into these fugues? I can't be sure what's causing the blackouts because I can't remember what happens right before them. My last memory before the drop off is coming to the library for an overdue study session on the supernatural. Whatever is going on, it's different than anything that's come before. I feel like my soul is only part way in and is leaking out where pieces of me have been torn away. Figuring out how to fix this latest supernatural sickness is hard to do when I can't stay conscious for half a day.

I knead my forehead to chase away the murkiness clouding my thoughts. Staying here, hiding in this castle of glass and marble, isn't going to help me sort out what's going on. I'm dizzy as if drugged when I stand and hit the wall as I stumble my way to the breakfast nook. My jacket and car keys aren't on the table where I thought I left them. I lean against the table to fight the sensation that I'm drifting away on a current I can't fight against. Did I leave them in my car?

I'm two steps out the front door when I see more than my jacket and keys are missing. The driveway is empty. My car is gone. That's not right. I know I drove here. There's a malformed memory of me driving down, the accelerator slick from blood.

"Going somewhere?" Salome crosses her arms in the foyer behind me. Her expression is a mix of amusement and sympathy. That ticks me off. I'm tired of people feeling sorry for me.

"Where's my car?" I ask.

"What are you talking about?"

"I drove here—" I stop when she shakes her head.

"I picked you up and drove you to Dr. Raim's," she says. "You called me, remember?"

"No, I drove here. I remember, I ..."

She frowns. The amusement in her expression is gone. There's only pity now.

"Are you sure you're doing alright?" she asks.

Something's wrong with my memory and that frightens me more than the haunting dead. I can't rely on what I see or hear, and losing faith that I at least remember events right even if I perceive them wrong shoves me over the last edge of stability into a sense of disorienting free fall.

"Remington?"

"I don't … I …" I don't feel right. The sick sensation of the ground falling away sets my head spinning. I grab for the door handle, seeking a physical anchor to stop myself from joining the crumbling ground.

"Hey, we'll sort it out." Salome steps forward and wraps her arms around me.

"What're you doing?"

"Making it better," she says and kisses me.

I still remember how to respond to that and much prefer how she feels against me than the sense of falling into nothingness.

"Better?" she asks.

"Are you sure I didn't drive here?" I ask.

Her lips press over mine and I chase after her when she pulls away, slow and teasing.

"Have you cleaned your stitches yet?" she asks.

"Where do you keep the medicine kit?" I'm pretty sure I'm remembering right in that she has one.

"I'll grab it and meet you in the master bathroom. Move the bathmats out first. I've noticed things get messy when you're involved."

***

The cool, damp cloth on my skin reminds me of the pulling tugs of the dead. Salome notices the shiver I can't repress.

"Was that of natural or unnatural origins?" She carefully dabs the sutures running up my side. I somehow got a solid slice over my lateral ribs that I can't twist to get to without straining a set of stitches on my lower abdomen.

"It's nothing." I grip the marble counter, hating that I'm so far removed from any semblance of control and reduced to becoming someone else's burden.

"Are you going to tell me what's bothering you? Or are you going to make me work for it?" she asks.

"Work for it. I prefer to play hard to get."

"Could've fooled me." She wrings out the cloth before moving to the next set of stitches. "I already have you home and half naked. If that's the work I'm supposed to be doing, most of it's already done."

"Thank you," I say.

"For what?"

"Helping." A lot of people in my life have done their best to help and had the very best intentions. In rare moments does it amount to anything more than a step above inconvenience.

A warm hand replaces the cool washcloth and her fingers trace up my chest. My leaning into her is all the invitation she needs. Her lips brush soft against my neck and I turn so she can meet mine.

"Why can't you be simpler?" she asks.

"I think I'm pretty simple." I slide my hands to follow her waist up and she gives an anticipating shiver.

"You're neurotic." She pauses for a deeper kiss. "Mulish. Needy."

I also listen to Christmas music year-round, drink directly from the juice carton, and don't look both ways when I cross the street.

"A goddamn mess," she says.

Judging by her throaty purr, I make up for that in other categories.

I'm not sure who stood first. I'm not much aware of anything beyond the feel of her, uncaring that we bump against the bathroom wall, the door jamb, her bedroom dresser. The world shrinks down until she's all that's there. The back of my leg hits the bed frame and we tumble down. The sheets smell like her, a smoky incense fit for impious rituals performed on the satin-draped altar. It'd be easy to disappear into it with her. Let everything else fade away. Forget about it all.

"Wait, wait. Stop." It hurts to push away. The longing hunger screams at me for denying it and the few inches I've put between me and Salome allows the cold void to remind me it's there and waiting.

"This is a bad idea." I shift farther back when she follows after me. Somewhere between here and the bathroom she lost her robe. That's all there was to lose.

"I can't think of a single reason why," she says.

There are plenty of reasons why, but it ain't the brain the blood is rushing to, so it's real difficult to articulate any. I go for the lowest and most obvious of them.

"I can count a few." I run a finger over a set of stitches. "There's one, there's two. Three. Four."

I sit up to leave and she places her hand over mine, sliding up my arm to reel me back in.

"Five," she counts and kisses me. "Six." A longer kiss I return. "Seven." Her lips linger and I feel them shape the word more than hear her whisper, "Stay."

Chapter 28

I reach across the bed to find Maria's already gotten up. Odd, usually I'm the one who has to harass her out of bed. I don't know what possessed her to agree to do a morning radio show. She comes from a family of night owls and doesn't have an early bird bone in her.

The sheets on her side are cool. She's been gone for a while. I sit up and stare around the bedroom. This isn't right. This isn't our room.

"Mar—" Her name catches and turns bitter in my mouth. The brain fog evaporates and I get walloped by a wave of empty regret. Dr. Day would have a thing or two to say about this. Chasing a dopamine drive, seeking solace in intimacy when faced with a reminder of loss.

I have a thing to say about it too. You done fucked up, Logan.

I don't see my clothes where I left them strewn across the floor. That almost convinces me to hold position. Staying in bed might be the best course of action seeing as how I somehow manage to make everything worse no matter what I do. But that's a coward's way of dealing with last night. Instead, I'll pretend nothing ever happened, there's nothing to talk about, sneak out of the house, walk to the nearest bus stop and never speak of this again.

I just need to find my clothes first.

Wrapping the bedsheets around my waist, I do a more thorough check of the bedroom and master bathroom for my clothes. Nothing.

After half a minute of rummaging through Salome's closet for something better tailored to the human form than sheets, I give up. Taking anything of hers to wear even for a short while creeps too close to intimate—a stupid outlook considering last night but I'm not about to break my stupid streak now.

Of course the moment I step out of Salome's room wearing only her bedsheets is the moment Jorge chooses to stroll on by.

"Looking for Salome?" he asks.

"Have you seen her?" My hackles rise to match each inch of his spreading smirk.

"Nope," he says and saunters off.

Well, I deserved that.

Fortunately, I don't see Lena in the kitchen, or any other house staff between Salome's room and the guest wing. Unfortunately, the guest bedroom I should have slept in has also been stripped of any spare clothes.

I might deserve that as well.

Rain patters down on the roof and skylights, a staccato *tap-tap-tap* that spreads into thick, watery sheets running down the windows to obscure the world beyond, distorting natural light and creating a disconnected claustrophobia. The room's speaker system sparks out white noise. It hasn't shaken off the muffled quality like it's waging war against an invisible enemy to get a smothered message through. The groaning static follows me through the house, each room's system hissing on when I walk by.

"... was found dead ... ksshhh ... foul play ... hssshk ..."

The speaker in the library snarls. Choking and spitting, it calls me over toward it.

"... to leave—shck-schk ... danger ..."

One hand cinching the sheets tight around me, I tap the cylindrical smart speaker with the other. The world drops away the moment my finger makes contact. A thousand voices roar up carrying flashes of visions I can't make sense of. One garbled voice almost breaches the surface of the warring static, a warning desperate to get through.

"What're you doing?" Salome leans against the door frame, arms crossed below a teasing smile.

"Looking for my clothes." I pick up the speaker and turn it over as if I'll find a supernatural switch.

"They're in the wash," she says.

"All of them?" To be fair, "all of them" is a set of scrubs and maybe a shirt and pants if they didn't get thrown out from being torn up and blood-soaked.

"It's not like you need them. You're not going anywhere." She walks over to rest a hand on my shoulder. "Really, what are you doing?"

"I told you, the radio talks to me," I say. "But I'm not crazy."

"I believe that first bit more than the second," she says.

I move away, unwilling to follow where noticing how nice she smells leads.

"What does it say to you?" she asks.

"It's partial to Johnny Cash, Sinatra, and Elvis," I say.

"And there're cryptic messages from the beyond hidden in the lyrics?"

"Not cryptic or hidden. I'm just really dumb."

Mentioning how stupid I am is the intended segue into

reestablishing the borders that last night obliterated. Salome interprets it as invitation to slide her hands beneath the bedsheets wrapped around my waist.

"Why do you always gotta be such a distracting nuisance?" I ask when I meant to tell her that as fun as that feels, we need to establish better boundaries.

"I'm distracting?" She cocks an eyebrow. "You're the one walking around in my bedsheets."

Her lips find mine and we're on the couch before the dropped speaker hits the floor. Reason, moral principles, and the bedsheets drop just as easy.

***

Darkness rolled in fast after the wind section joined the storm's symphony. The occasional lightning flash lights up the black sky as rain snaps a rataplan against the roof and windows. The drumming against the glass sounds a lot like the hiss of radio static.

"You're quiet," Salome says, sitting up and taking most of the sheets.

"I'm listening."

"To what?"

"The rain," I say. She's unbothered I'm late to react when she leans down to kiss me. The living intimacy she provides is a buffer that pushes the whispers and cold back to an almost forgettable distance. A defense I'm reluctant to let go.

I react much faster when a light hand taps at the door and I grab the little sheets left available to me. The storm has turned the windows into a massive rain-streaked mirror, reflecting the room to strip away any privacy the couch provides.

"Clothes are done," Lena says from the hall. She reaches a cautious hand in to show the scrubs.

"Thanks, you can leave them here," I say right as Salome says, "Go put them in my room."

Lena places them down beside the door before closing it. Salome looks irritated by this and her annoyance ticks up a couple more rungs when her phone hums. She sighs and slips back into her loungewear.

"Don't go anywhere." She steps out to take the call and the unease I've been trying to ignore settles in the space of her absence.

I mean to get up and grab the scrubs waiting at the door after she leaves. Instead, I lay unmoving as minutes of shame march by, holding me to the couch to stare blankly out into the thickening storm. It's only when the murmurings gain steam and Misery makes his presence felt does the want to escape the mounting sense of vulnerability motivate me to get dressed.

My skin is cold and crawling beneath the scrubs. The fecund smell of sex lingering in the library is an accusatory reminder encouraging my unease to shift into guilt. Guilt metastasizes into self-disgust for being too pathetic to say no to chasing fleeting comforts, and at my complete willingness to toss discipline and all higher safeguards out the window over the last couple days. How the hell am I supposed to control what comes through the veil when I can't be bothered to control myself?

I run an uninterested finger over the books stacked beside the couch. Researching the occult and studying up on the supernatural isn't going to solve the real problem here. That problem is me and my commitment to making every stupid choice I get the chance to. Lightning splits the sky and booming thunder adds a percussion bass to the rain's snare drum tapping. I weigh which is stupider, leaving now in this weather, or waiting until it blows over.

The door behind me creaks and I watch Salome's reflection come back into the room.

"Dr. Raim might have a lead," she says, placing two mugs down on the coffee table.

"Hmm."

"He'll come by tomorrow for a follow-up. And the parapsychologist can be here by Thursday—" She goes on about the plans she's making that I have no intention of sticking around for.

The rain slams hard on the windows. An angry hiss to match the murmurings. Both the storm and the murmurings sound as though they're separated from me by the thinnest layer of glass.

"You alright?" She places a hand on my shoulder.

"Fine." I scoot away to keep a healthy distance between us when she sits next to me.

"You should lie down," she says. "You're looking pale."

No, thanks, I think I'm done lying down for a while.

"I'd like a ride to the bus stop," I say.

"Why?"

"To go home."

"I don't think that's a good idea."

And staying here's a terrible idea. I don't like who I'm becoming.

Salome's phone buzzes again.

"Hold on, I'll be right back." She steps out into the hallway to take the call.

In want of something to do, I pick up the mug she left on the table. A sharp jab hits the back of my neck, I drop the mug, and it shatters on the floor. I clench my teeth, bracing for the second wave of Misery's haunting. His sobs echo out, cold hands rake at me, and the ice pick pain digs deeper into my neck.

"Please. Stop. Stop. Please ... please."

The room sways and the floor of Verkauf's unfinished apartments rise up to meet me as I fall. The woman standing above me is softened by the sedative drug. The needle she holds in hand shines sharp and clear. Salome's sitting room lurches back and I flinch away from the lights that are blinding after the gloom of the vision.

Misery sobs and shrieks, the little puzzle pieces click into place, and the sinking cold in my gut is one of realization, not supernatural influence. To be sure, I reach for the broken mug. The sharp pain I now know is a warning pierces my neck, Misery sobs, and the flashes of the same vision pour back over me.

Son of a bitch. The drink was drugged.

I assumed the confused fugues and memory gaps were rooted in a supernatural cause and overlooked all mundane possibilities. It's not a haunt, murmurings, or anything from behind the veil that's been causing the blackouts and lost time. Salome's been drugging me.

Son of a bitch. Son of a bitch. Son of a fucking bitch.

Discipline hasn't entirely been deserted as a cool calm earned through training settles in following this discovery. Salome's waiting in the hall and she doesn't quite succeed in suppressing her surprise I'm up and walking.

"Everything alright?" she asks when I stride past her.

"I dropped the mug," I say. "Gotta clean it up."

"Lena can do that."

"No, I got it." I use the glass decorations hanging from the walls to watch her. The moment her reflection steps out of the hall into the sitting room I pick up my pace, round the corner, and head straight for the front door. No need to be subtle or waste time with an elaborate evac plan. Just get out.

Movement catches in the glass lining the hall. A dark shape follows after me through the mirrors. The dull sepia hue spreading over the walls tries to throw me off-balance. I fight to keep my feet and senses as the stalking shape in the glass reaches out after me. I'm not going to let it win.

One of Salome's staff, Gianni, sits by the front door. He looks up when he sees me. I don't break stride and continue toward the kitchen to grab a handful of paper towels. Sager, another of Salome's staff, is stationed by the sliding doors leading to the deck. He follows after me a couple paces before dropping off to stay at his post. Exits are guarded, there are monsters in the mirrors, and no one in my corner knows where I am, so if I screw this up any further no one's going to find me. I'm gonna have to get a bit more creative with the escape plan.

Salome intercepts me in the hall, phone in hand, wearing an expression that spells trouble.

"Don't be difficult," she says.

"I thought that was part of my charm."

She holds up her phone to display a text message:

He knows. He knows. He knows. He knows.

"You think you're the only one who gets their information from unconventional sources?" she asks.

The coy confession should make my every muscle tense, chill my blood, and snap me to fight-or-flight readiness. My reaction is exasperation, not fear. I'm mostly angry at myself for being such an idiot. Hindsight is twenty-twenty and the clarity with which I'm seeing all the red flags ain't pretty. That the blackouts only occurred when I was at Salome's house should've tipped me off, but I missed it because I was too busy falling for her manipulations designed to isolate me.

"You've been drugging me," I say.

"You didn't leave me much choice and it's not like it was hurting you. Do you have any idea what you are?"

Sinner. Dumbass. Sagittarius.

"Those murmurings, they don't just speak to you," she says, feverish arousal burning in her eyes. "They speak through you, and are more than eager to tell me everything about anyone you come around." She takes a step forward and I take a step back. "You're more receptive when you've calmed down some, and even when you're not listening, you hear a hell of a lot more than they've ever told me."

My throat itches, still raw from someone—or rather something—speaking through me.

"Did you send something to do this?" I raise my bandaged arm. The darkness in the mirrors shifts closer to box me in. It's a fragment of the rotting presence that was at the Driskill, that clings to Jorge, and that attacked me at my apartment. No wonder Salome was so pissed when I dragged her away at the Driskill, she wasn't in danger from the fungal entity, they're on the same team, and I've been throwing them the game.

"I get what I want. I don't always get it how I expect. I wanted you to come back, and here you are." Her smile suggests I wouldn't be so angry if I could just see it her way. "I told you I knew people who'd kill or worse to have what you do. You have a gift, and it pisses me off you're dead set on wasting it. I was this close"—she holds up her finger and thumb—"to chaining you to a bedpost when you decided to leave after that dinner party. I really wanted to talk that night. You could've told me everything the murmurings told you about the other guests." She's getting more and more excited, tongue darting over her lips. "They'd tell you everything if you'd only listen."

She reaches her hand toward me and the shapes in the mirror reflect the motion. The glass bends to make a sinister *tink-tink-tink* as black, fungal hands stretch out to grab me. I turn and sprint to the front door—the smartest thing I've done in about a week. My relief that Gianni is gone from guarding the exit is short-lived when I find the door won't budge. The preternatural force reflected in the mirrors holds the door shut no matter how hard I tug.

"Remington," Salome scolds. She follows after me at a leisurely pace, confident I'm not going anywhere. The murmurings laugh and offer to whisper her sins to me.

I grab a vase from the foyer's credenza and hurl it at her. It should've hit her right in the face. It shatters on the wall directly behind her instead. I stare in dumb disbelief, letting her get too close as I try to make sense of what I just saw.

"Have you listened to anything I've said?" she asks. "Certain thresholds aren't crossed. Harm can't find me in my home."

I continue on the "not listening" tack and take a swing. My fist slams into the wall, completely missing her.

"Are you done?" She arches an eyebrow. "Because if you're going to keep acting tiresome, I'm going to get angry."

So I can't punch her teeth across the marble foyer. But I can gently grasp her shoulders. She's so confident in the powers that protect her that she doesn't even flinch. She forgets friends in low places—powerful as they might be—are in low places for a reason, and I'm willing to bet at the end of the day they're not friends at all.

Gentle as I can, I pick Salome up. No harm comes to her as I carry her over to the hallway coat closet. With absurd daintiness—particularly as she's screaming and thrashing, demanding I put her down, and doing her best to claw my eyes out—I gently tuck her into the closet and shut the door. No harm done.

I press myself against the door to prevent her from opening it as I hook my foot around the leg to the foyer credenza and drag it over. To be absolutely sure no harm comes to her and that she stays snug and safe in the closet, I wedge the credenza between the closet door and wall.

And look at that, no harm done.

"Remington!" she shrieks, pounding on the door. It jams against the credenza as she tries to force her way out.

She's going on such a tear—saying all manner of unladylike things as to what she's going to do to me when she gets out—I almost don't hear Gianni running up behind me. I duck to the side and he slams into the wall where I was a split second before. I put all my weight into a hook that sends his head into a wall's corner edge. That should've dropped him. He's not even fazed. I see the black corruption clinging to him in flashes. One moment he looks normal, the next he's consumed by dark rot. Must be an employee benefit that their low friends no longer need to hide.

Two-for-two on smart decisions, I sprint away from the front door and Gianni. I barely make it three strides before he grabs the back of my shirt. Good news is clothes tear easy and I rip away to smash a lamp into his face. The glass shattering on his skull does as much lasting damage as my fist. He charges right through and takes me to the floor. Not having his employee benefit of supernatural strength, I'm not as quick to shake off the back of my head smacking against the floor. Black, then white, bursts across my eyes and he's on top of me before I can see straight.

"Knock it off," he says, voice dispassionate as he hits me.

The open-handed blow to my already spinning head sends sharp ringing through my ears and stuns me out of struggling. He curls one of his hands over both my wrists, holding them down as easy as if I were a child. The other hand clamps down on my throat. I jerk to buck him off and roll away. He doesn't budge. He's impossibly strong and has me fully pinned.

"You're only making it harder on yourself," he says. He could snap my neck or rip out my windpipe using his one hand if he wanted. He's being gentle in simply stealing away my consciousness.

Lack of oxygen stifles my thrashing to weakening twitches, and restricted blood flow reels me away from the natural world. I see what he is now. Black fungi rolls off him, spilling from his eyes, bursting from his skin. It drifts from his lips in foul spores as he speaks. I can't hear him. Suffocation chokes out my senses. The murmurs are too loud. They have faces as they lean in close to cheer on the violence. The first feelers of unconsciousness crowd down on me.

I can't get free. I can't move.

Sight scorches red then disappears into black. I barely feel his hand tightening.

I can't breathe … can't. …

Air burns as it rushes down my throat. I cough and wheeze as I blindly crawl away, tears blurring my eyes. Hands pull me up and force me to stand.

"Run!" Lena's face wavers in and out of focus. "Run!"

A butcher knife protrudes from Gianni's chest and his neck is a bloody, hacked ruin. He lies unmoving. The blackness infesting him does not. It rolls off his corpse toward Lena and me, hungry for a new soul to feed from.

I can barely manage breathing, speaking is far beyond me, but Lena figures out what my rasping reluctance to move means.

"I made my choice," she says darkly. "I knew the consequences. As I do now. Go! Run!"

She has the same polluted appearance as Gianni, her veins tacky and rotted against her skin, and the same impossible strength as she yanks me to my feet. She throws open the deck's sliding glass door so hard it shatters.

"Run!"

I grab the knife from Gianni before I fling myself over the deck banister and plunge straight into the pool the next story down. The deep water slows me so I barely touch bottom, stopping me from breaking myself on the concrete. I don't waste time looking back as I haul myself out and stagger into a run. Angry yells carry from the house. I'm not going to have much of a head start.

The grass ends when I hit the tree line and the ground turns harsh and uneven. Rocks and thorns cut into my bare feet. The rain tears through the trees and the storm collapses the evening into a hungry darkness. My head pounds from being strangled, and drawing a full, pain-free breath won't be happening any time soon. I've probably consumed more sedative than food the last couple days and my reopened wounds weep warm beneath what's left of my shirt.

Physical ailments are the least of my problems. I've teetered too close to the veil and the natural world is losing the battle to hold back the hidden reality of fallen creation. The raging sky spoils to deepest black polluted by red like a corpse's marbling. There's a foulness to the rain. Something other than water bleeds from the putrid, red-streaked sky. The droplets are too slow to roll off my skin and an unnatural mist seeps through the weakening veil. One moment I'm running through storm-lashed trees and flooding backyards. The next I'm sprinting past looming shapes that groan and warp.

Keep it together. Don't fall through. Not yet.

I feel inhuman eyes on me. The murmurings thrill at the spectacle. Hands hidden by the unnatural dark reach out to drag me down. They laugh as I struggle, reminding me how pointless it all is. They tell me to give up. It'd be easier if I let them take me. The ground trembles, ready to swallow me whole should I accept the offer. I keep running.

Don't fall through. Don't fall through.

With a thrum that makes my bones shiver, the dying natural world slips away and doesn't return, leaving its fallen state unveiled in all its ugly terror.

"*Run.*" Lena's voice echoes after me, warning me of what will happen if I so much as falter. That I hear Lena as I do tells me exactly what happened to her.

Chapter 29

The maze of winding streets and homes separated by sprawling thickets would be hard to navigate in the natural dark and storm. Now it's impossible.

Trees warp and bend when I don't look straight at them. The ground shivers beneath my bare feet like a rotting corpse pulsating from carrion feeders devouring it from within. Lights muted by tainted rain and sepia shine out in square patches. Those might be the windows to houses. I don't run to them. Even if help were to be found behind those doors, I'm not inviting the darkness pursuing me upon an unsuspecting Good Samaritan.

I pause from my blind run to get some semblance of bearings.

"Run," Lena warns.

I think I'm standing on a sloping driveway and the towering mass of solid black stretching up to my left could be a house, but I can't confidently distinguish walls or roof against the cloaking dark. The mist's eerie, lifeless glow fails to illuminate what does not wish to be seen. Shapes creep among the shrouded trees and the murmurings hiss from the pockets of shadow.

"RUN."

An unseen hand grabs my arm and pulls me to the ground. My gasp cuts short as another hand clamps over my mouth. I can't see Lena as she holds me still. I only hear her warning whisper in my ear.

"Run. Run. Run."

Her grip relaxes when I stop struggling. The rain's furious roar can't fully muffle the approaching car on the road above, the hiss of wheels cutting through the small rivers drowning the streets. Lights arcing in a purposeful pattern sweep the warping trees. I slide down the embankment and press up against a low rock ledge for better cover as the figures wielding flashlights creep along the ridge to my right. The shade muddying the world does nothing to obstruct the light's search. Even through the distance and dark I can see the writhing fungal mass that's latched onto the closest man.

Lightning shoots the world blue and bright, banishing the sepia curtain for a brief second to give a clear glimpse of the physical world. I'm tucked against stone terracing on a steep hill leading down to a swollen creek. The large house behind me has no lights on behind the windows, probably an empty vacation home.

The flash fades and the world sinks back into ruin.

"Run. Run."

Lena's words are in contradiction to her tone, a begging whisper that I stay still and silent. I don't hear Misery. Maybe he left the moment I got it into my thick skull what Salome was doing, allowing Lena to take up first chair haunt-ist.

"Run."

Thunder rumbles and a second lightning strike grants another illuminating flash. Two men patrol the ridge to the right; their dark shapes stand obvious against the burn of blue light. I can't see the car driving on the road at the top of the hill. I only see the headlights reflecting off the heavy rain. The lightning flash fades and the surroundings tumble back beneath the sepia shroud. Salome's men are going to find me. Sooner or later, my senses are going to fail when I can't afford them to and each tick of the clock moves this game of cat and mouse further in their favor. If it comes down to a direct one-on-one fight, it's over. The devil's deal they made gives them the undisputed physical edge. They're stronger, faster, and I wouldn't rule out other heightened advantages.

But they can be killed. Lena proved that twice over.

"*Run,*" she says.

I doubt they're going to play as nice as Gianni did if they find me. That's fine. I have no intention of playing nice or fair.

I rip off the surviving tatters of my shirt, the pale fabric is a signal flare in these dark woods, and hide it beneath a foundation shrub. There's no shortage of mud to smear over me in diagonal lines to hide the bandages and my light-colored pants.

Following a road out isn't an option. Not only does Salome have men driving in search of me, but I'll bet she's got people watching the bridges as well where the winding streets bottleneck to lead over the Colorado River and back to Austin. Fording the offshoot creek is the fastest and best route I have to reach the relative safety of crowds and souls not in service to darker powers. Crossing the creek puts me at high risk of being seen, but staying on this north bank choked by unfriendlies guarantees I'll be found.

"*Run ... run.*"

I duck out from the rock terrace to take cover behind a

pool shed. I can't reliably see farther than a few strides in this unnatural dark, so I hold position, waiting for the split-second clarity lightning grants to get a better view of the terrain between me and the bank, and confirm that the swath of black at the bottom of the slope *is* the creek and nothing more sinister.

Lightning flashes, shining bright off the storm-bloated creek, and reveals a figure skulking lower down the slope between me and the water's edge. It's Sager. The rain has beaten his spiky hair into submission and fungal rot shivers over his skin. He traces the beam of his flashlight over the water and bank, looking for me to do exactly what I was planning on doing.

He liked the way he screamed. The look of fear. It made him a god—

"Run."

There's miles of creek bank to cover, and now that I know where Sager is, I can find an unguarded section. I'm ten feet away from the shed's cover when the porch lights flicker—on and off, on and off—and the entity croons, enjoying its interference in this game of hide-and-seek.

Sager turns and I barely outrun the flashlight's tracking sweep back behind the shed. On and off, on and off—the tattletale lights continue to broadcast my location.

She screamed louder. And louder. Begged him to stop.

A man's voice calls out and a second answers. Sager's bringing in backup, so I better do this dance number when it's just the two of us.

He liked the way she screamed. Her fear. It made him a god.

Sager isn't expecting me to come round the shed's corner and charge him straight on. He's closer than I thought, less than four strides. Black rot drifts from him as he raises his arm to block a strike, expecting me to go high. I drive the knife straight into his exposed leg. Femoral, aortic, subclavian—adrenaline aids my plunging the knife through each point. Red spurts from his slashed arteries to join the writhing black. He staggers back, eyes wide from the shock of realizing too late he misjudged his opponent.

And when he put his hands around her throat, she didn't scream again.

I slam the knife through Sager's neck and he gags on his own blood. The black corruption reaches out for me as he tumbles back into the mud. I leave him to bleed out and sprint down the rain-slick slope, sliding to a stop at the creek's edge. The water's higher and faster than it was a minute ago and churns from a force beyond the storm swelling its depth. It froths as if a hungry creature writhes beneath the surface. I step back. The dark water reminds me too much of the stream of screaming faces and the way Verkauf's hall buckled beneath the evil she invited in.

An ugly hush joins the rain's harsh rhythm as the entity creeps closer.

Logan, it calls.

It offers to make this all go away—all I need to do is step into the water. The sepia mist weaves a web around me. The bank's mud is unnaturally cool and all too willing to help me sink into it.

Come, it says, *it won't hurt.*

"RUN!"

Lena's warning jolts me back to avoid Jorge's lunge from the dark. I pivot to drive the knife through the corruption rolling off him and into his side. He doesn't flinch, doesn't even pause. He swings around and tackles me to the ground with rib-creaking force. A hard knee drives into my abdomen, cutting off my wheezing breath, and his weight sinks me deep into the muddy bank.

He wanted to see if he could do it, the murmurings hiss. *It was messier than he thought. But it was easy. So easy.*

Jorge pulls the knife out from his side with the casual indifference of removing a splinter. He's heavier than he has any right to be, weighed down by the black rot slithering off him. It latches onto my torso and neck, runs down my mouth and nose, clogging my throat.

It's not real, I tell myself, it's not really there, breathe, you can breathe.

I suck in a weak gasp through the black that tastes like spoiled meat and slam the heel of my hand into Jorge's nose. He blinks, shakes his head, and drives his entire bodyweight down through his knee into my diaphragm. I choke and he rolls me to shove my face down in the mud, forcing me into an omoplata submission hold. I can't reach him with my free arm, kick, or twist free, and all he has to do is shift his body weight to snap my shoulder.

"Yeah, I got him," he says into an earpiece. The black rot spreads out from him to wrap around me. "Just south of Canyon Terrace and Hollow. Bring the car around." He turns his attention back to me and shoves my head deeper into the mud. "How hard do you want to make this?"

I gag on the black rot flooding my nose and mouth.

He planned the next one. And he took his time with him.

"Settle down." He pushes into my shoulder, threatening to dislocate it. "She's gonna be pissed if you're too broken up."

Less mess. And even easier than the first.

An unnerving sucking sound gets us both to look up the slope. Sager's corpse sinks into the ground. The porch light shines in his open-eyed stare and casts an eerie glow over his descent into the yielding earth. The entity laughs and with a final, violent tug, the mud swallows Sager up entirely.

It'd be that easy, it says. *That quick.*

All I need to do is ask.

"Did you do that?" Fear sends cracks through Jorge's voice. From my position of face mostly buried in mud I see his smug smirk is gone. He looks wildly around, neck muscles tense, eyes wide.

"Did you do that?!" He drives his leg down so my shoulder screams.

"No," I gasp.

"Then what did? What—" he cuts off in a shocked cry. My shoulder cracks as he pushes off and away.

"What the fuck is this?" He claws at his arms and the dark corruption feeding off him. "What're you doing?!"

I don't get the chance to tell him it isn't me or puzzle over why he's getting a peek into the hidden reality behind the veil. I roll to avoid his kick and get back on my feet. Jorge holds up his shaking hands. Whatever he saw must be gone because fury replaces the fear twisting his features.

"You little shit! What did you do?"

I catch his punch and am lucky my arm doesn't break under the force. He grabs my throbbing arm, hurls me away as if I was a rag doll, and my ankle cracks when I land wrong on the muddy ground. The murmurings cheer when Jorge picks up the knife.

"You fucking son of a bitch." He advances toward me. "What the hell was that? What did you do to me?"

"RUN!"

Lightning strikes the tree closest him in a blinding burst. Bark explodes with uncanny precision and he roars in agony, clutching his ruined face. I'm running back up toward the road before I have my feet beneath me. Sharp pain shoots from my ankle but that's a problem for later.

I can barely see through the bloody rain and pay no mind to where I go so long as I keep running. The murmurings screech and snarl. The rain shifts from a storm-tossed frenzy to a heavy torrent streaking straight down without wind to break its course.

The entity circles and laughs.

Logan, it croons.

I ignore its calling, the hounding murmurs, and follow the advice of a single disembodied voice.

"Run. Run. Run ..."

***

Cold, both natural and unnatural, saps my strength. Exposure erodes the last of my reserves. The air cloys my lungs as I run like I'm sucking down poison.

Logan ...

My head is light, limbs heavy, my body a collection of new aches, reopened wounds, and dizzying fatigue. Each breath catches on my throat, raw from being strangled and stolen.

Give up, the entity says.

The sepia curtain refuses to lift no matter how far and long I run, and I have no idea how long that's been. Minutes, hours, miles, it doesn't matter. There's no escape. No end to the deadened sepia world. The entity's presence weighs heavier on me and each of my steps is slower than my last.

Logan.

It encourages me to fall and sink into the rotting earth. Just like Sager did.

The last of my strength sputters out and I go straight from running to a dead collapse. The ground shifts like a mass of worms beneath me, ready to take me under as the entity comes closer. I force myself to hands and knees, crawl to press my back against a tree, and curl into a pathetic defense against the sepia drowned world.

Give up.

An inhuman hand forms from the dark. All I need to do is take it and surrender to oblivion. It's a far less painful fate than what awaits if Salome finds me.

Headlights expand from pinpricks to distorted orbs and reveal how close I am to the road. They're going to see me. My legs don't respond when I tell them to stand and go back to running. Every injury, physical and otherwise, has caught up to me. I sit panting against the tree, unable to so much as crawl away as the headlights come closer. They're going to find me.

Unless I let the entity take me. Accepting the offered hand is the only way out.

Give up.

The car pulls to a stop, engine left idling as the driver exits. The sepia haze and rain render him unrecognizable. The car radio refuses to be silenced by the storm. It spits, hisses, and shrieks its fury. The entity retreats and the anger emanating from it rivals the radio's rage driving it away.

Square-face doesn't say anything. He picks me up like I'm a lost runaway kid. I don't care that it hurts like hell to be moved. I'm at the point I wouldn't care if all he planned to do was carry me out to the road to toss me down in front of the car and run me over. He tosses me into the back seat instead of the street. Asking where he's driving to demands energy I don't have.

The radio snarls out scolding static, berating me for being so stupid.

"Yeah, I know," I rasp. My voice is a ragged whisper from all the abuse and my throat is going to be black and blue tomorrow. As is the rest of me. Assuming I get to tomorrow.

Square-face turns the station dial in search for anything other than the raging static. He thumps his fist over the uncooperative radio.

"Don't bother," I say. "It does what it wants."

"Do you understand it?" he asks.

I press my hands over my ears. It does nothing to dampen the murmurings. I don't understand anything.

Chapter 30

The car pulls to a stop. The seat beneath me rumbles and goes still as Square-face shuts off the engine. The window is too far away for me to bother sitting up to see where we're at. Lying flat on the back seat is taking all my muster. I don't move; neither does Square-face. His jaw is clenched and he's staring straight ahead with an intensity that could bend steel.

Minutes tick by. His hands clench and unclench on the steering wheel. He's either figuring out how best to proceed or he's waiting for something. Maybe he's working for someone and needs their go ahead before moving forward. Or he could be working for *something* like Salome clearly is.

I stare at him, searching for any supernaturally revealed corruption. There's none I can see, but my senses are about as reliable as a broken clock, only right twice a day.

Square-face's mean, little eyes break from having a staring contest with the universe to glance back at me through the rearview mirror. He scowls at me, exits the driver's seat, and comes around to open the back door.

"Can you walk?" he asks. "I don't want to carry your sorry ass."

Yeah, I don't want that either.

My right leg doesn't want to take the weight. Pain bursts at the ankle and I wobble.

"I'm fine." I push Square-face's arm away when he reaches out to hold me up. The ankle isn't broken, it's just a bad sprain, and I've walked through worse.

He's parked outside a shabby one-story house in a low-income neighborhood. A rusted chain-link fence wraps around a yard of dead and dying grass and the house looks equally uninviting. The off-white paint is peeling and chipped, the front porch steps sag in the center, and there are chunks of wood missing around the door frame where someone must've used a crowbar to break in.

I hobble up the uneven porch stairs and am greeted by the smell of bachelorhood and cheap Mexican takeout. The kitchen is immediately to the right and Square-face pulls open one of the counter drawers to grab a pair of handcuffs.

"Cuff yourself to the table," he says, motioning to the bench table built into the wall.

The handcuffs are far from necessary. If I got into a pillow fight with a four-year-old I'd lose. Still, he was generous enough to give me a ride and I'm not in much of an arguing mood so I might as well observe house rules. I snap the cuffs around my left wrist and a table leg. Square-face doesn't bother to check to make sure they're secure. They're not. I could slip out easily. But again, the cuffs aren't necessary to keep me manageable.

Square-face looks even more uptight than usual as he puts on a pot of coffee. He won't meet my eye when he places a mug in front of me. Guess playing good cop isn't easy for him. I don't take the coffee. Call me paranoid, but I'm a lot more suspicious about accepting drinks than I used to be.

"Did she do that to you?" He nods at the ruined stitching on my arm and chest.

"In a roundabout sort of way," I say.

"What'd you do to piss her off?"

"Left."

"And you were stupid enough to go back to her?"

"I didn't know it was her."

Square-face stares at me in a way that says I continue to sink in his estimation of my intelligence. Well, forgive me for being the bright-eyed, bushy-tailed newcomer who doesn't know the rules and gets taken in at every turn 'cause he keeps thinking he can do something right.

A toilet flushes from within the house and a sink hisses into use.

"Who else is here?" I ask.

He doesn't answer and he doesn't have to. Glenny comes bounding down the hall.

"Oh my gosh, you look terrible!" she says and throws herself onto me. She's not graceful about the hug and drives a solid knee into my stomach. She doesn't let go as I grunt and cough. It takes more than my pain and her getting smeared in the mud covering me to deter her.

"What're you doing here?" I wheeze.

"Looking for you. What's wrong with your voice? Oh, and I'm still super mad at you!" she says. "Don't think you looking all sad and pitiful changes that!"

She's got a right to be mad. I shouldn't have yelled at her. That was out of line.

"No, dummy." She rolls her eyes. "I'm mad that you make bad choices! Next time a demon attacks you, call me. Or you could've called my dad, he would've helped. Don't go running off to some creepy witch chick you just met. I told you she was bad news and that you shouldn't see her!" She grabs me by the shoulders to shake me and ends up only moving herself back and forth in a passionate frenzy of disappointment. "You need to listen to me, Logan!"

"How did you get here?" I ask once she's done.

"I drove, duh. Also Kitty is spitting fire that you drove off after you promised her you wouldn't drive anymore."

"That's what she's mad at me about?"

"Well, that and other things. A lot of other things actually. You really—"

"How did you get involved with this guy?" I wave my hand at Square-face.

Glenny inhales half the oxygen in the room to go on one of her rapid-fire storytelling monologues. "Okay, so after you had your crazy episode—that's what Tyler called it, not me—I went through your stuff for clues and I found Mr. Campbell's business card in that suit jacket you left on the floor, which is going to really wrinkle it, you know? Don't worry, I hung it up for you. So anyway, I gave Mr. Campbell a call and he told me you were running around with this Salome person he's been tailing and that she's like a sock-puppet for the devil and he thought you might be in league with her and I told him, no, you're not in league with demons or anything like that, you just don't make good choices a lot of the time. And then I told him what Tyler said you did and that I thought you were in trouble and Mr. Campbell said he thought so too so I drove down and, oh my gosh, the radio would not stop freaking out the whole time so I knew it had to be bad. And then Mr. Campbell said he didn't know how to find you and I said that's okay, I'd just follow the radio. But then he said, no it was too dangerous for me to go and he didn't want me driving around with a baby—"

"You brought Titus?"

"Well, yeah, I wasn't just going to leave him. And he's fine, he's sleeping in the living room. Anyway, I told Mr. Campbell if he wanted to find you he should listen to the radio and it'd take him to you and it did, right?"

Square-face nods.

"So anyway, that's how we found you. Oh, and you're also in super massive big trouble because you've been declared mentally incompetent and I think your parents already got the ninety-day mandatory treatment or something like that."

Because being pursued by a batshit crazy woman whose business is run by making deals with the devil wasn't enough. I got no doubt if well-meaning folks manage to tuck me away in a padded cell, all they'll do is make it that much easier for Salome to find me. She didn't take our breakup well and made it abundantly clear she doesn't consider this relationship over.

"Yeah, I thought the same thing too," Glenny nods. "So I'm taking you to Aunt Cia's."

"Who?"

"Well, actually she's my great-aunt and her full name is Prudencia but she knows all about this sort of thing and lives in Louisiana so that should be far enough away, yeah?"

"And your aunt is okay with this?"

"Oh, I don't know, I haven't called her yet. But I think if we show up she'll say yes."

"And what about your parents?"

"Well, I told my dad someone needed to help you and he said, 'Don't you do anything stupid, Glen Ellen,' so I made sure to pack extra diapers for Titus and grabbed some clothes for you. Besides, I'm nineteen. I'm an adult. I don't need to ask their permission to do things."

"So he knows what you're doing?"

"Well, maybe. I left Dad and my sister a note because I knew they'd get all mad if I told them I was driving down to Austin to hire a private investigator to find you because you were in trouble and someone needed to bail you out. Oh, and my dad doesn't think you were trying to kill yourself or anything. When he got the call, he assumed you got wrapped up in something supernatural again, but he doesn't think your parents are ready to hear that yet. Don't worry, Dad still thinks you're an okay guy, you just have a bad habit of stepping straight into trouble."

Glenny plops down next to me and gives a dramatic exhale.

"So are you gonna tell me now please what you've been doing? I mean, holy moly, Logan, you're good at getting into messes, but this is ridiculous even for you."

"How did Salome pull you into this?" Square-face asks me, having patiently endured Glenny's tirade.

"I saw a haze monster stalking her, thought she needed help, and it went downhill from there," I say. How was I supposed to know I was stepping right in the middle of two women dragging demons into their catfight?

"You thought she needed help?" he asks, finding that a harder pill to swallow than the claim "I saw a haze monster."

"As I said, she was being stalked by a haze monster. It was the reasonable conclusion." And I gotta give credit where credit is due, Salome played me like a fiddle. I'll bet that night with the wine and the ice cream was all an act I swallowed hook, line, and sinker.

"Were you always this dumb?" Square-face gives me a look

that's uncannily similar to my father's constant expression of disappointment.

"That's not nice," Glenny says.

"I'd like to think a couple traumatic brain injuries had some role in it," I say.

"Is that what set you off?" he asks.

"What?"

"When you started seeing shit—ah, sorry," he adds to Glenny. "Is that when you started seeing things? A near-death experience pushed you too close and you never made it fully back?"

"No, he was hearing things before he almost died," Glenny says. I blast her a warning look that can't penetrate through her shields of indifference to my personal matters. "He told me he thinks it just kinda started on its own but he dismissed it all as stress and tinnitus until his last tour in Afghanistan pushed him over."

I've never told anyone that, so I suppose I thought it too loud when Glenny was around.

"And you have a family history of schizophrenia, yeah?" she asks. "So, I dunno, maybe it's genetic as well or something—"

Square-face's cell phone rings, stopping Glenny from sharing any more theories I've only thought and never spoken, and it's no coincidence that he has the same ringtone I do. Glenny changed mine to the Ghostbusters theme the moment I set it down within her arm's reach for more than a hot minute.

Square-face frowns before turning off his phone. It rings again and his frown deepens to Mariana Trench levels of depth.

"It's for me." I pull my hand out from the cuff to take the phone. I know who's on the other line.

"Put it on speaker," he says.

The screen flickers under the unnatural influence hiding the number. I wait until I see the button for speaker before setting the phone on the table.

"Remington." Salome's voice is twisted by electric chatter. "Where are you?"

I don't have anything to say, so I give her the floor to speak her piece.

"What do you think running away is going to do?" she asks.

"Cardio is good for the heart."

She laughs. "You're such a drama queen. You know I wouldn't kill you."

"Had me fooled."

Glenny looks like she'd smash the phone to smithereens if she had a baseball bat. Square-face keeps glancing out the windows, fingers tapping the holster on his hip. He mouths "keep her talking."

"If I wanted you dead, you would be," Salome says. "And I don't like chase games."

"Then don't play," I say.

She sighs, long, seductive, and one of the ugliest things I've ever heard. "I'll make this simple. Tell me where you are and we can figure this out to everyone's benefit. If not, for each day I waste looking for you, I'll have the good doctor Raim cut off another inch of your legs."

I have to put an arm out to stop Glenny—claws out and teeth bared—from grabbing the phone. I fully believe Salome means to follow through on that, but I'm too tired to come up with a clever response which is no one's fault but hers.

"That's not very ladylike." Square-face takes the phone, turns it off speaker, and jams it against his cauliflower ear. Sepia pulses like veins across my sight and the murmurs rustle in the silence of him listening to her reply. He waits a beat, then shakes his head. "He doesn't got any say in where he goes. He's not calling those shots any more than you are."

Straining to hear Salome's response only plunges me further into the faceless voices. I shiver and Glenny tosses me a sweatshirt from a duffel bag tucked beneath the kitchen table. She grins when I slip my hand out of the cuff for a second time to put the shirt on, then slip back in. Humor is thick in the air because Salome gets a laugh from Square-face. I didn't think he had a sense of humor.

"Like hell I am," he says. "That you want him that bad makes it worth it. Next time don't let your pets wander free."

This time I can easily hear Salome raging through the phone. Square-face taps a thumb on the screen to end the call.

"You kids better move," he says, square eyebrows furrowed as he tucks the phone into his jacket pocket.

"Can you give her a ride back to Encrucijada?" I ask. I'll borrow Glenny's car to drive to I don't know where, all that matters is it be somewhere far away to figure out what to do next.

Square-face ignores me and turns to Glenny. "You think your aunt can help him?"

Glenny nods. I shake my head.

"Glenny, go home. Please."

"We will," she says, bouncing into the living room to check Titus' diaper before picking up his car seat.

"No, you're gonna go home now," I say.

"What, you got a better idea of what to do?"

Nothing specific, but I know the only way to make this worse is to let Glenny get involved.

She pauses at the front door. "Okay, fine. I'll go home. *After* I drop you off at Aunt Cia's."

The crooked screen door swings shut behind her and Square-face steps up to loom over me, arms crossed. "You're gonna get in the car with that young lady and do as she says or you're going to enjoy a six-hour road trip in the trunk. And if I were your girlfriend, I might leave you in there for another six hours depending on how much more of a headache you want to give her."

I don't bother telling him Glenny isn't my girlfriend because the next line of questioning requires me clearing up that no, Titus is not mine.

"This isn't her business, and it's not your problem," I say.

"The moment you got involved with Trasmoz, you became my problem. And if you do anything that moves you back her way, I'm putting a bullet in you first 'cause that'd be a mercy considering what's after you."

"Why haven't you put a bullet in her yet?"

"Don't think I haven't tried, but she's got—"

"Friends in low places?"

He nods, realizes we're coming close to some shape of camaraderie, and doubles down on his scowl.

"Last time I'm gonna say it." He growls but some of his menace is gone. "Get in the car."

Six hours is a long time to spend in a car trunk. And it's a lot harder to make a break from a trunk than a proper car seat. My plan to ditch somewhere along I-10 is quickly dashed and it's a deep betrayal when Glenny is the one who handcuffs me to the car's door handle to be sure I stay put.

"I don't have to be psychic to know what you were thinking," she says and double-checks to make sure the cuffs are secure.

"You lied about going home after dropping me off," I say, once again figuring things out too late, "didn't you?"

"No. Well, okay maybe a little lie," she says. "But I knew you wouldn't get in the car if you thought I wasn't going home right away."

Confident I'm not going anywhere, she attends to her less needy charge, the four-month-old Titus. She buckles in his car seat and places a light kiss on his sleeping forehead before hopping into the driver's seat. She revs the engine and waves to Square-face on his lopsided porch before pulling away.

"If you want, we can argue about it," she says. "I mean, we got over seven hours of driving and I'm still super mad at you so we might as well fight now and get it over with."

Maria would put holds on arguments based on location. No arguing in the bedroom or the kitchen. If I wanted to fight with her, we had to take it to the living room, the garage, or wait until we could. Most times whatever we wanted to argue over simmered down to a discussion by then.

"And I wasn't completely lying," Glenny says. "We'll go home, it'll just take a little while. Maybe by then Dad can clear up everything on the legal end, yeah?"

"Run. Run. Run," Lena offers her advice.

Shapes move in the headlights and dark veins clutter my peripherals. The sepia hasn't lifted. It's softened, but refuses to yield its hold.

"Can you still see it?" Glenny asks.

"Yeah." The possibility that this might be a permanent change, a consequence of me looking too far beyond the veil to ever unsee it, turns my stomach. The radio squawks out static and spins through a couple stations before settling on Cash's rendition of "Trouble in Mind."

I roll my eyes. "Could you be any less subtle?"

The radio spits out what sounds like laughter, Glenny's hand finds mine, and for a brief moment the murmurings diminish, the night clears, and there looks to be more than gloom on the road ahead.

"We'll figure it out," she promises.

About the Author

When not reading or writing, S.K. Ehra can be found wandering the woods and, while skittish, is friendly when approached.

Subscribe to my Newsletter and receive *Gone,* a prequel short story to The Crossroads Series.

You can connect with me on:
- https://skehra.com
- https://twitter.com/SKEhraAuthor
- https://www.instagram.com/skehra_author

Subscribe to my newsletter:
- https://sendfox.com/skehraauthor

Also by S.K. Ehra

THE CROSSROADS SERIES
   CALL FROM THE CROSSROADS
   IN THE SERVICE OF SHADOWS

SHRINE AND SHADOW SERIES
   THE FOX AND THE DRAGON

* 9 7 9 8 9 8 5 1 5 2 2 1 0 *